"Don't act innocent with me," Will growled, shaking his left crutch at Ken. "Maybe it was Coach who made you starter, but you can't tell me you hadn't been wanting that for a long time. And what about Melissa? You moved in on her when I was laid up in the hospital!"

Will was pleased to see Ken's jaw muscles spasm at this last remark. Blindly tossing his helmet on a nearby bench, Ken narrowed his eyes and lifted his chin defiantly. "I never tried to steal Melissa from you," he said. "You were the one who pushed her away. She tried to stick by you, but you were too busy feeling sorry for yourself!"

Something dark and cold stirred within Will. For a second all he could do was glare at Ken with so much fury, he was halfway amazed the guy's skin didn't sizzle. Will knew on one level that Ken believed what he was saying. But on another, more subterranean, level, none of it mattered. And before he realized what was happening, he had dropped his crutches and was charging toward Ken, yelling at the top of his lungs.

Ken backed up, looking more shocked than scared. But before Will could reach him, a searing pain flared up in his right knee, making his entire body crumple. He fell to the ground with a sharp cry.

Don't miss any of the books in SWEET VALLEY HIGH
SENIOR YEAR, an exciting series from Bantam Books!

Visit the Official Sweet Valley Web Site on the Internet at:

www.sweetvalley.com

Francine Pascal's SVH senioryear

Playing Dirty

CREATED BY
FRANCINE PASCAL

BANTAM BOOKS
NEW YORK · TORONTO · LONDON · SYDNEY · AUCKLAND

RL: 6, AGES 012 AND UP

PLAYING DIRTY

A Bantam Book / March 2001

Sweet Valley High® is a registered trademark of Francine Pascal.
Conceived by Francine Pascal.
Cover photography by Michael Segal.

Produced by 17th Street Productions,
an Alloy Online, Inc. company.
33 West 17th Street
New York, NY 10011.

ISBN: 0-553-49343-4

Visit us on the Web! www.randomhouse.com/teens

Published simultaneously in the United States and Canada

Bantam Books is an imprint of Random House Children's Books, a
division of Random House, Inc. BANTAM BOOKS and the rooster
colophon are registered trademarks of Random House, Inc. Bantam Books,
1540 Broadway, New York, New York 10036.

PRINTED IN THE UNITED STATES OF AMERICA

OPM   0 9 8 7 6 5 4 3 2 1

To Mia Pascal Johansson

Ken Matthews

There has been way too much change this fall. Quitting football, Dad's hyperactive social life, going out with Maria, rejoining the team, getting my old position back, breaking up with Maria, hooking up with Melissa . . .

Lately I feel like I'm being sucked down the middle of a giant whirlpool. I just hope I come up for air soon. And when I do, I hope I still recognize everything around me.

Melissa Fox

Okay, so I changed boyfriends. I went from Will to Ken. But it doesn't have to make a huge difference in my life. They're both not, they're both football players, and Ken has the same future now that Will had a little while ago. So what's the problem?

Maybe there are a few differences. Like, I still love Will. And I don't love Ken.

But that doesn't have to matter. It can change. And even if I never feel the same way about Ken that I do about Will, Ken can give me what I need. Will can't anymore. So I just have to move on. Even if that means leaving Will behind.

TIA RAMIREZ

THIS HASN'T EXACTLY BEEN
THE BEST YEAR OF MY LIFE. I'M
THINKING I NEED A FRESH START.
MAYBE IF I CHANGE SOMETHING
ABOUT MYSELF, THINGS WILL GO
BETTER. BUT WHAT SHOULD I DO?
I COULD DYE MY HAIR PINK. OR
CHANGE MY NAME TO
"MORGANA" AND WEAR LOTS OF
BLACK. OR SUDDENLY BECOME
ULTIMATE STRAIGHT-A GIRL AND
SPEND ALL MY FREE TIME
STUDYING.

THEN AGAIN, MAYBE I SHOULD
JUST DEAL WITH MY NO-
BOYFRIEND, BEST-FRIEND-IN-
REHAB, INCREDIBLY MIXED-UP
LIFE AS IT IS. THE "NEW" ME
MIGHT NOT HAVE IT ANY EASIER.

Elizabeth Wakefield

At the beginning of the year, I promised myself I would be a new Elizabeth. Drastic changes. I was going to loosen up and have lots of fun. Great idea. Lately I've been convinced there are certain things people shouldn't be allowed to do until they're at least twenty-five.

Like fall in love.

CHAPTER
All Too Familiar
1

Jade Wu fixed her gaze on the back of the shaggy-haired guy walking a few paces in front of her. The hallway vibrated with the stampede of students eager to get home, but she'd had no trouble picking out Evan Plummer in the crowd. First there was that trademark dark hair, and then there was his slow, loping gait—as if he were gliding through a swimming pool. Jade liked that about him. In fact, it was probably number 127 on a list of things she liked about Evan.

All day long she had been keeping an eye out for him, and here he was, finally. Now that her dad had left town and her life was relatively problem-free, she could focus on other things—like snagging Evan and getting him to ask her out.

Jade smoothed her black, silky hair out of her face and briskly wove through the sea of people until she was right behind Evan. Then she purposefully crashed into him with her shoulder.

Evan stopped and whirled around, surprised, but

1

his expression immediately changed to a grin when he saw her. "Hey," he said. "I've been looking for you."

"Really?" Jade's pulse jumped, but she tried to keep her voice even. "What for?" she asked.

"I was wondering how your meeting went with the social worker yesterday," he said. He tilted his head, and his long, thick bangs swung to the side. Jade noted how his brow was furrowed in genuine concern.

Sweet, she thought. *The guy really seems to care.*

"It went great," she said. "My dad finally saw the light. He realized how Mom and I have this great connection and the worst thing for me would be for him to butt in and change that. He wants more visitation, stuff like that, but he's going to drop the custody suit."

"That's incredible!" Evan said, his brown eyes lighting up. "I'm so glad it worked out." His gaze locked on hers, and Jade's body practically buzzed with electricity. "You know, we should celebrate," he added.

Yes! Here it comes! It felt great to be back in the game again, back to flirting and soaking up attention from a hot guy. Only Evan was going to be more than just a fun time—she could sense it.

Since this "celebration" would be their first date, he'd probably try to impress her. Still, Evan was a down-to-earth kind of guy, so she could picture an intimate dinner in a vegetarian restaurant. But that was cool. As long as it was *intimate*.

"What'd you have in mind?" she asked, reaching down with one hand to smooth her short corduroy skirt.

He shrugged. "I don't know—whatever you want," he said.

Jade bit her lip. She needed him to set up the boundaries here, make it clear what he was asking for.

"What if we meet here after you're done with cheerleading and I'm finished with swim practice?" Evan continued. "We can swing by Healthy and have a couple of smoothies. My treat." He smiled, obviously pleased with his suggestion.

That's it? Jade squinted at him, searching his expression for some hidden meaning, but all she could see was friendliness. Genuine, *boring* friendliness. What was with this guy? Yeah, he'd told her he wasn't looking to jump into a relationship anytime soon, but wasn't he over that yet? Didn't he get what a great time they could have together?

"Jade?" he prompted when she didn't answer. "Sound okay?"

"Sure," she said, forcing herself to return his smile. "I'll meet you back here."

Evan nodded. "Cool. Later." He turned and loped away down the hall.

"Yeah, later," she called after him, moving to the side as a bunch of freshmen knocked into her arm as they passed by.

Free smoothie? Jade rubbed her elbow, frowning. That was *not* exactly what she'd had in mind.

Will Simmons stood outside the locker room, making circular designs in the dirt with the end of his crutches. He could hear the shouts, whistles, and crunching noises of football practice from the nearby playing field. The sounds were all too familiar—only this time they were muffled and distant, and without the accompanying soreness in his body.

Then again, there *was* pain. Having to witness the guys' practice and not be able to join in—to know that he'd never be able to join in again. All he could do was stand around, watching and listening like some sort of ghost.

He might as well be a ghost. His life as he knew it was totally over. No football, no college scholarship, no Melissa. Even his body felt foreign to him—as if it were a shoddy cage he was stuck inside.

"Good play!" a familiar voice cried from the sidelines. Coach Riley was obviously enjoying the new offense. An intense anger, tinged with envy, flooded Will's system. His body stiffened, and he almost lost his balance, which only made him madder.

He stomped the ends of his crutches into the ground, letting out a low growl. As if in response, his right knee suddenly started throbbing.

Will hobbled over to the locker room's brick wall and leaned against it, gasping in pain and frustration. Lately it seemed like everyone and everything was betraying him—his team, the Michigan scout, Melissa, even his own body.

A sudden rush of self-pity flooded through him. Will stared down at his own shadow spread out before him on the concrete. It looked like some alien creature with the hunched shoulders and two extra lines for the crutches. This wasn't him. This wasn't his life.

Will clenched his jaw and shut his eyes. Why had he let himself come here? He could have met up with Matt and Josh somewhere else. But no, he'd told them he'd wait for them here, just to prove that he could do it.

"All right, Matthews!" shouted someone from the field.

At the sound of the name Will's shoulders automatically went rigid. Ken must really be shining today. And practice wouldn't be over for another twenty to thirty minutes, which meant Will would have to listen to even more stupid cheers from the sidelines. He'd forced himself to do this because it was the *mature* thing to do. But maybe he wasn't exactly ready for the mature thing yet. And why should he be? It wasn't every day his entire future got flushed down the toilet and handed over to some jerk who didn't deserve any of it.

Ken Matthews unhooked his helmet, slid it off, and wiped the sweat out of his eyes with the back of his wrist. His passing arm throbbed, his left side hurt from getting slammed on that pass play, and his shoulder muscles felt like ball bearings. But Ken barely felt the pain. He was too focused on going over his plays in his mind, reviewing every moment.

"Okay, men," Coach Riley said, beginning his military-type march around the gathered players, "we've got an important play-off game twenty-four hours from now, and if what you've shown me today is the best you can do, you might as well kiss your helmets good-bye now. Because you won't be wearing them again after tomorrow."

Ken shifted uncomfortably. Coach was being a bit harsh. He'd thought they looked pretty good out there.

"Now, I've got to say," Coach went on, "defense looks solid. There are still some areas where we can improve, but overall I'm happy with the defensive effort. Offense, on the other hand . . ." He sighed and massaged his forehead. "I'm not really happy with our execution."

Ken could feel his cheeks heating up, and several guys looked right at him. Everyone knew Coach was talking about him in particular. Okay, so he'd made some key mistakes during practice. But he was working hard, and he knew what he needed to do in the game.

"We have been running these plays since day one," Coach continued, pacing and waving his hands as he spoke, "but you guys are acting like this is the first time we've trotted them out. After the last couple of games you'd think we'd have improved. But it still seems like your heads aren't in it." At this point Coach Riley swiveled around and stared right at Ken.

Ken's stomach churned. Coach didn't have to be so hard on him. Ken knew he'd been messing up lately, but Coach reaming him out in front of the team was only going to rattle him even more. Right now he needed to concentrate, without any outside pressures.

"All right, men. Hit the showers and get a lot of rest tonight. Tomorrow we're going to play a good, clean game. *No mistakes!*" Again he looked right at Ken as the others got up to leave.

Ken stood and fell in step with the retreating wave of players, unable to block out the echo of

Coach Riley's words in his head. What if he totally messed up in front of everyone? What if he ruined the team's chances for the finals? What if he lost his chance at a scholarship?

Stop it, he told himself as he bounded down the sloping sidewalk toward the locker room. *Forget everything and make yourself focus.*

That's what he would do. Dad always said he should shut everything out before a game. Ken remembered the countless pep talks his dad had given him over the years. "Just make a tunnel with a vision of a big win at the end," he would say. "Then tune the rest out."

Ken had always thought his dad was going a little over the top, but right now he needed that advice. "We're going to win. We're going to win," he chanted under his breath. A mental picture conjured up before his eyes. He could see the stadium quaking with excited fans, his teammates cheering all around him, and Coach Riley clapping him proudly on the back. His stomach pains started to ease up, and Coach Riley's exasperated voice slowly grew quiet.

"Will! All right! You stuck around." Josh Radinsky's deep voice broke Ken out of his thoughts. He glanced up and saw several of the El Carro teammates crowding around Will Simmons. Will's broad shoulders draped over two crutches, and his long, pale arms hung stiffly at his sides, grasping the handles. There was something so strange about seeing him that way, like watching a grizzly bear caught in a trap.

Ken hadn't even realized he was staring, but just then Will caught his gaze and looked back, obvious anger flashing in his light blue eyes. Once again Ken's gut seized up. Only this time it was with guilt—not tension over his playing.

Just stay focused, he told himself. *Don't let yourself get distracted.*

Ken quickly averted his eyes away from Will and stepped past him into the locker room. "We're going to win. We're going to win," he muttered.

Andy Marsden trudged through the front door of his house, tossed his dark green backpack onto the floor, and headed in the direction of the kitchen. School had left him with that heavy, groggy feeling he used to get after a long car trip with his family. But he was fairly certain a sixteen-ounce bottle of soda would supply him with just the right amount of sugar and caffeine to reactivate his mind and body.

He dragged the soles of his black Converse sneakers around the corner into the dining room, where his brother stood, hovering over the long teakwood table, an open can of Dr Pepper in his left hand.

"Hey! That better not be the last one," Andy warned him.

Ryan ignored him and pointed down at the table. "You got something in the mail," he said.

"Really?" Andy stepped closer and saw the long, flat box wrapped in brown paper. He immediately recognized the small, dainty writing on the package. Definitely a special delivery from Grandma.

That's weird. It's early for my birthday, he thought. Then again, Grandma did seem to operate on a totally different sense of time. To her, Andy was perpetually in eighth grade. He nearly gave her a heart attack during her last visit when he told her he'd be graduating in the spring.

"Open it," Ryan urged. "What do you think it is?"

An eager hope sprang up in Andy as an idea popped into his head. After months of hint dropping could she have actually bought him one of those cool, 128-bit gaming systems? He'd meant for it to be a Christmas present, but maybe she just couldn't wait to give it to him!

He lifted the package with both hands and gently shook it. Unfortunately the box was extremely light and offered no telltale rattling sounds. Andy sighed, then quickly removed the paper and lifted the lid off the box. Something soft and cushiony lay inside. It was bright red with blue diamonds across the front.

Andy lifted it up and saw that it was a sweater—a huge sweater. It hung down close to Andy's knees, and the sleeves passed his hands by several inches.

Ryan nearly doubled over with laughter. "You look like a psychedelic Charlie Brown!" he hooted. "I'll give you twenty dollars if you wear it to school!"

"Wear it? I was thinking I could go parachuting with it," Andy joked.

"Man, someone ought to remind her we live in California, where freezing weather only lasts about a week." Ryan turned and headed for the living room, shaking his head. "Grandma's nice and all, but sometimes she's a little clueless."

Andy nodded, then read the note pinned to the back of the sweater.

To My Almost Grown Grandson! Your mother told me you had a date with a nice girl named Six. Here's something to wear the next time you two go out. Hope I get to meet her soon!

Love, Grandma

Oops. Guess Grandma's not up on the latest news, Andy thought. He hadn't asked his parents if they'd told her, but now that he thought about it, he could see why they would have wanted to wait a little.

Make sure Andy was okay with making it more public that he was gay.

Maybe they'll put it in their Christmas letters, he thought wryly. He could just imagine it: "Bob got a promotion. Ryan's soccer team won their division. And we're so proud of Andy for coming out of the closet." Of course, knowing Grandma, she probably wouldn't get it. "You mean Ryan and Andy are still locking each other in closets? Tell them I said to play nice!"

Andy threw the sweater over his shoulder and trudged up the stairs to his room. Suddenly he felt incredibly tired. He'd figured once he told his friends and family, he could go back to his life and not have to deal with this constantly. But no. Every day little things happened that reminded him of what he was holding inside. It made him feel like a double agent—only not quite as exciting. And it was wearing him out.

Andy walked into his room and plopped down on the bed, staring at his reflection in the mirror over his dresser. He looked like the same guy he always was. He generally felt like the same guy. So why did this one issue have to butt into every other aspect of his life?

"Just forget it," he mumbled as he reached for the TV remote. All he needed was to focus on something—*anything*—that didn't have to do with relationships. Some lousy late afternoon programming should do the trick. He lay back on his bed and switched on the power.

"So, bachelor number one," said a blonde in a tight red dress, "what's your idea of the sexiest dinner you could serve me?"

Ookay, let's try something else, Andy thought, clicking the remote.

A guy wearing a T-shirt two sizes too small came on the screen. He reached out a muscular arm and pulled a black-haired woman up close to him. "Oh, Tabitha," he crooned. "You're the only woman I've ever loved."

"Oh, Brock!"

Oh, gross.

Andy turned off the power and threw the remote onto the floor. So much for avoiding the topic.

"You too, TV?" he moaned miserably, staring at his darkened Magnavox.

Will Simmons

When I was a kid, I saw this Disney movie about a girl who switches places with her mother for a day. It was like their spirits traded bodies or something, and they had to go through the whole day acting like the other person.

At the time I thought it was the coolest movie ever, and for the next few weeks I daydreamed about trading places with some of the older guys at school or Little League. I imagined how it would be to wake up one morning, look in the mirror, and see myself as someone else. Someone bigger, stronger, and cooler.

Lately that's just what it feels like, as if I've suddenly traded places with a stranger. Only instead of it being exciting, it's just scary. Scarier than anything I could imagine. I can't help thinking that this broken, lame excuse for a body actually belongs to someone else and that some other guy out there must have mine.

I know Ken Matthews doesn't have my body, but he has everything else that belongs to me. Meanwhile I'm left with nothing. And unlike that movie I saw, this won't be over at the end of the day.

CHAPTER
Subterranean
2

"Hey, Simmons. You don't have to stand *outside* the locker room, man," Josh said, gesturing into the open air. "Come in and hang out while Matt and I get ready. Then you want to go by First and Ten?"

Will didn't answer. He was too busy staring at Ken, trying to read the look on his face. Did the guy get what a piece of dirt he was? He almost seemed to—Will was pretty sure he could see guilt in Ken's eyes. But Ken quickly ducked his head and turned away, slinking into the locker room on the edge of a small group.

A coarse, raw anger welled up inside Will. *First he takes my spot on the team, then Melissa, and now he wants to pretend I don't exist? We'll see about that.*

Will shoved his crutch in front of the steel door to the locker room and pushed it back several inches. Then he forced his shoulder into the opening and struggled inside.

"Will? What's up, man?" Josh asked, following along behind him.

"Matthews thinks he can avoid me," Will muttered through his teeth. "I'm going to make him deal with me."

Several players stared at him curiously as he staggered between the rows of benches toward the back of Ken's jersey.

"Matthews! I'm talking to you!" he hollered as soon as he got within a few feet. "Don't try to hide from me!"

The entire locker room grew silent. Will watched, quietly fuming, as Ken slowly turned around. This time Ken didn't bow his head shamefully. Instead he stared at Will straight on. Will locked his eyes onto Ken's and found, to his horror, that they were filled with pity.

All at once an intense fury flamed up inside Will—a wild, uncontrollable flash that normally would have made him charge forward, knocking over people and things. But unfortunately his limbs wouldn't obey.

"What makes you think you can walk past me like I'm nothing!" Will spat, leaning as far forward as his crutches would allow. "You think you're better than me now? You think you can just sit on your butt all season and then suddenly take over the team?"

Ken's eyebrows lowered in confusion. "I didn't

take over the team, Will," he said calmly. "Coach put me in after you got hurt. You know that."

His cool demeanor only angered Will even more. Will wanted to see Ken lose it. He only needed some sign of weakness—a shout or threat or stomp or punch. But Ken just kept staring at him with that calm, detached expression.

"Don't act innocent with me," Will growled, shaking his left crutch at Ken. "Maybe it was Coach who made you starter, but you can't tell me you hadn't been wanting that for a long time. And what about Melissa? You moved in on her when I was laid up in the hospital!"

Will was pleased to see Ken's jaw muscles spasm at this last remark. Blindly tossing his helmet on a nearby bench, Ken narrowed his eyes and lifted his chin defiantly. "I never tried to steal Melissa from you," he said. "You were the one who pushed her away. She tried to stick by you, but you were too busy feeling sorry for yourself!"

Something dark and cold stirred within Will. For a second all he could do was glare at Ken with so much fury, he was halfway amazed the guy's skin didn't sizzle. Will knew on one level that Ken believed what he was saying. But on another, more subterranean, level, none of it mattered. And before he realized what was happening, he had dropped his crutches and was charging toward Ken, yelling at the top of his lungs.

Ken backed up, looking more shocked than scared. But before Will could reach him, a searing pain flared up in his right knee, making his entire body crumple. He fell to the cement floor with a sharp cry.

"Hey! Take it easy!" Matt said, kneeling on his left-hand side.

Josh immediately appeared on his right. "Are you okay?" he asked.

Will was too out of it to answer. He lay propped on his elbows, gasping and writhing in agony. His knee throbbed, but strangely enough, most of the pain seemed to be traveling from the pit of his chest.

"Let's get you up before Coach comes," Josh said.

With Josh and Matt on either side of him, Will felt himself being raised up. Everything blurred in front of him as they steered him through the locker room. But he did manage to catch yet another guilt-stricken look on Ken's face.

They hobbled through the double steel doors into the sunshine. Matt held Will steady as Josh handed him back his crutches.

"Are you going to be okay?" Matt asked once Will was supporting himself again.

Will shut his eyes and nodded weakly. He didn't want to tell them how bad he really felt—completely wasted and dying from embarrassment, not to mention the new collection of aches and pains he'd just added to his body.

"Don't do it, man," Josh muttered. "Don't waste your knee going after that snake."

"Yeah. Get better and *then* you can kick his butt," Matt added.

Will gave another, more vigorous nod. "Thanks, guys," he mumbled.

Josh peered at him closely. "You sure you're going to be all right?"

"Yes, I'm sure!" Will barked. "Go back inside. I just need some space. That's all."

"Okay," Josh replied. He and Matt lingered uneasily for a few seconds longer before finally heading back into the locker room.

Will sighed heavily and leaned back against the brick wall. He couldn't believe he'd just lost it in front of everyone like that. Then, to make things worse, he practically had to be carried out the door by his two best friends.

If only he had managed to land a good blow on Matthews. That would have made it all worth it. If he couldn't play football again or get his girlfriend back or even get *close* to being the way he was before, at least he deserved to see Matthews receive a giant punch in the face.

Will knew the best thing was just to let this all go before it drove him out of his mind. But he couldn't. Revenge was all he had left.

Jade squinted at the large piece of white butcher paper and slowly connected the lines on the large, cubed Y she was drawing on the giant run-through for the game. Behind her she could hear Jessica Wakefield burst out laughing for about the twentieth time since practice began.

"So then I opened the box, and it was this beaded necklace that spelled out 'Jess' with all these pink hearts around it," Jade heard Jessica say. "Jeremy actually sat down with his sisters and the three of them made it together with this jewelry kit the girls have!" Jessica started giggling again, and Jade had to close her eyes and clench her fists to avoid saying something snide. After all, it wasn't Jessica's fault she was so irritatingly happy. And it wasn't Jessica's fault that Evan seemed far more interested in being Jade's *buddy* than an actual boyfriend. She should just push aside her jealousy and get a grip.

Jade took a deep breath and relaxed her fierce grasp on the pencil. But when she opened her eyes again, she saw that she'd managed to make a long stray streak across the paper, turning the Y into a lopsided X.

"Great!" she snapped, a little more loudly than she'd intended.

She turned to find the rest of the squad staring at her. Jessica, Tia, and Annie had matching surprised expressions, while Melissa Fox and her followers, Cherie, Lila, Amy, and Gina, were smirking in amusement.

Jade winced. "Just broke my pencil point," she said, forcing a cheery smile. "That's all." Jade hoped Melissa's radar wouldn't detect how annoyed she really was. The girl was a master at twisting other people's pain to her own advantage.

"Sorry you guys have to stay late and finish up the run-through," Melissa said, her voice oozing fake sympathy. "We've already finished our spirit posters. What do you say, girls? Think we deserve a trip to House of Java?"

"Sounds perfect," Gina replied.

The group stood and headed out the gym doors, whispering to each other on their way out. Jade shook her head. Those girls were all serious freaks.

"I didn't realize we were in some sort of spirit-poster race," Jessica commented once the doors had closed behind them.

"No kidding," Jade agreed.

"Um, Jade?" Annie asked, scooting up beside her. "Are you sure you're really okay?"

"Of course," she said brightly. "Why?"

"Well . . ." Annie knit her brow and gestured down at the butcher paper. "Because you lettered out '*Sweat* Valley' instead of 'Sweet Valley.'"

Jade stared down at her work. Sure enough, there was a slightly crooked but unmistakable capital *A* where the second *E* should be. "Great!" she yelled again. What was wrong with her? She had volunteered to draw out the letters instead of painting so she wouldn't get messed up for her pseudo-date with Evan. But maybe she should have taken on something more mindless.

"What's going on with you?" Tia asked, peering at her anxiously.

"You really don't seem like yourself," Annie said, looking genuinely worried.

"Yeah, what's up?" Jessica chimed in.

Jade nervously fiddled with the silver ring on her left pinkie. Maybe she should just go ahead and spill it. After all, Jessica's relationship bliss might be annoying, but it did prove she knew her stuff when it came to guys. And even though Tia had gone through a tough time recently, she and Annie weren't bad in that department either. Maybe they could lend some advice.

"It's . . . it's this guy I like," Jade began. Immediately the other three leaned in closer.

"Yeah?" Tia asked, her large, brown eyes flashing with curiosity. "Who is it?"

Jade bit her thumbnail and glanced over at Jessica's expectant face. How would she take this? After all, both she *and* her twin sister had histories with Evan. Besides, first Jeremy and now Evan? It probably looked like Jade only had a thing for Jessica's ex-boyfriends.

"Oh, you know," Jade replied with a shrug. "Just some guy."

"Jade! You can tell us!" Annie urged.

"Yeah. Come on," Jessica added. "Melissa and her troop are long gone, and you can trust us not to blab it around school."

Jade sighed and continued twisting her ring back and forth. She really did want some help with this. Besides, the fact that Evan *was* one of Jessica's exes might give her some special insight into the matter. It was worth a shot.

She took a deep breath. "It's Evan," she replied, smiling weakly.

"I knew it," Jessica squealed. She grinned. "You guys are so perfect for each other!"

"Yeah, I can see it, actually," Tia added. "So what's the problem?"

Jade ran her fingers through her dark hair. "I don't know," she said. "I can't seem to get him to think of me as more than just a friend."

Jessica frowned. "Are you flirting?"

"Are you kidding?" Jade laughed. "I *know* how to flirt. And believe me, I'm turning it on full power. But for some reason it's . . . not working." She scowled and stared down at her lap. She hated having to admit her failure.

Tia tapped a finger against her chin. "That's weird. I don't think he's gone after anyone else. At least, not since that thing with Elizabeth." She tilted her head toward Jessica. "Do you think he's still hung up on her?"

Jessica frowned and shook her head. "No. I'm pretty sure that's way over. He told me he was done with girls on the rebound from the loves of their lives." She paused, then leaned forward. "Jade, that's probably it," she said. "Evan must think you're not over Jeremy. I mean, he does know everything that, um, happened with the three of us."

Jade pressed her lips together. Evan *had* mentioned something like that to her too, but could he really think she was still into Jeremy? She shook her head. "I don't know, Jess. I'm pretty sure I'm dropping enough hints that I like *him*, not Jeremy. I'm practically all over him."

Tia's mouth curled into a smile. "Um, Jade, don't take this the wrong way or anything, but you're kind of known as a major flirt."

Jade glanced over at Annie, who scrunched her

face up into an apologetic smile. "She's right," Annie said. "He might not exactly feel singled out."

Jade felt a flash of hurt, but she knew deep down that her friends were right. That really was how she *used* to be. Before Evan and Jeremy, she considered any guy fair game—whether any of them were involved with other people or not.

"So what do I do?" Jade asked, frustrated. "I mean, I can't exactly *stop* flirting. Right?"

Jessica tilted her head, thinking it over. "Maybe you just need to change your message," she suggested.

"Like what?" Jade asked.

"Okay, listen." Jessica pushed aside a couple of paint cans and inched up closer to Jade. "You've been dropping all sorts of hints that you're totally into him, but Evan hasn't bought it, right? He just assumes you're goofing around like usual."

Jade flinched. Jessica didn't have to make her sound like a complete bimbo. "Get to the point, Jess," she snapped.

Jessica ignored Jade's tone. "Well, instead of throwing out clues that you like him, you should drop hints that you're totally over Jeremy."

"Hey, yeah," Tia remarked. "That's a great idea."

Jessica beamed. "So what do you think, Jade? Can you do that?"

A sly smile slowly crept across Jade's face. She

had to admit, Jessica was on to something. Jade had never made it totally clear to Evan that she was over Jeremy. Maybe once he got the picture, he'd finally get that she was just waiting for him to ask her out.

Just a few more feet until the bathroom, Tia told herself as she continued striding down the hallway. Thick dabs of paint were already drying on her arms and legs, making her itch all over. She couldn't wait to get cleaned up and then head home.

Normally she enjoyed sitting around gossiping with her friends while they painted run-throughs and spirit posters for the upcoming games—but not today. First there were Jessica's happy ramblings and then Jade's love-life problems. Tia was getting really tired of relationship talk. Since her own personal life has been a wreck for so long, her "understanding-friend" reserves had been a bit low.

A long streak of red on her right shin suddenly started itching fiercely. Tia stopped in midstride and bent down to scratch it.

"Hey, Tia," came a deep male voice. "What are you doing?"

Tia stood back up and found herself face-to-face with Ted Masters, another old El Carro student who got transferred to Sweet Valley this year. She'd known him since fifth grade, and he'd even hung out with her and her friends once in a while. He was nice. Cute, too, with short, black hair, retro sideburns, and a funky sense of fashion.

"Hey, Ted," she said, forcing a polite smile. "I just got out of cheerleading practice, and we were painting signs," she explained. "I guess we kind of painted ourselves too. Or at least I did."

He grinned and gestured at her stained outfit. "I like the look," he said.

"Yeah, right," she muttered. "So why are you still here so late?" She knew Ted would never be on a sports team.

Ted frowned. "I had to make up a trig exam." He waved a pencil at Tia, then threw it up in the air and caught it. "But has anyone ever told you how sexy you look when one eyebrow goes up like that?"

Tia held back a sigh. She knew Ted was totally harmless, and on another day she probably would have bantered right back with him, but not now. Today she just didn't have the time or energy for his lame jokes.

She shook her head. "Later, Ted," she answered, brushing past him and resuming her trek toward the bathroom.

"Whoa," he exclaimed. "Hey. Come back, Tee. I was just having some fun."

Tia lifted the back of her hand in a half wave and kept walking.

28

"Whatever, Tia," he called out. "You know, you used to be a fun person, but you've really changed this year."

A burning sensation welled up in the pit of Tia's stomach. She really didn't mean to be so cold to him. But after going through one guy disaster after another these past few months, playing around with someone like Ted just didn't seem fun anymore.

Ted was right about one thing, though. Things were really different this year. And not all for the better.

Tia pushed open the bathroom door and walked over to the sink, then started rinsing off the paint. If only she could hit rewind and go back to the way things used to be. Lately everyone seemed so focused on the future. The counselors were lecturing about applying to college. The class officers were voting on a song and motto for the graduation ceremonies. Even the freshman class was raising money with a dumb fortune-telling booth. They were charging fifty cents to ask a question of their special Magic 8 Ball, which was supposedly on loan from Madame Nirvana, some local psychic kook. During lunch they had a huge line. Everyone wanted glimpses into their futures. Not Tia, though. What she'd really pay for was a chance to go back into the past.

Tia rubbed off the last of the paint, then shut off the faucet and grabbed some paper towels to dry off her skin. She pictured her life the way it used to be. There she was, sitting with the old crowd on the front lawn of El Carro High during lunch—her head in Angel's lap as he fed her french fries one by one, Andy sharing some dumb theory that the groundskeepers were actually the principal's paid spies, Conner slouched against the big oak tree, not saying much of anything unless it was to rag on Andy. For three years they'd hung out like that, just the four of them. Occasionally others would join them, like Ted or Evan or Rebecca Collins.

Tia smiled as she remembered how Conner used to cringe whenever Rebecca showed up. He said it was a miracle the girl swallowed any food at all, considering how much she talked. But Tia liked her.

I haven't heard from her in a while, she realized. Rebecca had been one of the El Carro students who ended up at Big Mesa instead of Sweet Valley. *I should give her a call, maybe even get together with her soon.*

Tia walked out of the bathroom, letting the door swing shut behind her. *In fact, why wait? Why not call her now?* Rebecca might be just the person to snap her out of this funk.

Tia jogged over to the pay phones. She jammed some change into the coin slot and dialed Rebecca's number. After a couple of rings a familiar voice answered.

"Hey, Becca! It's Tee!"

"Tia?" Rebecca paused. "Oh my God. How *are* you? I haven't seen you guys in forever."

"I know," Tia said. "That's actually why I called. Look, I know it's late notice, but . . . do you want to meet this afternoon for coffee at House of Java? Or do you have other plans?"

Rebecca laughed. "Yeah, my social calendar's just *bursting* with activity," she joked. "I'm sitting here outlining a research paper for government. I think you can tear me away. How about I meet you in twenty minutes?"

"Sounds good," Tia said. "Do you know where House of Java is?"

"Yeah, I'll be there. Hey, I can't wait to hear all the gossip about everyone. It'll be like old times."

I hope so, Tia thought. It was just what she needed.

MAGIC 8 BALL QUESTIONS

Jade Wu: Will Evan and I go out soon?
Answer: Signs point to yes.

Elizabeth Wakefield: Is Conner coming
back soon?
Answer: Outlook fuzzy.

Maria Slater: Will I ever get over Ken?
Answer: Very doubtful.

melissa Fox: Will Ken and I have
a great future together?
Answer: Outlook not so good.

Ken Matthews: Will we win the game
tomorrow?
Answer: Very likely.

Jessica Wakefield: Should I wear my new sheer black dress Saturday on my date with Jeremy?
    Answer: Signs point to yes.

Andy Marsden: Will I ever feel normal?
    Answer: Ask again later.

CHAPTER
Wavelengths
3

"Will, good, you're still here," Josh said as he came out of the locker room, followed by Matt.

Will greeted them with a nod. As they walked out, a small amount of steam came with them, and Will could hear the echoes of the other guys' voices inside, laughing and talking.

The three of them headed toward the school parking lot, just like they always used to after practice, with Will in the middle, flanked by Josh and Matt. Only now Will staggered along on crutches, causing the other two to slow their strides. Will couldn't help feeling like some deadweight they had to haul around.

His heart was still hammering after his confrontation with Ken, but at least he was back in control. For a while back there in the locker room, he felt like he was in real danger of losing his sanity—just one more thing for Ken to steal from him.

"Man, I wish I could have clobbered Matthews," Will muttered through clenched teeth. "The guy is asking for a serious pounding."

"Yeah, I can't believe he tried to just shut you out like that," Matt muttered, veering onto the grass to give Will more room on the sidewalk.

Josh shook his head. "We shouldn't even think about that waste of space. Before long, when Will's back in game shape, Coach'll kick Matthews back on his butt. Back to the sidelines, where he belongs."

"Man, I can't wait till you call the plays again," Matt said, jogging around to face Will. "So what do you think? Another week or two, maybe?"

Will stopped dead. He couldn't bear to listen to another word. His entire chest felt like it was caving in. For once he was glad he had crutches. He gripped them hard and leaned forward with his eyes shut, breathing heavily.

"Will?" Josh asked, a note of uneasiness in his voice. "What's up, man?"

"You okay?" Matt asked.

"It's not going to happen," Will practically whispered.

"What?" Josh stepped closer. "What's not going to happen?"

"Me!" Will shouted, straightening up and staring Josh right in the face. "My future! I'm never going to play football again! Don't you understand? There won't be any big Will Simmons comeback. Ever."

He stared at his friends' frozen expressions, feeling completely drained. Lately it seemed his main emotions were a thunderous rage followed by a heavy dose of self-pity. But the worst times were when he felt nothing at all, just a dark, vast emptiness.

"What are you talking about, Will?" Josh finally said. "I thought you wanted to come back. I thought that's what all the physical therapy was about."

Will sighed. "I'll walk and run eventually. But my therapist said I'll never be able to play again. She told me yesterday—I was just fooling myself about the whole thing." He watched as his friends' faces slowly sagged with sympathy.

"Oh, man. That's rough," Josh said.

"Um, yeah. Sorry, man," Matt added, hunching his shoulders. "And sorry about all that stuff we said. We were just trying to talk you up and—"

"It's cool," Will said, holding up a hand. "Don't worry about it." If there was one word he couldn't stand to hear right now, it was *sorry*. He felt bad enough without his friends pitying him. All it did was make him feel weak and useless. What he needed was for them to make him feel strong again. If that was even possible.

"So . . . is there anything we can do?" Josh asked, scratching the back of his neck.

"Yeah, man. Anything you want," Matt chimed in. "Just ask."

Will looked out toward the empty football field, a

chilly wind breezing across his face. "Anything I want," he repeated. Then he glanced at Matt. "Right now what I want more than anything is for Matthews to get a taste of his own medicine. For him to see what it's like to lose everything—like I have."

Matt and Josh exchanged glances, each of their faces hardening.

"You're right," Josh muttered. "It isn't fair."

Matt nodded, his jaw muscles twitching. "I'd love to see that guy get taken down a few notches."

"Too bad there's no way to do it," Will said. He took another glance at his friends' angry expressions, feeling slightly better. It was good to have a team behind him still—even if they couldn't help him win.

Tia took a giant sip of her third mocha latte and set it back down on its saucer. Her hand shook slightly, spilling a few droplets of the latte onto the glass tabletop. She grabbed a napkin and quickly wiped it up, then wadded the napkin into a ball and tried to throw it into a trash can. Unfortunately she threw wide, causing it to land on a nearby customer's plate of chocolate scones.

"Sorry," she called out, giving a meek little wave. Then, as she brought her hand back down, she knocked her cup, spilling her drink again.

Ookay. Definitely time to lay off the caffeine, she

thought, cleaning up the mess with fresh napkins. This time she walked over to the trash can.

Sinking back down onto her plush maroon chair, Tia absently tugged at the fringe trim, wondering why she was suddenly so manic. It was just Becca—someone she'd known for years.

But that was it exactly. What if she wasn't "just Becca" anymore? Tia hadn't seen her in months, so for all she knew, Rebecca could be totally different. And after all the things that had come undone this year, Tia didn't think she could handle another change.

"Hi, Tee! Oh my God! You look fantastic!"

Tia glanced up and saw Rebecca breeze by the other customers to reach her table. Her anxiety vaporized when she caught sight of her friend's familiar round, green eyes, wild brown curls, and constellation of freckles scattered across her nose and cheeks. And that huge, warm smile.

"Becca! I'm so glad you came!" She jumped up and hugged her tightly, then pulled her toward the front counter. "Come on, let me buy you a drink."

"Forget that," Rebecca said, tugging her back toward the table. She threw down her large leather bag and plopped down in an overstuffed armchair across from Tia's seat. "I want to know about everything that's happened this year. I've been hearing some stuff, but I have no idea what to believe. Did you and Angel really break up?"

An old pang squeezed Tia's heart. "Yeah, we did," she mumbled, staring down at her hands.

"No way! Not you guys!" Rebecca exclaimed. "What happened?"

"It's a long story." Taking a deep breath, Tia launched into as concise a summary as possible of how shaky things were after Angel left for Stanford, how she got carried away with Trent, and how they finally realized the long-distance thing just wasn't working. Rebecca listened silently, her eyes filling with sympathy.

"But you guys can try to reconnect during the break, right?" she asked.

Tia swallowed. "He's already hooked up with someone else."

"Oh, Tee." Rebecca shook her head. "You really have been through a lot."

Tia sighed. "Becca, you have no clue how insane it's been." She paused. "I even ended up kissing Conner," she admitted, avoiding her friend's gaze. "But we're not together or anything."

Rebecca drew in a sharp breath. "That's major," she said. "You know, I always thought there was something more between you. Kind of like I always thought there might be a little Rachel-and-Ross sort of thing between me and Andy."

Tia's eyes widened. Obviously Rebecca hadn't heard *all* the big news about their group.

Rebecca's smile faltered. "What?" she asked. "Why are you looking at me like that? Okay, so I'm no Jennifer Aniston, but you don't have to seem so shocked. You knew I had a silly crush on Andy."

"Um . . . Rebecca . . . there's something else that happened this year," Tia began. She stopped, wondering if Andy would have a problem with her telling Rebecca. But he wanted his friends to know—he hadn't said anything about keeping it a secret. "Well, it didn't really *happen*," she added. "I guess it was something that had always been there. It's more like . . . it finally *revealed* itself."

Rebecca squinted. "What are you talking about? You're not making any sense."

Tia shifted in her chair. Rebecca *had* always carried a little minitorch for Andy. She hoped this wouldn't be too big a blow.

"Tee? Tell me. What's up?" Rebecca pressed. "Is Andy okay?"

"Andy's gay," Tia blurted out.

Rebecca's mouth dropped open slightly. "No," she said. "Seriously?"

Tia nodded, waiting to see how Rebecca would respond.

Rebecca narrowed her eyes, quiet for a second.

Then she started to smile. "I can't believe we didn't see that coming," she said. "I mean, first of all, he didn't fall for my irresistible self, right? Hello, the signs were all there."

Tia laughed. "So . . . you're okay with this?" she asked. "I know it can kind of suck when there's a little part of you that believes you'll still end up with someone and then you find out it's really not going to happen." *More than "kind of" suck,* she added silently, thinking about all the disappointments she'd had in the past couple of months.

"Oh, no, I'm fine, really," Rebecca said. "In fact, I actually think I know the perfect guy for Andy."

Tia blinked. "You what?"

"My cousin," Rebecca explained. "He just recently told our family that he's gay. He's sweet, cute, sort of goofy. Definitely a match."

Tia didn't know what to say. Rebecca was taking this news much more easily than she had. Wasn't it a pretty big shock? And then on top of it, Rebecca knew another teenage guy in the area who was openly gay? Maybe Tia was severely in the dark here, but it seemed pretty impressive that Rebecca knew two guys who had it all figured out so young.

"Come on, Tia," Rebecca urged, leaning across the table. "It wouldn't hurt to set up one little date, would it? Don't you think Andy deserves it?"

Tia frowned. Of course Andy deserved it. Somehow ever since he'd told her he was gay, all she'd thought about was what that *meant* in some big sense—and not the fact that the guy could use a date.

"You're right. Let's do it," Tia said. "You talk to your cousin, and I'll work it out with Andy."

"Great!" Rebecca grinned. "This will be so much fun."

Tia smiled. After all, if she couldn't fix her own love life, maybe she could at least help Andy out with his.

Jade pulled her Nissan into the parking lot of Healthy, searching the lot for Evan's beat-up blue Volvo. Sure enough, there it was—right by the store's front door.

She reached up and adjusted her rearview mirror so she could check out her reflection. *Poor guy,* she thought, using her fingertips to smooth the eye makeup she'd applied after practice. *All along he probably thought I was still hung up on Jeremy. I can't believe I was actually worried he didn't like me.*

She grabbed a tissue out of her faux-tiger-skin purse and blotted her lipstick, then threw the tissue on a pile of empty fast-food wrappers in the passenger seat. Time to set things straight. All she had to do was inject a few well-timed hints into the conversation. Then maybe they could meet at a *real* restaurant—for a *real* date.

"Hey, Jade," Evan greeted her as she entered. He was leaning against the polished chrome counter, talking with a wholesome-looking girl standing behind the cash register. She looked like a Jewel clone in a forest green apron.

Jade locked eyes with Evan and walked up next to him. "Hey, yourself," she murmured. No way was he going to leave here thinking she was interested in anyone but him.

"Can I get you something?" the girl asked Jade.

"I already ordered. Go ahead and tell Sasha what you want," Evan said, nodding toward the hippie girl. "Get anything you like."

"Really?" Jade raised her eyebrows and tugged playfully at Evan's hemp shirt. "*Anything* I want?"

"Sure," he replied with a warm smile. "I'm buying, remember?"

"Right," she said, frustrated that he wasn't picking up on her message. She squinted up at the colorful chalkboard listing of food items. "Okay, then. I'll take a mango-passion-fruit smoothie with extra protein powder."

Evan's mouth fell open. "You're kidding. That's *exactly* what I ordered."

"Oh, couples always order alike," Sasha remarked as she scooped yogurt into a blender. "They just click onto the same wavelength."

43

Jade grinned. She could have hugged Sasha for her observation. Evan had to see this as a sign, right? How could he not know there was something between them?

Evan laughed lightly. "Sorry to blow your theory, but we're not a couple," he told Sasha. "She and I are just good friends. That's all."

"Oh," Sasha said. She shrugged. "Okay, whatever." Then she turned and activated the blender full blast.

Jade felt her face go bright red. What was Evan's deal? He sure went out of his way to correct the girl, as if it were some major, life-threatening mistake. Talk about humiliating. *That's it,* she thought. *Time to straighten this out.*

"You know, I used to come to this place a lot when Jessica worked here," Jade yelled over the blender.

"Really?" Evan shouted back, right as the blender stopped. His voice reverberated throughout the small parlor, causing a couple of girls sitting in the back to stare at him in surprise. He and Jade laughed.

"Anyway," Jade continued as they grabbed their drinks from Sasha and sat down at a wicker dinette set along the far wall. "She and I would hang out if it wasn't too busy. Jessica was always obsessing over some new guy. Always having some sort of minidrama, you know?"

Evan nodded as he sipped his smoothie. With his long bangs hanging in front of his eyes, Jade couldn't even be certain he was listening.

"Well, at least Jessica *used* to be that way," she added. "She's been so blissed out lately since she and Jeremy got serious." Jade smiled and tried to make her voice sound as warm and sincere as possible. "I'm really, *really* happy for her. Jeremy is just the greatest guy. So sweet and understanding. I think he's going to be so good for Jessica. Don't you think so?" There. No way would she be this mature about Jeremy's new relationship if she still had a thing for him.

Evan leaned his elbow on the chair's armrest and pushed his hair off his face. "Um, yeah," he replied. "I guess so."

She could tell his brain was still at full tilt, trying to make sense of her statement. *Good,* she thought. *Any second now he'll figure it out.*

Slowly the kinks smoothed out from Evan's forehead and a grin crept across his face. "So, come on. Out with it," he said, slouching back in his seat.

"What?" Jade asked, blinking. She was glad he'd finally picked up on her hints, but there was no way she was going to admit her feelings just yet. *He* had to go first. She leaned forward to meet Evan's gaze, her whole body humming with anticipation.

Evan looked into her eyes, his expression growing more serious. "You know what I mean," he said, tilting his head slightly. Jade felt a shiver travel down

45

her spine. "You must be so relieved that this whole mess with your dad is over."

"Mess with my dad?" Jade repeated blankly, feeling like she'd just been doused with cold water.

"Yeah," Evan said with a chuckle. "That's what we're here celebrating, isn't it? The fact that it's all over?"

"Exactly," she said through a forced smile. What did it take to get through to this guy? It was sweet for him to listen to her problems and all, but this whole concerned-friend bit needed to be turned up a thousand degrees. It was time to drop another clue.

"But that's just it," she added quickly. "It's over, so let's leave it in the past. That's how I celebrate. I never dwell on the past. Not me. Once something's over with, I move on. Just like that." She snapped her fingers in the air for added effect.

"Okay. That's cool," Evan said. "We'll just talk about something else, then." He settled back in his chair and sipped his drink.

Jade fought the urge to bang her head against the table. She had thought this was going to be so easy. Maybe she needed to be more direct with her comments about Jeremy.

She let her gaze drift behind Evan, and her eyes slowly focused on the large chrome clock on the wall. She had only twenty minutes until her shift at Guido's began. If she was going to make it clear she was over

Jeremy, she needed to do it right now. There was no way she could risk showing up late and losing another job.

"Thanks for the smoothie," she said, grabbing her purse from next to her. "I'm sorry, but I actually have to take off kind of early. I didn't realize what time it was, and if I'm even one minute late to work, my boss will freak."

Evan frowned. "What a drag."

"Oh, he's not all that bad," she said, thinking fast. "I like this job a lot more than working at House of Java. That place was just way too intense, you know?" She paused. "I don't miss that place at all. Or *anything* about it."

Evan squinted through his bangs at her, looking a little confused. "That's cool," he said, starting to smile. Was he finally getting the idea?

Too bad she couldn't stick around long enough to make sure. "Well," she said, hopping up from her chair. "See you tomorrow."

"Yeah, sorry you couldn't stay longer," he said. "We'll have to try again another time."

"Okay, sure," she said, returning his smile. She turned and headed out. *Maybe I should have kissed him good-bye,* she thought as she hurried over to her car outside. *No, I'll leave him with something to look forward to. Now that everything's been taken care of, it won't be long.*

47

Evan Plummer

I'm basically a very straightforward person, which is good, I think. I tell people exactly how I feel. No coded messages. But there is a downside. Since I don't drop hints, I'm not really good at translating them.

Then again, some things girls say seem really obvious to me. For example, "How do I look?" is always a way of saying, "Lavish me with praise right now."

And maybe I'm still a novice, but when a girl suddenly shifts the conversation to the topic of her ex-boyfriend—not just once, but <u>twice</u>—it's a pretty blatant clue that she's not over him. In fact, I'm guessing that's exactly what I'm supposed to pick up on.

So when Jade tells me, "Jeremy is just the greatest guy. He's going to be so good for Jessica," I figure it's really a polite way to say, "I can't come right out and tell you this, but I'm never getting over the amazing and wonderful Jeremy Aames."

Jade is cool, but I have to keep things casual. I can't get burned by another confused rebound girl.

CHAPTER

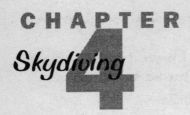

Skydiving

Ken's bed creaked as he sat up from the sprawled position he'd been in for the last hour. Pushing himself up against his headboard, he massaged his right shoulder and let out a long yawn.

After the frustrating practice, Coach Riley's lecture, and then his crazy encounter with Will in the locker room, all Ken could do was go home and collapse onto his bed. He'd tried to do the tunnel-imagery thing, but all he could see was Coach's angry face and Will charging at him like a bucking bull. Now his stress was reaching danger levels again.

"Son? Hey. Can I come in, buddy?"

Ken glanced up and saw his dad's face peering around the door to his room.

"Sure," Ken replied, rubbing his eyes.

Mr. Matthews pushed the door all the way open and walked in, sitting down at the foot of the bed. "How'd practice go?" he asked.

"Fine," Ken lied. No need to tell him about Will or all the mistakes Coach called him on. His dad would just ask a bunch of questions and give all sorts of unwanted advice.

"So . . ." Mr. Matthews glanced around Ken's room as if seeing it for the first time. "Psyching yourself up for the big game tomorrow?"

Ken lifted his shoulders in a slight shrug. "Guess I'm ready as I'll ever be."

His father frowned. "That's not good enough. You've got to *feel* it. You should be in here visualizing how you're going to stomp the Raiders."

"Right." Ken rolled his eyes to the ceiling. Obviously there was no stopping his dad from spouting the usual lines. He wished the guy would get a clue, though. Right now football was the last thing Ken wanted to discuss.

"Listen. I know what I'm talking about," his dad continued. "I've been watching Raider films at work this week, and that cornerback, Huxley, is someone to be reckoned with. He's shaken up a lot of offenses this year. You've got to be into this one hundred percent."

Ken sighed. There was a time when he considered his dad's job as a sportswriter for the *Tribune* a plus. All last season Ken was guaranteed prime coverage, and it was good to get the inside scoop on the other teams. But right now he was tired of people giving him pointers and spelling out worst-case scenarios. He just couldn't take any more stress.

Mr. Matthews rubbed his hands together. "I don't think I need to remind you how important this game is. Krubowski will be watching your every move. One mistake and you could lose a great scholarship." He leaned forward, elbows on his knees, and slowly blew out his breath. "I don't make that much at the paper, and tuition is ridiculous. This could be our big chance. We've got to be ready."

We? Ken wondered. Our *big chance?* He hated it when his dad talked as if he were going to be right there on the field beside him, guiding his every move. His own college-football career had been cut short by an injury, and he'd had to settle for writing about other people's successes in sports.

No pressure there, Ken thought sarcastically. *Play lousy tomorrow and I end up messing up my life* and *my dad's.*

He wished his father would just leave. Why didn't people realize they were only making it harder for him? He didn't even get this much advice from people after Olivia died.

It wasn't that Ken didn't love football. He loved being back on the team, having his dad back in his life, and being a big hero at school. For a while it had actually seemed like football was going to give him back everything he'd missed and thought he'd lost forever. Only now he wasn't so sure.

All he wanted now was to have someone—*anyone*—talk to him about something other than football. Someone who'd understand all the stress he was under and just *listen* to him instead of jumping in with their own opinion every six seconds. Someone like Maria . . .

He shook his head. How could he even think that? Maria had quit on him when things in his life were finally coming together. But still, he could tell himself that a million times—he had, in fact—and it didn't make him miss her less.

Suddenly the phone rang, jolting him out of his thoughts.

"You know," he said to his dad, "this could be Mr. Krubowski. He said he might call to answer some questions I had about Michigan. Could I take this in private?"

"Of course," his dad said, leaping to his feet. He reached over and clapped Ken on the back. "Tell him how stellar you're going to be tomorrow," he added before leaving the room.

Finally, Ken thought, taking a deep breath. He grabbed the phone. "Hello?" he said.

"Well, *that* took forever!" Ken's heart dropped as Melissa's high-pitched, angry voice cut through the receiver.

"Hey, Melissa." Ken couldn't even pretend to sound

happy to hear from her. "Sorry about that. I was just talking to my dad about—"

"Where *were* you today?"

"Huh?"

She sighed—loudly. "I said, *where were you?* Why didn't you meet me after practice?"

"Um . . ." Meet her after practice? He searched his memory for a reference but came up completely blank. "Did we have plans?" he asked.

"No," she said. "But it's sort of a given, don't you think? Being a couple, it should be understood that we'll hang out after our practices."

Ken rubbed his forehead with his free hand. Did she even realize she was piling more stress on him when he needed it the least? Did *anyone* realize the strain he was under? "Look, I'm sorry. I was beat and came home to rest. I wouldn't have been good company anyway." Hopefully she'd get the clue and back off.

"Well, think about how *I* was feeling," she responded. "I got out of practice early and hung out with my friends. They wanted to go to the mall, but I made them bring me by the school to look for you. Then we got there, and your car was gone! Think about how embarrassed I was! Stood up by my own boyfriend."

How could I stand you up if we didn't have plans? Ken wanted to yell, but he just didn't have the strength. After dealing with practice, his coach, Will, and his father, this whole relationship thing was draining any energy he had left. In fact, it was getting increasingly harder to deny that he just wasn't into it. At first Melissa had seemed so excited about his football career, and he felt like she knew exactly how to support him. Now it was becoming pretty clear that she was more concerned about what she could get out of it. Here it was, the night before a big game, and she didn't even care that he was totally burnt out.

"I said I was sorry, Melissa," Ken said. "Look, I have to go. That Michigan scout might call. Besides, I need to eat some dinner and crash so I'll be rested up for the game."

There was a pause on the other end. "Okay. You're right," Melissa said, sounding more subdued. "I know you don't want to make any mistakes tomorrow and mess up our chance to go to Michigan."

"Yeah," he muttered. He half listened as she crooned some sugary good-bye and then hung up. He just had to push her out of his mind. There wasn't any time to figure things out now, not with the play-offs starting.

Unfortunately, his dad and Coach Riley were right. He needed to focus on football and nothing else. His whole future depended on it.

*   *   *

Andy frantically jabbed the red button on his control pad and blew up the giant green carnivorous insect on his video screen. His neck ached with tension, his eyes were starting to blur, and his wrists felt like they might snap at any moment. But at least he wasn't thinking about anything remotely relationship oriented. Nothing like a violent video game to cure that.

"Ha! Get your final gasp of methane!" Andy shouted gleefully. "That's what you get when you deal with a first-warrior-class space commando!"

"Andy? Andy!" his mother called from the doorway.

Andy hit pause and turned around to face her. "That's Commander Neutron to you, madam," he said.

Mrs. Marsden rolled her eyes. "Sir, there's a signal coming through from Earth on line one. Didn't you hear the communication module ringing?"

Andy slouched down. "Sorry. Guess I had the volume too loud." He set down the video controls and turned off his television. "I'll patch myself through, Lieutenant. You're relieved of duty."

His mother rolled her eyes again but smiled before walking away.

Andy snatched up the cordless phone from his floor and hit the talk button. "Marsden's gossip central," he answered.

"Andy? It's Tia."

"Tee!" Andy stood up and walked around his room, stretching his stiff legs. "Hey, what's up?"

"You're in a good mood," Tia replied.

"You should be too. I just saved our galaxy from marauding mutant grasshoppers."

"So that's what that squishy-sounding noise was," Tia played along. "Hey, listen. I've got some news."

Andy frowned at his sallow complexion in the mirror. "Yeah? What is it?" he asked. "News" according to Tia could be anything from someone's new radical hairstyle to a blowout beach party to running into a Ryan Phillippe look-alike at the mall.

"I saw Rebecca today. We had coffee at House of Java."

"Really? Wow, how's she doing?" This really was news. He hadn't seen their friend Rebecca Collins since summer break. He'd always *meant* to keep in touch, but things just kept coming up, one drama after the other, since the new school year started.

"She's okay. She says Big Mesa has a good art scene. And you won't believe who she went to homecoming with."

"Who?"

"Lenny Boyden. Remember him? The guy who wet his pants during show-and-tell when we were in third grade?"

"Really? I hope he's got the bladder-control problem solved."

Tia laughed. "Oh, yeah. He's a big track star now. But it didn't work out. Rebecca said he was too macho. There's a turnaround, right?"

Andy sat down on the bed, chuckling. He suddenly felt incredibly nostalgic for their old El Carro crowd. It seemed strange to think about how changed everything—and every*one*—was now.

"Listen," Tia continued. "Rebecca told me some other interesting news."

"Yeah?" Andy shifted uncomfortably. He recognized Tia's tone. It was usually reserved for asking monumental favors.

"I told her about your, um—what you realized," Tia went on. "That's okay, isn't it?"

"Yeah, sure," Andy replied. That was one less person he'd have to tell. "How did she react?"

"Oh, fine. Surprised for, like, half a second, and then she acted like we were all idiots for not guessing it a long time ago. But she also had an idea."

"Tee? What kind of idea?" He did *not* like the sound of this.

"Well, she mentioned that her cousin Dale recently went through the same thing."

Andy waited for her to explain why she was bringing it up, but she was silent, obviously expecting some kind of response from him.

Does she think I'm keeping stats on the number of

gay teens in the area? he wondered. Still, it was hard to be annoyed. He knew Tia was just trying to connect with him on this. Maybe she was even trying to make up for being too distracted to help much during his long period of confusion.

"Um . . . good?" Andy eventually replied. "Good for him, I guess."

"Yeah. So anyway, we sort of thought it would be cool to have you guys meet."

Andy frowned and ran his fingers through his red curls. "Why? Do you want me to mentor the guy or something? Seems to me he already has this figured out."

"No!" Tia laughed. "I mean, you should meet as in *dating!*"

Total panic tore through Andy's gut. *"You're setting me up?"* he exclaimed. What was she *thinking?*

"Come on, Andy," Tia urged. "It's not like some stranger out of the personal ads. This is Becca's cousin. He sounds like a really cool guy. In fact, he sounds perfect for you."

"Really, Tee," Andy said, his voice cracking. "Don't do this."

"But why not?"

"Because . . . because I'm so not ready for this. I mean, just because I'm gay doesn't mean I want to go on a date with some guy."

Tia snorted. "Um, Andy? Isn't that exactly what it means?"

"No! I mean, yes. I mean . . ." Andy's brain felt like it was skydiving. Thoughts were hurtling through at breakneck speed, but he was unable to grasp any of them.

"It'll be fun," Tia went on. "Just one date. You've got to try this *sometime,* Andy. And I bet you guys end up hitting it off. Then you'll thank me."

Andy slumped down onto the floor with one hand grasping the phone and the other clutching a handful of hair. He couldn't believe Tia was doing this to him. Why was this such a big deal to her anyway? He hadn't heard her sound this excited in a long time.

He knew she was restless ever since Conner left. And Angel, the only other person in the world who could handle her, was away at college. Andy had few defenses against Hurricane Tia. When she got inspired to do something, nothing short of an imperialist government takeover could stop her, if that.

Still, he couldn't let her push him around. He knew she was only trying to help him in her own warped way, but he had to make her stop.

"I said no, Tee," he said, trying to make his voice low and forceful. Instead he ended up barking out the words a bit more loudly and abruptly than he'd meant to—sounding amazingly like Conner.

Tia didn't respond, but he could picture the hurt in her big, brown eyes.

"Look, I'm just not up for it, okay?" Andy said, going back to his normal squeaky tone. "Could you please call Rebecca and tell her thanks, but no thanks?"

"Yeah. Okay. Whatever," Tia replied.

Andy heard his mother calling him from downstairs.

"Hey, I've gotta go," Andy said quickly. "I think it's time for dinner. But I'll see you tomorrow, right?"

"Fine," Tia mumbled. "Bye."

Andy switched off the phone and took a deep breath. It was obvious he'd offended Tia. He'd probably pay for it tomorrow with her cold-shoulder treatment. Still, it had to be better than going out on a blind date.

A date. The word practically made him start to shake. *A date with a guy.*

Somehow he'd rather face ten-foot-high mutant grasshoppers.

Tia slammed down the phone and flopped back onto her bed. She couldn't believe Andy. After she went out of her way to set him up with his dream date, he turned her down flat. So much for trying to help.

Okay, so maybe she had been a little bit pushy. But so what? Andy never took action about anything in life. If she left it up to him, he'd probably start looking around for prospective dates around retirement age.

She'd really wanted him to be thrilled about this whole setup thing. She'd figured he'd be nervous but excited and full of lots of questions. Then she could have been his go-to girl for advice on what to wear, what to say, when to call, etc. Only now that he'd given the idea a big thumbs-down, she was left to stew over her own lousy love life.

"Tia?" Her mother knocked on the door as she entered the room, a move that always seriously irritated Tia.

"What?" Tia asked with a sigh.

Mrs. Ramirez held up an envelope. "You got a letter from Conner today. He must have sent it from—"

Before her mother could even finish her sentence, Tia leaped off her bed and grabbed the envelope, her bad mood completely dissolving.

"I can't believe it," she said, staring down at Conner's messy scrawl.

She hadn't heard from Conner since he checked himself into the clinic. For weeks she'd been dying to know how he was but wasn't sure if she should contact him. Conner was so closed off already, and rehab was probably only making it worse.

"I'll let you read that in private," Mrs. Ramirez said, smiling. Tia had to give her points for at least figuring out that much.

As soon as her mother shut the door, Tia ripped open the envelope. She gasped softly as she pulled out two whole pages of notebook paper. It was unbelievable. Tia couldn't remember ever seeing so many words from Conner—written *or* spoken. Even his song lyrics were sparse and to the point.

This is good, she thought. A warm feeling spread throughout her body as she quickly scanned the paragraphs. Conner would never go on like this if he were upset. So this had to be a good sign. She fell back onto the bed and began to read:

Tee,

Hey. Just wanted you to know that I'm still alive. The food here makes me miss the school cafeteria, and you don't get a lot of space. But really it's not all that bad. I've even met a couple of cool people.

The big news—I'm going to get out of here sometime next week. I guess they're impressed enough with my progress to send me home. I'll still continue my therapy on an outpatient basis, but at least the shock treatments and rubber room/straitjacket stuff is all over with. (Joking.)

Tia's heart swelled. He was coming back! He was better! Not only did he sound like his old self, he actually seemed a little more *together* than usual. He was even cracking jokes. This was good. This was very, very good.

She sucked in her breath and continued reading:

Anyway, I also want to tell you that I feel real bad about the way I treated you before. I was a monumental jerk, and I'm sorry. I know my drinking doesn't excuse the stuff I said and did, but for the record, I

64

didn't mean any of those things. I was tapped out, and I couldn't handle the stress. I thought the drinks would keep me from losing it, but it only tapped me out more. And it always seemed like you were there right when I was getting ready to snap.

When I came apart, you were at ground zero. I don't even entirely remember the things I said to you, but I'm sure they weren't pretty. You deserve better than that, and I hope I can somehow make it up to you. You were the only person who saw what was really wrong. And you dug right in trying to help me, even when I fought you on it. Thanks. Seems like too little to say, but thanks.

A lump rose up in Tia's throat. She'd never thought she'd get an actual written apology from Conner. Just getting the letter was more than she'd hoped for. He could have talked about his shoelaces for two pages, and she'd still have been thrilled to hear from him.

I hope you and Liz are still friends and that she's doing all right. I've been thinking a lot about how I screwed that up. I know, I know. Typical Conner. It was only a matter of time. But this was different.

I'm sure she's still too freaked out by everything that happened to even think about me anymore, and I don't blame her. She was good for me. But I'm not sure I was ever good for her.

Tia pressed the letter to her chest and frowned up at the ceiling. Conner obviously missed Elizabeth. In fact, being away seemed to have made his feelings for her even stronger.

Of course, idiot. He loves her, Tia thought, feeling a slight twinge.

It bugged her to realize Conner could still tug at her heart that way. But if there was one thing she'd learned in the past few weeks, it was that she and Conner were only destined to be friends—nothing more. They didn't have that thing he and Elizabeth did. That special we-belong-together thing.

Tia rolled over and burrowed her face into her pillow. She used to feel that way about Angel—that they were meant for each other. And now that it was over, she wasn't sure what she missed most—Angel or that feeling of living her destiny. Would she ever find anyone else she truly belonged with? Or was she doomed to spend all of her free evenings with Andy and the girls?

Andy! Tia sat up abruptly. What was it Conner had said? That he appreciated how she'd hung in there and helped him even when he didn't want her to?

Tia reached for her phone and quickly dialed Rebecca's number.

"Hello?"

"Hey, Becca? It's Tee. Listen, we're all clear with the setup for Andy."

"Really?" Rebecca said. "So he was into the idea?"

"Well," Tia began. She paused, licking her lips. "He's not quite ready for a private date, so we're doing a group thing instead. Why don't you come to the Sweet Valley play-off game tomorrow night and bring Dale?"

There was a brief silence. "He said no, didn't he?"

Tia sighed. "Sort of," she replied. "But he's just scared. That's why I think it'll be better this way with everyone around. You'll be there, and I'm sure some of our other friends will show up. I'll have to cheer during the game, but we can hang out together afterward."

"I don't know, Tee," Rebecca said. "If he's not up for this, maybe we shouldn't force him."

"We're not forcing him," Tia protested. "It's not even a date. It's a bunch of us hanging out. Dale will just happen to show up with you. Andy can't say no to that, right?"

"I guess not," Rebecca replied. She didn't sound too convinced. "But I'm only doing this because I want to see you guys."

"I know," Tia replied. "So I'll see you at the game!"

And just like Conner, Andy would thank her later.

Will lay back on his bed, propping his head and knee with pillows. Then he grabbed the remote control off his nightstand and turned on the TV. He had already finished his homework and done his strengthening exercises. Now he had nothing better to do than veg out. It was amazing how much free time he had now that he had no life.

He flipped through the channels, catching one-second bits of news reports and sitcom reruns. Finally something caught his eye—a shot of a football player running in slow motion. Will stared transfixed at the guy's smooth motion as he easily dodged his opponents. One hand tightly embraced the football against his chest, the other stretched out in front of him, hand flexed upward, to ward off tackles. As the man moved past the camera, Will focused in on how his well-toned arm and leg muscles pushed his limbs forward in an effortless glide.

That used to be me. He remembered the thrill of running back to launch the perfect pass or racing for the first down on a quarterback sneak. On the field he had always been completely focused on the game, but at times he'd take a moment and enjoy the feel of it all. The strength and power of his body. The precision of his throws.

He *used* to play sports. Now he watched them on TV while lying in his bed like an invalid. Will could almost feel his muscles going soft.

"Forget this," he said, lifting the remote toward the set.

He was just about to change the channel when two giant defenders slammed into the slo-mo superstar from each side, sandwiching him in a fierce tackle.

"*Ouch!*" came an unseen announcer's voice. "Now here's another play. Watch this tackle on Michael Irvin of the Dallas Cowboys."

Again Will watched a slow-motion shot of Irvin jumping up to catch the football. Just as he came down onto his feet, an opposing player soared like a missile from the left side of the screen and crashed into him, stripping him of the ball.

This must be one of those world's-most-dangerous-tackles type of shows, Will thought. *Just my luck.*

He used to hate stuff like this. These programs always made football look like some crazed circus instead of the tough sport that it was. But now that he knew exactly what those players had felt, he was mesmerized by the morbid images on the screen.

"And here's the play that ended the football career of Joe Theisman of the Washington Redskins," the announcer called cheerily, as if presenting a game-show prize. "*Boom! Yee-ouch!*" he added dramatically as Lawrence Taylor from the New York Giants sacked Theisman from behind, shattering Theisman's leg.

Career-ending play. The words echoed through Will's mind, and the images in front of him blurred. Just one play, one lousy little play, and everything changed.

Will's throat constricted, and his breath came out in ragged bursts. Meanwhile the jaunty announcer cried out again as a poor running back was sent somersaulting onto the turf. Will felt like he was going to lose his mind. He glanced wildly around the room, trying to focus on something, anything, that would free him from this feeling. Eventually his eyes rested on a framed photo on his nightstand. It was a picture of him and Melissa at their junior prom. Will couldn't believe the smiling guy in the black suit could be him. And Liss . . . she looked incredible, her face all lit up with a wide smile. Only the longer he looked at it, the more she seemed to be sneering at him.

Will took a deep breath and sat back against his pillows. At least he wasn't feeling pathetic anymore. Now he just felt angry—a red-hot rage aimed right at Ken Matthews.

Ken was the reason he was turning into a couch potato. Ken had stepped right into Will's life as if it were a stopped subway car, kicking Will onto the tracks. Now Ken got a free ride to glory while Will got flattened to a pulp, over and over and over.

Again the voice-over announcer's cheerful tone

cut through Will's thoughts. "How about this for a quarterback sack?" he sang out. "Absolutely no protection here!"

Will glanced over at the screen and saw the QB get thrown onto his head after his two offensive tackles each missed their blocks.

At least that *didn't happen to me,* Will told himself. No matter what, he could always count on Matt and Josh to do their jobs. Only now it was Ken they were out there protecting, not him. And that guy wasn't worthy of their loyalty. In fact, he probably just took it all for granted.

Will couldn't help but wish that instead of two stellar tackles like Matt and Josh, Ken had those lame-os from the TV play instead—two dorks who couldn't block a doorway. Maybe then Ken would find out what it felt like to get taken down hard.

He smiled at the mental image of Ken collapsing under an avalanche of giant defenders. *Now, that would be a play worth prime time,* he thought, clicking the off button on his TV remote. *Too bad it won't ever happen.*

Senior Poll Category #9
Most Radical

Jessica Wakefield: Evan Plummer.

Elizabeth Wakefield: Evan Plummer.

melissa fox: Josh Radinsky. He made us all walk out of our history class last year when the teacher assigned homework over prom weekend.

Will Simmons: Josh Radinsky. That history-class walkout was awesome.

Maria Slater: Evan Plummer. He's the only one who sees football for the mindless waste of time it really is.

TIA RAMIREZ: CONNER MCDERMOTT. YES, CONNER. RADICAL <u>CAN</u> MEAN UNUSUAL, TOO, RIGHT?

Jade Wu: Evan Plummer. Duh.

Evan Plummer: Define <u>radical</u>.

Andy Marsden: Radical? Who's radical? Certainly not me. Nothing at all radical about me. Just an average guy with an average lifestyle who certainly doesn't need any press coverage right now. But hey, thanks for asking.

CHAPTER 5

The Freaking Can Begin

The second the bell rang after first period on Friday morning, crowds of students spilled into the corridor. As everyone rushed to get to their next classes, Jade stood rooted in the middle of the hall, causing the tide to split around her. She checked to make certain the beaded strands in her hair hadn't come loose, straightened her shoulders, and waited for the burst of confidence she needed for her next move.

This was the time she usually ran into Evan, and she couldn't waste the opportunity. All last night at work she'd mentally rehearsed their next encounter. Now that she'd made it clear that she was over Jeremy and ready to move on, Evan would have to be more receptive to her flirting. After all the hints she'd dropped, she was anxious to get things started. In fact, she'd even made up her mind that *she'd* make the first move. Knowing Evan, he'd probably love that.

She rounded the corner of the hall where his locker was and immediately spotted him. He was leaning against the trophy case, deep in conversation with a couple of guys from the swim team. His long, blunt-cut hair bounced around his square jaw as he talked, and his muscular arms sliced at the air around him. He was so intense and extreme about everything. She could only imagine what that intensity would be like in a kiss. . . .

"You can't buy that brand, Ronnie," she overheard him saying as she got closer. "Those shoes are cranked out in Asian sweatshops by underpaid slaves. You pay ninety bucks, and they get four cents an hour!"

"Hey, Greenpeace boy. Take a break already!" Jade teased, joining the group. Evan's head jerked in her direction. Instantly the tension drained from his face, replaced by a wide grin.

"Hey," he said. "What's up?"

Jade shrugged. "Um, can I talk to you for a sec? I have a quick question."

"Sure." Evan pushed himself off the trophy case and took a step toward her. "Catch you later," he told his friends. They nodded, then started off down the hallway together.

"So, what's up?" Evan asked, stuffing his hands into the pockets of his woven parka.

Jade inched up closer to him, hoping he'd catch a whiff of her new musky perfume. "Well, I was thinking," she began, tilting her head. "I know you don't have much to do with football unless you're protesting it as society's way of condoning violence, right?"

Evan smiled. "Usually, yeah," he agreed. "Let's just say I'm not a regular fan at the games."

"Well, what if you showed up tonight to support the *cheerleaders*—one in particular—instead of the football players?" Jade asked. "*We* aren't violent. At least—not normally," she joked.

He smiled and rubbed his chin as if deep in thought. "I suppose that's only a minor violation of my code," he said. "One I'd be willing to break."

"Great." Jade tried to suppress her silly grin. This had been too easy! "And then we can hang out afterward," she added softly, moving yet another inch into his airspace.

Evan nodded. "Sounds cool," he said. "In fact, why don't we get a group together? I'll call up some of my El Carro buddies at Big Mesa. You'll get along great with them."

It no longer took any effort to keep from smiling. He wanted to invite his *friends?* What kind of a date was that?

The warning bell for the next period rang, and students all around them picked up their speed. Evan hoisted his backpack onto his shoulder. "I'd better go," he said. "If I'm late to marine biology one more time, they'll dissect *me* during lab. But I'll see you later tonight, okay?"

"Yeah. Sure," Jade replied. But Evan was already jogging down the hallway.

Okay, where exactly did I go wrong? Hadn't she been totally in-your-face obvious yesterday?

As students whizzed past her, Jade trudged toward her own second-period class. "Forget it," she mumbled. It was time to stop being so subtle. It certainly wasn't working. Besides, subtlety wasn't really her style anyway.

Tonight at the game she'd find a way to make things clear. She didn't know how yet, but it would be big.

Finish paper for French class? Check. *Fill out final paperwork for Senate scholarship?* Check. *Learn lines for theater?* Almost there.

Maria frowned down at her to-do list as she zoomed through the hallway on her way to third period. It was insane. Every time she checked something off, it seemed like two more things had to be added. Then again, she was good at juggling tasks. She actually felt more restless and stressed when she didn't have anything to do.

Besides, right now she not only liked being busy, she *needed* to be busy. She welcomed anything that would take her mind off Ken Matthews and Melissa Fox. Otherwise any free second of the day would be spent feeling sorry for herself.

It wasn't like she hadn't survived breakups before—even messy ones. But for some reason, she couldn't stop hurting whenever she saw Ken, especially when he was with his new *love*—Melissa. Maria had tried all her usual remedies. She'd eaten loads of Ben & Jerry's ice cream. She'd bad-mouthed the male gender with Tia and Elizabeth (Jessica had tried to join in, but the girl was still swooning over Jeremy way too much to be convincing). And she'd even sunk into total dorkdom and ritually burned a photo of the two of them together. Unfortunately, nothing had worked.

Let's see . . . turn in advertising money to Oracle *office?* Maria's finger continued down her list of things to do. *Finish writing sports cutlines for Walt while he's out with mono?*

Maria was just about to flip a page in her date book when she collided with something. She raised her head and saw a small freshman guy, who instantly crouched down on his knees to begin gathering the papers and books scattered around him.

"Why don't you look where you're going?" he mumbled.

Maria frowned. "Sorry," she said. She stooped to

recover a couple of folders that had flown in her direction.

He grabbed them out of her hands, still scowling. "I don't need any help," he snapped.

"Ookay," she said. Clearly this guy had a serious attitude problem. Maria stood back up, straightening her skirt.

Just as she started to head back down the hall, a familiar figure caught her eye, and she froze.

Ken. Walking right toward her. Maria's chest tightened, as if it were suddenly caving inward. Then slowly she focused in on the expression on his face. Something was really wrong.

She'd seen Ken look out of it before. At the beginning of the year he was so messed up over Olivia's death, he basically walked around like a zombie for several weeks. This was nothing like that, but it wasn't good. His face was pale and cramped up with tension, and as he moved, Maria noticed how hunched and rigid looking his shoulders were. Even his eyes had visible dark circles under them, and they were staring blankly into the distance—which was probably the only reason he hadn't seen Maria yet.

It must be that stupid play-off game, Maria realized. She'd heard a few kids in history earlier make some comments to Ken about how they knew he'd pull in a victory for them tonight. Even then he'd looked kind of stressed. The entire school was in a state of near hysteria over the fact that Sweet Valley made the play-offs. It was all anyone could talk about.

Maybe I should say something to him, Maria thought. *That wouldn't be any big deal, would it?*

She knew she was supposed to be angry at him. And she was—definitely. But still, even if he'd been a jerk to her, the guy didn't deserve to self-destruct. Right?

Maria bit her lip, quickly forcing herself to start moving toward him. Then, before she could talk herself out of it, she sucked in her breath and stepped right in front of his path. His head raised up, and his eyes focused right on her. For a split second their gazes locked, and Maria could feel a warm, tingling sensation spread throughout her body.

They were only a few feet away from each other. Maria steadied herself, trying to think what to say that would calm him down.

"Ken! There you are!"

At the sound of the shrill voice Maria's body stiffened. She didn't even have to turn around to know Melissa was behind her. Sure enough, in seconds Melissa breezed past her and up to Ken. She immediately hooked herself onto the left side of his body, draping her arm on his shoulder and murmuring something into his ear.

Maria turned and veered around the happy couple, striding away as quickly as she could. What was she thinking? The guy basically cut her out of his life. And now just because he looked a little stressed, she suddenly felt the need to cheer him up?

No. He was Melissa's problem now, not hers. She had too much on her mind as it was without taking on the problems of an ex-boyfriend. From now on she would just focus on her to-do list and not let anything—or anyone—distract her.

"I'm so glad we ran into each other," Melissa practically purred into Ken's ear. "I have so much to tell you." She was standing so close to him that she had to throw her head way back to meet his gaze. Still, it amazed him how her tiny grip was managing to drag him down the hallway.

"Really?" Ken replied, trying to sound interested while he searched for Maria out of the corner of his eye. But there was no sign of her short, dark curls anywhere.

Great. He'd been almost certain she was about to say something to him, before Melissa showed up and sent her flying off down the hall. Even that one second of looking into her eyes had made his breath catch.

"Ken? Ken!" Melissa let go of his arm and gave his shoulders a rough shake.

"What?" he asked, staring down into her narrowed, ice blue eyes.

"You haven't heard a word I said, have you?"

Ken hesitated. Should he tell the truth here? Either way it seemed like he'd be in for it. "I'm sorry," he said. He reached up to rub his eyes. "I'm just out of it. What were you saying?"

But Melissa only glared harder. "You'd better not zone out like that during the game," she warned. "Too much is riding on this. If we want to have guaranteed spots at Michigan, then you can't blow this. You know Hank Krubowski is going to be there."

Ken's stomach clenched. Why'd she have to bring that up? This was *not* what he needed right now.

"Don't start, okay?" he said, gritting his teeth. He shut his eyes and massaged the back of his neck. "You're getting all worked up about nothing."

"Nothing?" Melissa's voice hissed like acid on metal. "Our entire future is at stake, and you call it *nothing*? This is not the time to space out, Ken. I'm depending on you."

"Well, maybe you shouldn't depend on me!" he barked. By now most of the students had already entered their classrooms, and his voice echoed through a nearly empty hallway. "Maybe you and everyone else shouldn't pile their dreams on my shoulders. Because I don't need them. I'm not even sure I *want* the future of a college football star. In fact, I'm not even sure I want your future tied up with my future! All I want is for all this stress to be over with!"

Melissa leaned against the wall and watched him with a cold, unwavering stare. "Feel better now?" she challenged. She paused, folding her arms across her chest. "Good," she continued when he didn't respond. "Well, then, back to what I was saying. After the game tonight we should meet on the field and maybe even try to sneak up close to Mr. Krubowski. Then we can—"

"Wait a minute. Whoa." Ken shook his head. For the first time in weeks he knew what he needed to do. He needed to get out.

Melissa raised her eyebrows. "Yes?" she prompted.

Ken took a quick breath and made himself meet her steely gaze. It seemed like lately she was always looking at him that way. He couldn't even believe that when they'd first gotten together, he'd only seen a delicate, fragile quality behind Melissa's eyes. It was that quality he'd connected with. But now he wondered if he'd been seeing the real Melissa or just a version of her she'd wanted him to see.

"Look, this isn't working out," he said. "I'm sorry

to do it here, like this, but I think we need to cool things between us for a while. Maybe even for good."

A flash of hurt crossed Melissa's face, immediately replaced by a blank, hard expression. "Oh. I see," she said flatly. Then, with a flounce of brown hair, she turned and walked away.

Ken watched as she disappeared down the corridor. *That was easy,* he thought, feeling just the slightest bit disquieted.

He hadn't expected to break up with her—it just sort of came out on its own. But maybe that was a good thing. If he had taken the time to think, he probably wouldn't have gone through with it.

The final bell rang, and Ken turned to head for class. Cutting things off with Melissa had definitely been the right thing to do. And it felt good to finally be honest with *someone* about how he felt.

He just hoped everything could go that smoothly at the game tonight.

I can't believe that just happened, Melissa thought as she walked slowly down the hallway, struggling to remain in control. *I can't believe Ken just dumped me.*

The worst part was how he'd just thrown this at her with no warning. It wasn't a huge surprise to her that he wasn't happy. She wasn't exactly thrilled about the way things were going either. The guy wasn't at all tuned in to her, and he didn't have a clue how to be romantic. But still, she could have worked with him on that. She had the rest of the year and college to show him how she needed to be treated. Even Will had required some work when they started going out.

Will! Melissa gripped her books tighter as it hit her that Will was in her next class. She had to get it together. No way was she going to lose it in front of him.

Melissa plastered a big smile on her face as she entered the classroom, relieved to see the back of her teacher's head as he scrawled away on the blackboard. She slid into her usual seat without having to answer for being late.

"What happened? Why were you late?" Lila Fowler whispered, leaning across the aisle between their chairs.

Melissa could see Will's head pivot slightly in her direction. He was definitely listening.

"Oh, you know," she said to Lila, letting her voice take on a teasing note. "Ken and I got a little . . . carried away in the hall."

"Got it," Lila replied with a smile. "Spare me the details." She shifted back in her seat, and Melissa cast another glance in Will's direction. His lips were pulled into a tight frown. Score one. Now she just had to keep it up for the rest of class.

It wasn't easy, but somehow she did manage to maintain the phony smile for an entire forty-five minutes. Finally, after what felt like forever, the bell rang. Melissa jumped out of her seat and headed for the door. But just as she started down the aisle, Will's crutch came down in front of her, blocking her path.

"Wait," he said.

No, not now, she thought. Will was the only person who'd ever been able to see through her, and she wasn't sure she could keep up this act much longer. But she raised her eyes to meet his, willing herself not to cave. "What is it, Will?" she asked.

Will glanced around them, waiting for the other students to get out of earshot. Then he narrowed his eyes at her. "You know, one of these days you're going to see you made the wrong choice."

Melissa felt a quick stab of pain. There was no way he could realize that she *already* knew that. "Whatever, Will," she said, rolling her eyes. "Just let me go."

"I mean it," he insisted. "You're gonna realize Matthews isn't as hot as he thinks. In fact, I bet you find that out soon. *Real* soon."

Melissa frowned. What exactly did Will mean by that? Then again, why should she even care? Ken had treated her like dirt. He deserved whatever Will had planned for him.

"I doubt that will ever happen," Melissa lied. "But

you keep on fooling yourself if you want to." Before he could react, she cut between two desks and stalked up the next aisle.

As soon as she was out of the classroom, she started to race down the hallway, her breath coming out in short gasps. There was no holding it back—she needed privacy, now. She made it to the girls' bathroom, relieved to find it empty. Then, leaning back against the cold wall, she finally let herself feel the emotions she'd been holding back for nearly an hour.

Will's right, she thought, squeezing her eyes shut. She had been fooling herself. She'd never really felt anything for Ken. And obviously it was the same for him if he could break things off so easily. Will was the one she wanted—he'd always been, and he probably always would be.

But so what? There was no way she was crawling back to him—not after everything he'd put her through and the cruel things he'd said to her.

Suddenly the door swung open, and Melissa straightened. She blinked, clearing her eyes.

I've got to get a grip, she told herself. *I can't freak out. Not now. And definitely not here.* First she had to get through the rest of the day and the football game. Then the freaking could begin.

Jade Wu

A Few Not-So-Subtle Ways to Tell Evan How I Feel

1. Use Coach Laufeld's megaphone.
2. Hire a skywriter.
3. Put a neon sign on the field.
4. Storm the press box at the game and use the PA system.
5. Tattoo the words onto my body.

All of the above—just in case.

CHAPTER

A Plan

Andy slammed his locker door shut and spun around, smacking right into a sophomore couple making out in back of him.

"Um . . . sorry," he mumbled. He ducked his head and stepped around them, rounding the corner into the main hallway.

With his eyes still averted, he didn't see another happy twosome embracing until he'd bumped right into them too.

"Hey!" the blond girl exclaimed, lifting her head off her boyfriend's chest long enough to scowl at Andy.

"Oops. Excuse me," Andy said, his face sizzling.

He turned and blended into the river of students heading down the hallway.

As he walked, he noticed several other pairs of students snuggling in corners and behind doorways. Had they always been around? Or was today Smooch-Your-Locker-Neighbor Day or something? Maybe the cafeteria served up fried-fat-laden aphrodisiacs for breakfast this morning.

Do I have to be constantly *reminded?* Andy wondered. What was with these people anyway? There was much more to life than finding a willing grope partner. There was stuff like . . . NASCAR racing. And Starbucks. And . . .

Who was he fooling? Just because he didn't want to think about dating didn't mean the rest of the world didn't. In fact, he was pretty sure everyone else thought about it 24/7. Which meant he was the only weirdo loser on the planet.

"Oh, come on," he muttered under his breath as a hand-holding couple walking in front of him made him slow to a snail's pace. Where were those dried-up, nosy teachers when you needed them? There had to be one nearby who could lecture all these people against public displays of affection.

Maybe that was *his* destiny. Maybe he'd never get his act together and would end up doomed to harass anyone who actually had a social life. Andy shook his head as he imagined himself as a skinny old man, shaking his cane at every lovey-dovey couple that crossed his path.

It wasn't as if he didn't *want* to be happy with someone. He just needed to totally redefine everything he'd ever thought on the topic. Looking for a date was hard enough as a straight guy, but being gay added a whole new scary dimension to the situation.

How was he even supposed to let a guy know he was interested? He remembered this one annoying guy at a Big Mesa party who'd claimed to be a long-lost cousin of Leonardo DiCaprio's. Somehow the guy managed to insert that fact into every single conversation he got into. It drove everyone crazy. But Andy didn't have to do that with being gay, did he? Maybe he could introduce himself by saying, "Hi, I'm Andy, and I'm gay." Or officially change his name to Andy Gay Marsden. Or he could just use it as a greeting. Whenever someone said, "Hi," he could respond, "Gay!"

Or maybe I should just let Tia fix me up, he thought. He sighed and shifted his backpack higher onto his shoulder. *What am I so scared of anyway?*

All Tia wanted was to see him happy. She was right—irritatingly right—when she said he was going to have to go on a date eventually. And if she set him up with that Dale guy, it would save him the trouble—and possibly the embarrassment—of meeting someone on his own. At least he knew for sure the guy was gay. And he was Rebecca's cousin, so the odds were good that he'd be cool.

Besides, even if things didn't work out, it would be nice just to know he wasn't the only guy on the planet going through this stuff.

*   *   *

Tia walked into the cafeteria on full alert, searching for Elizabeth. She spotted her pretty quickly, sitting at a corner table and digging halfheartedly through her soggy salad. Even better—she was alone. No Andy in sight.

"Hey, just the girl I'm looking for," Tia said as she plunked down in the chair opposite Elizabeth. She dusted some crumbs off the table and propped her elbows on the surface. "Listen, I need your help with something."

Elizabeth frowned. "Sounds serious. What's up?"

Tia checked the vicinity for Andy. Still no sign of him. "It's about Andy," she confessed, leaning across the table. "I'm going to set him up on a date with this friend of mine's cousin."

"Um, does Andy know about this?" Elizabeth asked.

"Of course," Tia replied. That wasn't a total lie— she *had* told him about the date.

"So then what do you need me for?" Elizabeth asked, shaking a few strands of blond hair out of her face.

Tia paused, chewing on her lip. "Okay, maybe he wasn't too excited about the idea," she admitted. "But I think I can make it work. I asked my friend Rebecca to show up with her cousin at the game tonight. I figured then you and some of our other friends can come with Andy, and it'll feel like a big group thing instead of a blind-date thing." She put on her best pleading expression.

"I don't know. . . ." Elizabeth trailed her fork through her salad. "I'm not even sure I want to go to the game. And Andy will totally see through this. Besides, how do you know he'll hit it off with this guy anyway?"

"I just do," Tia said. How could she explain her gut instinct to someone who highlighted all of her lecture notes before a major test? "Look, I just want to help Andy out. I mean, we're there for him and all, but I thought it would be good if he could meet someone dealing with the same stuff."

Elizabeth shrugged. "I guess you're right," she said. She paused, her eyes clouding over. "Being lonely does suck," she added.

Tia nodded. "So . . . you'll help me?"

Elizabeth sighed. "Yeah, sure. What do you want me to do?"

"Okay, all I need is for you to talk Andy into meeting you at the game," Tia said. "He has to sit with someone besides me since I'll be cheering."

"All right. I'll try. Maybe I can get Maria and Megan to come too. Then it will really feel like a group thing."

Tia grinned. "This is so great! He's going to be thanking us later, I promise."

"Who's going to thank you for what later?"

Tia whirled around and saw Andy standing behind her, holding one of the cafeteria's ugly orange trays.

"Um, Angel is going to thank Liz and me for . . . the cookies we're going to send him." It was weak, especially since she'd barely heard from Angel lately and Andy knew it. But it was the best she could do.

Andy rolled his eyes. "Whatever you say," he said. He dropped his tray down on the table and sat down next to Elizabeth. "Hey, listen, Tee," he said. "I've been thinking about it, and, well, maybe I do want to meet Rebecca's cousin."

Tia practically choked on the fry she'd just put in her mouth. "Really?" she said. She exchanged an amused glance with Elizabeth. "That's great! What changed your mind?"

Andy shrugged. "I don't know. I guess I realized you were right, and why not? But I'm still not sure how this would all work."

"Well . . ." Tia shot another glance at Elizabeth. "You know, Liz said she was going to the game tonight with a couple of friends. Maybe you could meet up with them and then we could get Rebecca and Dale to come. Then it would be a low-pressure kind of thing, right?"

Andy's eyes darted back and forth between them.

"That idea sure came fast," he said. "Almost as if *some-one* had it planned all along. Don't you think so, Liz?"

Elizabeth shrugged, keeping her gaze focused on her plate. Clearly she hadn't inherited the same acting ability her twin had.

"You never called Rebecca to cancel the whole thing, did you?" Andy asked.

"I did *call* Rebecca," Tia said. "But really, Andy, it doesn't matter. You're going to have the best time."

"Yeah, well, I hope so," he said, tapping his fingertips on the table.

"Don't worry, Andy," Elizabeth chimed in. "I'll be there. And I'm pretty sure I can convince Maria to come along too. And Megan."

"Thanks, Liz," Andy said. "I really appreciate it."

"Hey, no problem. It's not like my own love life is too active right now," she replied, hunching her shoulders slightly as she went back to her salad.

Suddenly Tia remembered Conner's letter. "Hey, Liz? I meant to tell you, I got a letter from Conner yesterday. He sounds much better. In fact, he said he's coming home next week!"

"Next week?" Elizabeth dropped her fork back down, looking up at Tia with a strange expression. "That's . . . great."

"What's wrong?" Tia asked. "I thought you'd be psyched."

"I am," Elizabeth said, sounding exactly the opposite. "I mean, I'm glad he's doing so much better."

"But?" Andy prompted. "You're glad he's better, *but* . . ."

"But nothing," she said. "I'm happy he's better. *Period*. End of story." She flashed them a wide, fake grin and went back to cutting up her tomato.

Yet another example of Elizabeth's lack of acting skills, Tia thought.

"Liz?" Tia began, trying to catch her gaze. "You know, it's okay if you're nervous about seeing Conner again."

Elizabeth let out a short, awkward laugh. "What? No, I'm fine. Anyway, it shouldn't matter how I feel. He and I broke up, remember? And the fact that he wrote you instead of me only proves that he meant it when he said he wanted me out of his life. So let's just drop it, okay?"

Tia sucked in her breath. That was it, wasn't it? *Great job, moron,* she scolded herself. *Blab about the letter and make her feel left out.* She had to explain that it wasn't what Elizabeth was thinking.

"No, Liz, you don't understand," she argued. "The whole second half of his letter was about you. It's so obvious that he's totally not over you at all."

A flicker of hope came into Elizabeth's eyes, and Tia knew she had it right. Just because they'd broken up didn't mean things were over. Not by a long shot.

"Did—Did he say that?" Elizabeth asked softly.

Tia cringed. "Um, not exactly. But I could tell he *meant* it. Come on, Liz, I know him better than anybody." She stopped, realizing that she was not doing this well. "I mean, I've known him *longer* than anybody."

"Look, Tia. It's all right," Elizabeth said, giving her a small smile. "You don't have to convince me of anything. I said I was fine, and I meant it. I've moved on, and so has he." She stood and picked up her tray. "But actually, I've got to do some work in the *Oracle* office. Deadlines, you know. So I'll see you guys later, at the game, okay?"

"Yeah, okay," Tia said. She slumped down in her seat as Elizabeth hurried across the cafeteria. "The worst part is that I was trying to cheer her up," she told Andy.

Will sat stiffly in the cafeteria chair, his leg propped on the seat beside him. He had thought lunch would never come today. He'd been so anxious for the chance to just sit alone and think without the constant noise of teachers and students yammering.

Of course, he wasn't exactly alone. Josh and Matt were sitting across from him. But they obviously got the idea that Will wasn't in a social mood. While they talked and flirted with some girls at the table next to theirs, Will took his frustration out on a basket of french fries.

Why did I say that crazy stuff to Melissa? he wondered as he picked up a limp fry and twisted it between his hands. He hadn't meant to freak out on her. In fact, he had tried as hard as he could to keep himself together during class. But there was just something about seeing her so happy while his own life lay in pieces that set him off.

Will grabbed another fry, broke it in two, and clenched each half between his fingers. He knew he had to cool off before he completely snapped, but he wasn't sure how. The thing was, he couldn't do much of anything. He had never ever felt this powerless before, and it scared him. If only he could take some sort of action, maybe then he'd feel better.

"You know, on that thirty-two-X counterreverse we've got to make sure we're sealing off the defensive end," Will heard Josh telling Matt.

"I'll take care of that defensive end," Matt replied. "You just make sure you pull and get out there in front of that receiver."

Football. Will flinched. He was the one who'd started the tradition of using lunch to get in game mode. Only now he was out of the loop.

Will squashed another fry as he thought about

Ken. Was *he* focusing on the game at all right now? Probably not. He was probably off making out with Melissa, surrounded by admirers, while his offense did all the mental prep.

"It's just not fair," Will muttered.

"What's not fair?" Josh asked, turning to face him.

Will shifted, realizing he'd said his last thought out loud. "It's Matthews," he admitted. "I just hate how that guy gets away with everything. He steals my spot on the team *and* Melissa, and everyone treats him like he's some hero. Meanwhile you guys are the ones sitting here planning the plays for tonight."

"Yeah, you're right," Matt said. "You did all the hard work getting us to the play-offs, and he gets all the glory."

Josh narrowed his eyes. "I can't stand that guy," he said. "He's not even a decent QB, right, Matt?"

"He sucks," came Matt's muffled reply as he chewed a handful of onion rings.

Will sighed. It was cool of his friends to try to make him feel better by cutting on Ken, but he couldn't completely buy into it. Ken wasn't a bad quarterback. Will was better, but Ken was still okay. Will just wished he could knock the attitude out of the guy somehow.

If only something really awful could happen to

Ken—something so incredibly humiliating, he'd never want to show his face in public again. And if only Will could have a ringside seat when it happened. He'd even bring a camcorder and capture it on tape. Then whenever he felt like it, he could watch it over and over again in slow motion—just like the plays on that lousy football show.

Will sat up straighter as something clicked into place in his mind. Remembering the gruesome TV tackles, he superimposed Ken's face on the shot of the quarterback getting sacked when his lame teammates left him exposed. Suddenly he knew exactly how he could get his revenge.

"Wait, I know what we can do," he said, leaning forward with excitement. "I know how we can bring Mr. Superstar down a few notches."

Josh's eyebrows raised. "How?" he asked.

Will paused, realizing just how much he was asking of his friends. But they'd offered to help—however they could.

"You guys are his protection, right? So . . . just *unprotect* him during a key play. Let him deal with a bad tackle, get his face rubbed in it in front of everyone. He'll feel like such an idiot!"

Matt and Josh stared back at him with equally shocked expressions.

"You want us to purposely screw up?" Josh asked,

his eyes wide. "Are you insane? Coach'll kick our butts!"

"And it could cost us the game," Matt pointed out.

Will shook his head. "I'm only talking about one play. Both of you could miss your blocks and let Ken doll get creamed. You could make it look like you didn't do it on purpose. Just fall backward when the defenders rush you, and everyone will think they overpowered you."

"And everyone will think we're lame," Josh mumbled.

"Just one lousy play!" Will almost yelled. He glanced around, then lowered his voice to a whisper. "Look, you want the guy to get what he deserves, right? Well, this is the best way. He'll get shoved on his butt in front of the whole school *and* the Michigan scout."

Josh's jaw twitched. Then he let out a deep breath. "You forget that we're going to have scouts checking *us* out too," he pointed out. "I mean, sure, it'd be cool to see Matthews get clobbered, but it's not worth it if we end up looking like screwups."

"Yeah. And it sort of goes against the all-for-one team thing, you know?" Matt added, shrugging apologetically at Will.

Will clenched his hands into fists, trying to stay calm. Now that he had this image in his head, he couldn't shake it. He had to find a way to make it happen.

"Wait," he said, "what if instead of acting like their defense took you down, you just mess up on the snap and blame it on Ken? Stay in your stance for an extra count. By the time he sets up to pass, the defensive ends will be in the backfield with him and"—Will smashed his right fist into his left hand—"Ken won't know what hit him. Then you can swear to Coach that *he* was the one who got the count wrong."

"What if we lose because of this?" Josh asked. "Or what if Ken gets really hurt?"

The thought of Ken getting injured didn't bother Will much, but he knew the chances were slim anyway. Tackles like the one that had taken out his knee weren't standard in high-school ball. No, he'd just gotten *lucky*.

"That won't happen," he assured Josh. "Besides, even if the guy has to sit out a play or two to get his balance back, Larry Reimer's the third stringer. Larry's good enough to step in, *and* he's from El Carro. He's one of us."

Matt nodded, obviously persuaded by that last part. Matt had always hated playing with the Sweet Valley guys. But Josh still didn't look convinced.

"Come on, Josh, please?" Will begged. "Think about everything I've done for you. I always stick with you, no matter what. And like Matt said, I *did* lead you guys to a winning season, right?" He paused, deciding to pull out the pity card. "Look, even if it doesn't fly, at least *you* get to play football again."

Josh winced. "Yeah, okay," he said, sounding less than psyched. "I'll do it. But just one play—that's it."

"Deal," Will replied. He exhaled slowly and wiped his french-fry-greased hands on the legs of his jeans. A strange sense of peace came over him. The anger was still there, but at least now he had a plan. A focus.

"Okay. We have to make sure we have it all straight," Will said. The guys leaned forward, listening closely. For a split second Will was again reminded of when they used to spend their lunches like this, drilling play strategies before a big game. Except this play was designed to fail.

Jessica Wakefield

Why is everyone so down on me just because I'm happy? Why can't they just be happy <u>for</u> me?

I mean, it's not my fault they don't have boyfriends right now. It's not like I caused it or anything. (Okay, well, I guess I did a little with Jade and Jeremy, but that doesn't really count.)

Yeah, I'm sorry that Liz, Tia, Maria, and Jade are all going through the bitter thing. But I can't exactly break up with Jeremy just to show I can relate. I try not to gush, and I try to keep the dopey smile off my face when I'm around them — I really do.

The thing is, I've been where they are. I've been dumped. I've been tricked. I've been rejected. That's why I'm going to enjoy every moment of this.

And why I deserve it too.

CHAPTER 7
In the Zone

Elizabeth squinted at the black type on the computer screen. *That's not right,* she thought. *I'm pretty sure there's only one* e *in* judgment. She quickly highlighted the word and hit the spell check. Suddenly her computer made a harsh buzzing sound, and an error message appeared on the screen.

"What did I do?" she said out loud. As if in response, another message warning flashed on the screen, telling her to restart.

She groaned as it hit her that she hadn't saved her work, which meant even if she got the computer restarted okay, everything would be lost. *This* was what she got for coming back to the *Oracle* office after school to put in an extra half hour editing her articles. Okay, so maybe fifteen minutes of that had been spent trying to decide if she needed a comma after an opening phrase, but still. And she couldn't even remember if she'd kept the stupid comma or not!

At least it beat going home and listening to Jessica babble about Jeremy. If she had to stare at her twin's bright, beaming smile one more time, she'd rip her teeth out. It wasn't as if she didn't want her sister to have a deliriously wonderful love life. She just wished she didn't have to witness it. All it did was remind her how messed up things were with Conner. Or, actually, *without* Conner.

Elizabeth shut her eyes, remembering what Tia had told her at lunch today. When she'd heard he was coming back, she'd felt a sharp, rushing sensation in her chest, as if something chained up inside her had suddenly been let loose. She kept telling herself it was nothing—she was just taken off guard. Conner McDermott was part of her past. She still cared about what happened to him, but she wasn't about to fool herself into thinking they could go back to the way they were before his drinking got out of hand.

Then again, if she really believed that, why did it feel like her heart had been swelling up inside her ever since Tia mentioned him? And why did it bug her so much that Conner had written to Tia instead of her?

She sighed and flopped her head against the keyboard, causing another harsh buzzing sound from the computer. "Oh, shut up," she mumbled.

"Um . . . you talking to me?"

Elizabeth immediately sat up and pivoted around

in her chair to find Maria standing in the doorway. Maria gave her a small, understanding smile.

"The computer froze up on me. *Again*," Elizabeth explained as she stretched her arms up above her head. "Hey, I didn't know you were still around. I tried to call you at home."

Maria tossed her backpack on the table by the door. "I told Mr. Collins I'd cover for Walt while he's out with mono," she explained. "He was supposed to leave me Walt's assignment in my mailbox."

"That was nice of you," Elizabeth commented. Actually, it was amazingly generous. She knew how swamped Maria was lately. The girl probably had ten free seconds a day, if that much. But she also knew Maria liked to keep busy when she was upset. And Maria wasn't nearly as over Ken as she wanted everyone to think.

"Hey, guys!" Megan Sandborn breezed into the room, happily distracting Elizabeth from having to face how familiar that last thought was.

"Hey," Elizabeth greeted her. "You're still around too?"

"Mom just dropped me off so I could finish up my article," Megan said, twirling a strand of her strawberry blond hair around her finger. "I thought I'd be the only one here, but I'm glad I'm not."

"Why do you need to finish your piece up here?"

Elizabeth asked. "Is your computer acting crazy too?" She cast a quick glare at her screen. The computer was still going through the restarting process.

Megan shrugged and slunk down into a nearby chair. "It was just . . . you know . . . too quiet at home."

Elizabeth tilted her head, feeling a pang of guilt. There she was feeling bad for herself, but all of this was a thousand times harder on Conner's little sister.

"No way," Maria said, interrupting Elizabeth's thoughts. She turned in Maria's direction and saw her standing in front of the staff mailboxes, clutching a sheet of notebook paper in front of her panic-stricken face. "I don't believe this!"

"What? What is it?" Megan asked.

Maria slumped against the wall. "It's this note from Mr. Collins," she said, crumpling the paper in her fist. "He wants me to cover the game tonight while Walt's sick. I figured I'd be writing cutlines or something, but *this?*" Again she waved the note in the air. "I don't think I can do it." She looked over at Elizabeth, her dark eyes filling with pain. "Liz, I can't handle watching Ken play football while his new girlfriend struts around on the sidelines. What am I going to do?"

Elizabeth's guilt intensified. At lunch she'd promised Andy she could get Maria to come to the game without even making the connection that it would only rub Maria's face in the cause of her depression. But maybe it still could help Maria just to be around her friends, out having fun. Ken was only one player on two huge football teams.

"You know what?" she said. "I think you should go."

Maria's jaw dropped. "What? Are you crazy?"

"That's what I was trying to call you about," Elizabeth explained. "I'm going to the game after I finish up here, and I think you should come with me. Both of you."

"No way!" Maria said, folding her arms across her chest. "Football's the reason Ken and I broke up. Why would I want to give the stupid team my support?"

"Because it's Andy you'll be supporting," Elizabeth said.

Maria frowned. "Since when does Andy play football?"

Elizabeth laughed. There was an interesting picture. "No, he's being set up on a blind date," she told her. "And he wants us all to go as a group so it won't be so awkward. I told him I could get both of you to come with me."

"I'll go," Megan said. "I don't have anything planned anyway. And it sounds like fun."

They both turned their gazes to Maria. "Come

on, Maria. Please? You have to do it for Mr. Collins now anyway."

Maria slouched forward. "I don't know," she mumbled. "I guess you're right—I do need to do the dumb article anyway. I might as well sit with you guys."

"Great," Elizabeth said. "Then it's all set."

"Ladies and gentlemen, get on your feet for your Sweet Valley High Gladiators!" the announcer called out.

Ken could hear the roar of the crowd and the rumble of their feet against the bleachers. Then, as acting team captain, he gave the signal and the entire team was off, racing across the field.

Normally Ken liked to jog along slowly and let the big bruisers tear up the run-through. But not tonight. Tonight he wanted to feel it. He charged across the turf and hit the giant Ream the Raiders! sign along with the first wave of guys. Instantly he felt the paper give, and he crashed through with a satisfying rip.

The rest of the team followed and regrouped in a giant huddle at the fifty-yard line. Todd Wilkins raised his left fist in the air and hollered, "What time is it?"

"Game time!" the rest of the team answered.

"What time is it?" Todd shouted again.

"Game time!"

111

The group jumped up and down, repeating the chant, each time increasing the tempo and volume. It was something new the team had added this year to get themselves fired up for games. During his weeks on the bench Ken had thought they looked idiotic—like human stove-top popcorn or something. But tonight, as he stood in the middle of it all, he had to admit it was cool. And it really did whip them up.

Afterward he trotted over to the sidelines with the rest of the team, enjoying the weight of his uniform on his body and the feel of his cleats bouncing against the grass. He was totally revved up. In fact, he couldn't remember ever feeling this ready to play. Strangely enough, it helped to *not* take his dad's advice about blocking everything out. Instead he channeled it all in. He let himself feel the sound vibrations thrown off by the crowd and breathed his lungs full of the crisp fall air. Tonight was going to be a win. He could sense it.

He restlessly paced up and down in front of the bench as the other team won the toss and their offense took the field.

"Come on! Go!" he called out toward the defensive players. He had to do something while waiting for his turn with the ball, and yelling seemed to power up the electric charge running through his veins.

As he wandered down the sidelines watching the

game, Ken caught sight of Melissa shouting out the "Gladiator Power" rally cry with the other cheerleaders. Immediately he felt a slight surge of guilt as he remembered blowing up at her. He knew it had been the right thing to do, but he still couldn't help wondering if she was all right.

When the cheer was over, the squad whooped and clapped and performed various limb-twisting jumps. Melissa did a back handspring topped off by a high split in the air. Afterward she walked back up to the edge of the track to grab her water bottle. Just as she was about to take a drink, she glanced his way, and her eyes met Ken's. Ken tried to give her a friendly smile, figuring it was a good time to show he didn't want any bitterness between them.

Melissa paused for a fraction of a second before tilting back her head for a long sip. Then, without acknowledging Ken at all, she rejoined the squad for the next cheer.

Okay. So obviously she didn't feel like staying friends.

What did you expect? Ken asked himself. *A good-bye present?* He shook his head and turned his attention back to the game. All the excitement about playing tonight must have warped his senses. But he couldn't let that distract him now, not when he felt more ready to play than he'd ever felt in his life. It was time to push everything except football out of his mind.

The crowd behind him cheered as a Raider wide receiver missed a long pass. The intense volume coming from the stands seemed to penetrate Ken's body and accelerate his heartbeat. For a second he considered checking the crowd for Hank Krubowski or his dad, but he forced himself to keep his eyes on the field.

Don't go there, Ken scolded himself. *Just keep your focus on the now and show them all some stellar ball playing.*

Once again the bleachers shook with cheers, and Ken looked up in time to see the Raider running back get pushed back for a loss of five yards. "Yeah! Way to go, D!" he cried.

Now it was fourth down and seven, and they were nowhere near field-goal range. They'd have to punt for sure. Then finally it would be Sweet Valley's ball. *His* ball. The heels of Ken's feet bounced in anticipation.

After the Raiders punted and the ball was downed at the twenty-yard line, Ken and the rest of the offense jogged onto the field. Behind him he could hear the crowd roar to a new level. Ken shut his eyes and gave himself one second to feel the jolts of energy flow through him, then he joined the rest of the guys in the huddle.

"All right, let's show them how we do things," he

said, meeting their gazes. "Todd, you'll do a crossing pattern over the middle. The twenty-seven-Z cross. Snap on two. Got it?"

Todd nodded. "Break!" called out the team, clapping. Then they all jogged to the line and got into formation.

As Ken planted himself behind the line and glanced downfield, he could feel himself go deep into "the zone." It always happened this way during a game. As soon as he got into position, the sounds of the crowd seemed to disappear. The words of the announcer no longer reached his eardrums, and his sight constricted down to the playing field in front of them. It was as if he were a preprogrammed cyborg, built only to play football.

This time was no different. Ken felt like he was watching himself from someplace back inside his brain. He heard himself call for the snap, felt himself drop back, and was aware of his arm lifting back for the pass. Looking downfield, he saw that Todd was right where he should be. Ken focused on Todd's jersey and launched the ball into the air. It hung in the air for a few seconds, soaring with a gentle spiral, before falling right into Todd's waiting hands. Todd clutched it to his chest and ran for another eleven-yard gain before getting tackled.

Then, as if someone turned off a mute button,

the sounds of the crowd cheering once again reached Ken's ears.

A first down on the first play of the game! He was definitely in the zone.

"So after a couple of years of growing my hair out to get that long, straight, Marcia Brady look, I read in *Cosmo* that a short, bobbed cut is the style now. And that's how I had it before I grew it out!" Rebecca waved her arms in frustration.

"I know what you mean," Elizabeth jumped in. "I spent eighty dollars on Sedona makeup—and that was *after* my employee discount. Now 'natural' is in." She shook her head. "It's like, thanks a lot. I only had that look for seventeen years!"

Andy watched as Rebecca, Maria, and Megan all nodded in unison. He sneaked a glance at Dale, Rebecca's cousin, who was sitting on the bleacher just above him on the left. Dale seemed equally amused by the conversation. He was grinning, his light brown eyes sparkling with laughter. Andy had to admit the guy was good-looking—a sort of skinny David Boreanaz type without the mumble. And he seemed nice too. Of course, Andy hadn't had much of a chance to really talk to him since they'd arrived.

Dale leaned over to where the four girls had their

heads together. "You know, I always wondered," he said. "Who exactly decides what's 'in' and what's 'out'?"

"Dale, what are you talking about?" Rebecca asked, her voice tinged with irritation.

"I mean, whose job is it to tell everyone what to wear and how to do their hair? Is it the designers? The media? Or is there some little old lady in Barstow that hands down the verdicts every year?"

Andy smiled. A sense of humor too. Good sign.

"Come on," Rebecca said, rolling her eyes.

"No, I'm serious," Dale went on. "I want to know who decides all these important things. Andy? Do you know?"

Andy rubbed his chin thoughtfully. "You know, I'm pretty sure it's Joan Rivers," he said.

Dale laughed, and the others just groaned.

"Don't listen to them," Rebecca said, dismissing Dale and Andy with a wave of her hand. "So like I was saying . . ."

Her voice was immediately drowned out by the rest of the crowd's thundering cheers. Andy turned and saw that Sweet Valley had scored another touchdown. That made two so far, plus a field goal, and halftime was only a few minutes away. It was obvious to even Andy that Ken was having a great game. He had almost commented on it the last time they scored, but he could tell Maria was doing her best to avoid any mention of Ken—even though she was taking notes for the paper's write-up.

"Did you guys hear the new dress code at Lago Vista doesn't even allow tattoos or body jewelry?" he heard Megan say. She scooted up closer to Maria while Rebecca and Elizabeth leaned forward to tighten the circle.

That left Andy and Dale alone, out in the open. Andy realized this was the perfect opportunity for the two of them to get to know each other—in fact, he wondered if the girls were excluding them on purpose. He figured he should make conversation with the guy, but he just couldn't think of an opening statement that wouldn't sound lame.

Dale bent forward toward Andy. "I guess they didn't appreciate our views on fashion," he said.

"Great wisdom is often ignored in its time," Andy replied, grateful Dale had made the first comment.

Dale laughed, and Andy felt some of the tension ease. But as soon as Dale's chuckles faded, the silence was back, and he still didn't know how to fill it.

Luckily right at that moment Sweet Valley ran the ball in for the third touchdown of the half and the crowd exploded into loud cheers.

"What happened?" Dale asked, craning his head to see over the spectators jumping up and down in front of them. "Was it a pass? I didn't see it."

"They ran the ball in," Andy replied. "The Raiders have that stellar cornerback, so Ken's been avoiding the long-pass plays."

Dale stared at him admiringly. "You really know your game, huh?"

Andy blinked. "Me? No way. All I know I learned from Nintendo. My brother has the latest John Madden. Of course, he usually clobbers me on it. But then I get to beat him on Spacehaunt."

"You're kidding me, right? That's my favorite game."

"Seriously?" Andy's eyebrows raised. "I thought I was the only guy outside of Hong Kong who played that game."

Dale smiled and shook his head. "No, I've been into it for years. In fact"—he hunched his shoulders self-consciously—"I'm sort of a sci-fi/fantasy nutcase."

"Me too!" Andy said. "I get so much trouble about that. Most people outgrow the Tolkien phase by high school. Not me. Tia says anytime I see an elf, I go all sappy."

"Really?" Dale inched forward. "Rebecca has forbidden me to quote any more lines from *Star Wars* when I'm around her. She says it's like stamping a giant *L* on my forehead."

"You should forbid her to talk about hairstyles," Andy joked, tilting his head toward the girls.

"No kidding!" Dale said, smiling.

Andy grinned. Suddenly his uneasiness was completely gone. In fact, talking with Dale was a lot like talking with Rebecca. They both had that same easy humor about them—even if their conversation topics were totally different.

The stands stood and cheered as the announcer called the end of the first half and the team ran off the field.

"I'm going to run and get a soda before the lines get too long," Rebecca announced, jumping to her feet. "Anyone want to come with me?"

Dale stood. "I'll go," he said, then turned to Andy. "Can I grab you a drink while I'm there?"

"Um . . . sure," Andy replied. "Dr Pepper?"

"No problem," Dale said, smiling.

As soon as Dale and Rebecca were out of sight, Elizabeth, Maria, and Megan immediately swarmed him. He was about to ask if their medication had just kicked in when a familiar voice rang out in the near distance.

"Wait! Wait for me!" It was Tia. He glanced over and saw her scramble over the bleachers. Eventually she reached them. "I've only got a few minutes while the marching band plays," she said breathlessly. "So, come on! Tell me! How do you like Dale?"

"Um, I don't know," Andy responded. He looked

around at all the eager faces watching him. "It's not even the second half. I have no idea how I feel about all this yet."

The girls looked at each other and shrugged.

"Yeah, you're right," Tia conceded. "You just keep on taking it slow. But be careful. Guys can really let you down sometimes."

Will slouched at the end of the team bench as he watched the Gladiators emerge onto the field from the locker room. Not surprisingly, Ken was jogging confidently at the head of the pack, his chin up and eyes focused with newly fired-up attitude. Coach must have recharged the team with one of his pep talks. Will was so glad he didn't limp back there with them. If he had sat there and listened to everyone praise Ken like some big superhero, he would have hurled right on the spot.

A wave of cheers rose up from one end of the stands to the other as the spectators caught sight of the team returning. A few people even shouted Ken's name.

"Yeah, you just keep it up, Matthews," Will muttered under his breath. "Keep making those big plays and thinking no one can touch you."

He had to admit Ken was on a streak, though. The guy did hit twelve of fourteen passes. Pretty stellar. He had two incompletions, but one of those was picked off by that star cornerback, Huxley, when he jumped that out route. Considering Huxley had done far more damage in other games, that wasn't bad. As much as he hated to admit it, Will had never had a first half go so well when he played.

"Who cares," Will grumbled, angry at himself. After everything that had happened, Ken didn't deserve to have Will admiring his stats. So he had an incredible first half. Fine. Let him get all cocky and complacent. It would only make it hurt worse when he got taken down.

By now the team had assembled on the sidelines. Will tried not to make eye contact with Matt and Josh, afraid that any exchanged glances could tip someone off. Instead he looked out onto the field and nervously jiggled his good leg. It wouldn't be long now. He, Matt, and Josh had decided that the first passing play of the second half would be when it happened.

The Raiders kicked the ball down to the Gladiators' fifteen-yard line. Will watched as Ken and the rest of the offense took the field. He thought he saw a faint smirk on Matt's face, while Josh stayed as cool as stone.

Will's heart hammered against his rib cage as he

watched Ken huddle up with the others. His palms started sweating, and the skin of his leg itched uncomfortably under his brace. *Come on. Come on,* he thought. *Just slam him and get it over with.*

Unfortunately, the first play went to the running back. Obviously Ken was going to stick with the same strategy that worked in the first half and avoid the pass plays until he really needed them. Will's hands balled into fists.

Why am I losing it? he wondered. *What am I so afraid of?*

Nothing. He wasn't afraid of anything. He was just eager to see Ken get a sample of what he'd been going through.

All of a sudden a voice from behind cut through his thoughts. "I'm standing here on Gladiator Field at one of the most hotly contested games in the local division play-offs."

Will leaned back slightly and saw a short guy in slacks and a sports jacket talking into a microphone just a few yards away. Will recognized him as a sports reporter for one of the local TV stations. Cool. Maybe they'd capture Ken doll's wipeout on tape and play it during the news.

"It's the beginning of the second half, and Ken Matthews has just started the first drive for the Sweet Valley Gladiators," the man went on. "While some people predicted the Raiders would easily trounce the Gladiators with the help of their all-district cornerback, Eric Huxley, that has not been the case so far. Huxley did intercept the ball once for a Raider touchdown during the first half, but the Gladiators still managed to rack up a twenty-four to fourteen lead over the Raiders by halftime, due in large part to the levelheaded playing of their second-string quarterback, Ken Matthews."

A burning sensation welled up in Will's stomach. This was not what he wanted to hear right now. It was bad enough having to watch Ken on a hot streak without listening to some TV guy rave about it. He slouched forward and tried to concentrate on the game, but still the reporter's voice cut through.

"Matthews, who was Sweet Valley's starting quarterback last year, quit the team before the season officially began due to personal reasons. He later rejoined as a second stringer to new quarterback Will Simmons. For most of the season Matthews cheered his team on from the bench until a knee injury forced Simmons out and put Matthews back in as the starter. Still, it was Matthews's unwavering support as a sideliner and his loyalty to the team that earned him this year's Spirit Award. You've got to admire dedication like this. I'll be back later with more highlights. Back to you in the studio, Bob."

As Will sat there, trying not to listen, the dull pain in his gut slowly grew to a raging fire. Snatches of words from the reporter's commentary seemed to stick in his chest. *Unwavering support . . . loyalty to the team . . . dedication . . .*

When Matthews couldn't play football, he toughed it out, Will couldn't help thinking. *And now look at me. Am I hanging in there, cheering everyone on? No. Instead I set Matthews and the team up for disaster.*

An intense guilt gnawed its way through Will. What had he been thinking? Taking Ken down wouldn't make him feel better. It would just make everything worse. In fact, he *already* felt worse.

What do I do? he wondered, looking out onto the football field.

Maybe Ken wouldn't pass on this drive. Then Will could tell Josh and Matt to call it off when they came back to the sidelines.

"Don't throw the ball, Matthews," he whispered. "Don't throw the stupid ball."

Josh Radinsky

I don't care what anyone says—football is more than just a game. In high school football is everything. It tells you who has power and who doesn't. Football has done more good for me than just about anything. Except maybe Will.

If it weren't for him, I'd probably be a few rungs down still. That's why I hate to see him so caught up on this revenge kick.

I'm no friend of Matthews, but he's part of the team. During a game the <u>other</u> <u>team</u> is supposed to be the bad guys, not your own quarterback. Which means this stupid plan of Will's almost goes too far.

Still, he's my friend, and I owe him. I guess friendship doesn't have rules the way football does. But then again, maybe it should.

CHAPTER 8
Something Missing

"When it comes to *winning*, we're second to *none!*" Jade shouted at the top of her lungs, drowning out the rest of the squad. As they struck their end-of-cheer poses, she quickly glanced up at Evan to see if he was watching. He wasn't, of course.

Jade exhaled sharply. What did she have to do to get his attention? Start up some chant against wearing fur?

But the problem wasn't her volume or her cheering. The problem was the tall, blond bimbo sitting to Evan's left. Sitting practically on his *lap*.

Evan had showed up here with her and some guy Jade didn't know. She wasn't sure why they'd bothered to bring the guy, though, since Evan had spent almost the entire game talking and laughing with Barbie doll. Every time Jade looked up there (which occurred an average of once every three-point-two seconds), Barbie would be hanging all over him—talking, giggling, tossing back her long, glossy blond hair. Jade was surprised anyone could hear their cheers over the girl's screeching laughter.

"Gladiatorrrrr *a-ttack!*" Tia called out.

The rest of the squad instantly stood in a triangular formation, joining in the cheer. Everyone except for Jade, who had been too busy giving Evan's friend the evil eye. By the time she tried to catch up, she was completely out of step and kept accidentally thrusting her arm in Cherie Reese's face.

"What's your problem?" Cherie hissed as soon as the cheer was over.

"Sorry," Jade replied. "I wasn't ready."

"You know, we're all getting sick of your lame mistakes." Cherie shook her head. "All night you've been too loud and way off your marks. You can't even get the words right. On defense you yelled push *her* back instead of push *them* back."

Jade glared back at Cherie. "Hey, I said I was sorry, okay?"

Cherie's eyes narrowed, and she seemed ready to go into major witch mode, but just then Tia signaled for the start of the next cheer.

All I have to do is hang on for the last half of the game. Then I can tell Evan how I feel, Jade reassured herself.

From the corner of her eye she could see the tall blonde burst out laughing, giving Evan a playful shove.

Okay. First I might have to beat that girl to death, she added silently. Then *I will definitely tell him how I feel.*

Ken shook his head as the Sweet Valley running back, Vince Givens, emerged from underneath a pile of Raider players. Two running plays and they'd only managed a gain of five yards. It was definitely time to throw the ball.

The only thing that worried him was that cornerback, Huxley. He had managed to pick off a pass in the first half—one of only two bad offensive plays in an otherwise perfect game. If it wasn't for Huxley, Ken would be on fire. Still, they were up by ten points, and Ken hadn't let those interceptions rattle him. He could risk a passing play for sure.

"All right," he said as the rest of the guys huddled up around him. "Let's give this ball some frequent-flier miles. Todd, go long. Slot right, eighty-six-Y streak, with snap on two. Got it?"

"Break!" the others chanted, and headed for the line.

As Ken called the signal, he wasn't surprised to see the defense cheating up toward the line of scrimmage. He had figured they'd blitz. Once the ball was in his hands, he immediately dropped back for the pass, searching for Todd.

Just like before, Ken switched to autopilot mode.

But as he moved, his brain kept telling him something was missing. Normally, to his right, he would be seeing the giant number 79 on the back side of Matt's jersey. Only Matt wasn't there. Out of the corner of his eye he thought he could see Matt still in his three-point stance at the line. But that couldn't be right, could it?

Ken didn't have time to figure it out, though. Just at that moment a giant Raider-blue 94 was charging at him on the right. Ken tried desperately to launch his pass before the guy reached him, but as he started to propel his arm forward, he felt another icy realization—there was no one protecting his left side either. He was totally alone. And another blue blur was heading toward him from that direction too.

The next thing Ken knew, a shoulder pad and helmet came crashing into his left side, jarring him off his feet and popping the ball from his hand.

No! Not a fumble, Ken thought, still in midair.

Before he could try to retrieve the ball, there was another sudden blow to his gut, and his body went hurtling backward. Ken felt the sharp impact of the ground underneath, followed by the crushing weight of players on top. Then it was all over.

That's weird, he thought as harsh, throbbing pain surged through him. *I can't breathe. It really, really hurts to breathe.*

*　　　*　　　*

Will winced as he watched Ken go down, his stomach twisted up with nausea.

"Oh, no," he muttered, staring at the pile of players that lay where Ken had just been standing.

He'd never imagined Ken would get slammed so badly. It looked worse than any of the replays on that lame TV show. After Ken got knocked off his feet by the guy on the left, the player on the right came in low with his tackle. Will couldn't tell for sure from where he was sitting, but it looked like Ken's knee could have been torn up too. Just like his.

In fact, seeing it happen triggered a memory of his own crushing tackle. Will's body seemed to hurt all over again, and he could almost taste that bitter mixture of turf and blood.

An entire hush came over the Sweet Valley side of the stadium, and few people seemed to notice that the Raider defensive end who recovered the fumble was now high stepping into the end zone. It was as if they too had a weird sense of déjà vu.

"Come on! Get up!" Will pleaded, still keeping his eye on the heap of fallen players. But there was no sign of Ken yet. By now the crowd was muttering and getting to its feet, and the guys on the sidelines were creeping to the edge of the field for a better look. Will straggled to a standing position to see over them.

Finally the pile of players picked themselves up one by one. As they stood, they revealed Ken still lying on the ground in an oddly contorted position. He didn't seem to be moving at all.

Will sucked in his breath and prayed for Ken to get up, or sit, or wiggle his legs—any sort of sign that he might be okay. But Ken just lay there.

He's hurt bad, Will thought as a cold numbness spilled through his body. *And it's all because of me.*

All he'd wanted was for Ken to feel some of the same fear and humiliation that he'd experienced. To regain some sense of the power he'd lost. He never wished for the guy to get seriously injured.

Or did he? Had there been some small part of him that had actually wanted this to happen? Could he be that rotten of a person?

Come on, Matthews, Will thought, craning his head as other players moved into his field of vision. *You've got to be okay.*

As the coach and team doctor rushed out onto the field, Will squeezed the crutches at his side. *Let him be all right,* he pleaded silently, *and I'll make it up to him somehow. I swear I'll do whatever it takes. Just let him be okay.*

"Oh my God—he's not moving," Maria said. She clasped her hand over her mouth as Coach Riley signaled for the team doctor. A second later Doc Tyler ran out onto the field, clutching a black medic bag. The two men bent over Ken's limp frame, blocking him from sight.

"Don't worry, Maria. I'm sure he'll be okay," Elizabeth said.

"Yeah," Andy echoed, giving her an uncertain pat on the shoulder. "Stuff like this happens all the time. Just another day on the job for a football player."

Maria stood and stretched her neck to look over the other spectators. Something was wrong. He'd have gotten up by now if he was really okay. If she could just get close enough to see.

"I'm going down there," she announced. She took off down the bleachers before anyone could respond. A million emotions were rushing through her, but she blocked them out, focusing on just getting to Ken.

She reached the bottom of the bleacher steps and slid underneath the metal railing to the track below.

"Maria? What are you doing?" It was Tia. Maria recognized her voice, even though she didn't turn to look.

"Hey!" another cheerleader called out. "You aren't supposed to be down here!"

But Maria ignored them both and kept on running downfield. The entire Sweet Valley team was standing along the sidelines. Maria couldn't see past them, and her vision was further blurred by the hot tears welling up in her eyes.

What if he's unconscious? she wondered. *What if he has a severe concussion or internal bleeding or a ruptured spleen?* Suddenly every critical diagnosis she'd ever heard on an episode of *ER* was jamming up her thoughts. Her heart rammed against her rib cage as she quickened her pace. She just had to get near him. That was all.

Maria reached the Gladiator bench and pushed in between a couple of players. She was just about to rush out onto the field when a movement caught her eye—Ken was getting to his feet.

Behind her the home crowd cheered loudly as Ken, supported on one side by Coach Riley and on the other by Doc Tyler, walked tentatively toward the sidelines.

He's okay! Maria told herself, her breath restarting in sharp gasps. Ken's face was contorted with pain, but there was no sign of blood. And although his movements were slow and cautious, all his limbs seemed to be functioning properly.

As Ken reached the edge of the field, several players circled him, cheering him on. Ken blinked, staring around him, and all of a sudden his gaze locked on Maria. His eyes widened in dazed confusion for a fraction of a second before the rest of the team swarmed in between them.

All at once Maria felt like she'd been yanked from a deep trance. She glanced around, noticing a few players shooting her curious stares.

What am I doing here? She blushed, then spun around and headed back to the stands.

The intense relief she'd felt a second ago, seeing that Ken was okay, was quickly replaced by a feeling of total embarrassment. How could she let herself get carried away like that? Ken already made it clear that this mindless, ridiculous, dangerous sport meant more to him than she did. So how could she still care so much about him?

The only option she had was to not *let* herself care. If Ken wanted to go on risking his neck in this dumb game, let him. She didn't have to worry about him anymore.

Or at least, she didn't have to watch.

Megan Sandborn

Things to Do Before
Conner Comes Home

1. Put those T-shirts I borrowed back in his drawer.
2. Tune his stereo system back to that lame alt-rock station he likes.
3. Load up on Doritos, root beer, Twinkies, and other nonaddictive, nonalcoholic snacks Conner likes. (Hmmm. Then again, Twinkies might be addictive.)
4. Remember to give him space.
5. Remind Mom to give him space.
6. Think of some urgent reason why Elizabeth might have to stop by.

CHAPTER

The Right Spin

9

"Everybody back away," Coach Riley grunted at the other players. "Give the guy some air."

Ken winced as Coach Riley and Doc Tyler gingerly eased him onto the bench. It was getting a little easier to take breaths, and he wasn't in as much pain anymore. But he had to be disoriented or something because he'd been sure he saw Maria standing with the rest of the team a second ago.

"It doesn't look like any ribs are broken," Doc Tyler said while jabbing Ken's chest and stomach. "But I think you need to sit out the next few plays." He shone a small light into each of Ken's eyes. "There's no sign of a head contusion," Doc continued, zipping up his medical kit. "And you said your vision's fine. That guy really knocked the wind out of you, though. Just rest here and let the backup take over while you shake it off and regain your balance."

Ken nodded, and Doc walked over to Coach Riley. He muttered something to Coach as they stood watching the Raiders kicker score an extra point.

"Hey—you okay?" Todd Wilkins asked, sitting down next to Ken.

"Yeah, I guess," Ken said. "I got lucky."

"You sure did. And you know, a certain someone seemed pretty scared for you. She raced all the way down to the field to see you."

"What?" Ken snapped his head around to search the sidelines and instantly felt a dull, twisting pain in his side.

"Whoa. Take it easy," Todd said, grabbing hold of Ken's arm. "Sit still or Doc won't let you back in the game."

"So, Maria was really here?" Ken asked.

"Yep," Todd answered. "She took off once she saw you back on your feet."

Ken faced the field again and rubbed his sore side. So he hadn't hallucinated it. Maria really had been there. Did that mean she still cared about him?

"Wilkins! Get out there! Offense is on!"

"Feel better quick," Todd mumbled before fastening his helmet and jogging onto the field.

For the next few plays Ken could only sit on the bench, shifting uncomfortably. His left ribs still hurt, but it was more excruciating to watch Larry Reimer, the third-string quarterback, mess up play after play. Thanks to Ken's fumble, which had resulted in a touchdown for the Raiders, Sweet Valley's ten-point lead had been whittled down to three. And the Raiders seemed more fired up than ever.

In between downs he continued checking around for Maria but couldn't catch sight of her anywhere. He did, however, spot Hank Krubowski sitting in the stands, frowning down at the clipboard in his hand. Ken immediately spun back around, slouching. No doubt there were a few unflattering things about Ken's last play written down there.

Why'd he have to get sacked anyway? He'd been in the zone up to that point. And why weren't Josh and Matt there to protect him? Ken reviewed the play in his head. He could remember the lineup and the snap going off without a hitch, but as he dropped back for the pass, Matt seemed to remain in his three-point stance. Maybe Josh too. Was he imagining it all? Or had they totally messed up on the count?

A whistle blew, and the Sweet Valley punter ran out onto the field. Poor Larry went four downs with only a two-yard gain. Ken didn't feel all that much better, but he knew he had to get back out there soon. Not only for the team's sake, but also to prove to Krubowski—and everyone else—that he still had some game in him.

But first he had to talk to Matt and Josh and figure out what happened.

As soon as the offensive line wandered off the field, Ken took a deep breath and hoisted himself off the bench. Then he walked over to where Matt and Josh were standing off to the side of the group.

"Hey, guys. I need to ask you something," he said as he approached.

"Hey, how are you holding up?" Josh asked, his eyes narrow.

"I'm getting there," Ken said, managing a weak smile. "But I need to know, what happened?"

"What are you talking about?" Matt asked, his voice a little high.

Ken frowned. "I mean, what went wrong on the pass play? When I dropped back into the pocket, I could have sworn you were still in formation. Where were you guys?"

Matt took a step toward Ken and opened his mouth to say something, but Josh held a hand up in front of him. "You told us to move on three," Josh said calmly to Ken. "But you moved on two."

"No, I didn't." Ken shook his head. "I said two."

"You said three," Josh repeated, stone-faced.

Ken put his fingers up against his temples. Was he losing his mind? First the sack. Then Maria. Now this. "Why would I do that, Josh? We *always* run that play on two."

"What are you saying?" Matt blurted out. "Are you calling us liars?"

"What is going on here?" Coach Riley suddenly appeared next to them, his typically pink-tinged face even more red than usual.

"Matthews thinks we let him get sacked on purpose!" Matt hollered.

"What? No, I didn't—I never said they did it on purpose," Ken tried to explain. "But they keep saying I told them to snap on three when I know it was two."

"It *was* two," Todd Wilkins said from behind. Ken noticed the rest of the offense had closed in around them and were listening in.

"Yeah, they set him up!" someone else yelled out.

"You don't know that. Besides, it was just one play!" shouted one of the El Carro guys.

"It scored the Raiders a touchdown!" came another voice.

All at once everyone started shouting. The El Carro players yelled at the Sweet Valley guys, and the Sweet Valley guys yelled back. Coach Riley barked at them to be quiet and focus on the game, but no one seemed to listen. Ken's head swam as the commotion grew louder and louder.

Suddenly a familiar voice cut through the din. "Stop it! I said, *stop it!* Will you guys just shut up?"

One by one the players all turned toward the voice and immediately grew silent. Ken glanced up to see Will, leaning on his crutches, facing them all.

"Get with it, guys. The real fight is out there." Will jerked his head toward the playing field behind him. Gripping his crutches, he hobbled toward the group, facing a small knot of El Carro players. "We were tight at our old school, and you need to be tight here. If you guys want to make it to the championship, you have to back Matthews one hundred percent."

A few of the players gazed down at their feet, nodding. Matt's mouth fell open in total shock, and Will didn't even glance in Josh's direction.

Yeah, okay, Will thought. *I know I shouldn't be talking.* But at least he'd finally realized what a mistake they'd made and was ready to try and fix it.

"You heard the guy," Coach Riley said. "Go walk it off and get back into game mode. We've got the rest of the half to go, and we're only up by three!"

As the players splintered off, Coach gave Will a short nod and walked back over to where his assistants stood watching the game. Will knew a gesture like that was high praise coming from Coach. He should be psyched—but he still just felt like a jerk.

Will turned and met Ken's confused stare. He

took a deep breath, realizing that somehow all the rage wasn't there anymore when he looked at him. He still didn't like the guy. But the thing was, Will liked himself even less right now.

"Look, Ken, I think we need to talk," Will said, rocking slightly on his crutches.

Ken's brow furrowed. "Ookay," he replied, drawing out the word as if it were more of a question than a response. "What's up?"

Will glanced around at Josh, Matt, and some other nearby players. "Over here," he said, nodding toward a more vacant spot on the sidelines.

Ken hesitated for a second. Then he gave a small shrug and ambled toward him. They walked a few yards down from the Sweet Valley bench and turned to face each other.

"So . . . what did you want to say?" Ken asked.

"I just wanted to share some pointers with you," Will replied. He poked the ends of his crutches into the soft turf. "I played Huxley a lot last year, and I know his moves. If you want a guaranteed win, you've got to trust me on this."

He met Ken's gaze straight on, waiting to see if he had Ken's trust.

"All right," Ken said after a brief pause. "What do you know?"

"You remember how Huxley jumped the out

route and picked you off in the first half?" Will asked.

Ken blew out his breath. "Sure. Cost me a touch-down."

"Well, run that same formation on the next drive but audible to an out and up," Will explained. "Just give him a hard pump fake, and I guarantee you Huxley will bite on it. That should leave Todd wide open."

A slight grin slowly crept across Ken's face. "Yeah?"

"Worked for me every time," Will said. A lump of nostalgia rose up in his throat. He thought about those thrilling moments on the El Carro playing field, back when he had two working knees and a loyal girlfriend cheering him on from the sidelines. It seemed strange to remember it—as if it had happened to someone else entirely. In a way, maybe it had.

Will cleared his throat and stared out into the distance, pretending to be very interested in the Raider quarterback's next play. He could feel Ken's eyes on him, studying him intently, but no way was he going to let on how pathetic he felt.

"Thanks, Will," Ken said.

Will finally turned and met his eye. "Yeah, well. Don't thank me till you beat him." He gripped his crutches and turned to go.

"Hey, Will, wait." Ken cracked his knuckles and stared down at his cleats. "I know a lot of bad stuff has gone down between us, but . . . what do you say we call a truce?"

Will lifted the corner of his mouth in a half smile. "Sounds good."

What is that *all about?* Melissa wondered. She slowly inched backward to get a better view of Ken and Will as she stepped in time to the cheer.

First of all, they'd managed to talk this long without either of them throwing a punch. But even weirder—she could have sworn she'd seen Will smile.

Ever since the accident Will had walked around with a constant scowl on his face, as if the tackle had somehow rearranged his features as well as the tendons in his knee. No one could cheer him up—not Matt and Josh, not his family, not even Melissa.

But now he was smiling at Ken. At *Ken!*

"*We* know that *you* know that *we* know we're *number one!*"

The rest of the squad whooped and shouted as the cheer ended, but instead of doing her usual set of jumps Melissa walked over to their pile of equipment along the track and took a long drink from her water bottle.

"What do you think's going on there, Liss?" Lila asked, coming up behind her.

Melissa cringed. She hated it when Lila called her that. "Liss" had always been Will's name for her. It wasn't right when anyone else used it.

"I don't know," Melissa answered. "They've been talking for a while."

"Do you think they're fighting?" Cherie asked as she, Gina, and Amy came up on Melissa's left.

Melissa shrugged. "They don't look mad."

"God, that's weird!" Gina exclaimed.

"Yeah," Cherie agreed. "I wish we knew what was going on."

"Why don't you sneak over there and ask Ken after Will leaves?" Gina asked Melissa.

A heavy sensation filled Melissa's stomach. She still hadn't told anyone Ken broke up with her. She just couldn't—not yet. Not until she found the right spin to put on it.

"No, I don't think so," she said. "We agreed not to talk during the game so he can concentrate," she lied.

Lila nudged them and flashed a grin. "*I'll* find out," she said.

Before they could react, Lila headed toward the football team's bench and leaned in toward one of the players. After a couple of minutes she strolled back over to them, her smile even more smug.

"He said that Will was giving Ken some advice," she said.

Melissa swallowed. Will was being a good sport? After all that stuff he'd said to her today? It didn't seem possible. Will's basic instinct was to fight anyone who had more power than he did, not *help* them.

"Looks like Ken's feeling better," Gina observed. "For a while there I thought he was dead meat."

"Good thing he's not," Lila said, studying her glittery lavender nail polish. "Then Melissa would have had to go out with Larry Reimer."

Melissa whirled around and glared at her, shocked that the girl had actually shown some guts for once. It wasn't a good time for it.

"God, Lila, that's low," Cherie said.

Lila raised her eyebrows and stared at Cherie for a second. Then she swiveled toward Melissa, her expression filling with fake regret. "I'm sorry, Liss. You know I was just joking."

"No big deal," Melissa replied, keeping a note of warning in her tone. Inside, her heart pounded like mad. How dare that spoiled tramp make her out to be some boyfriend day trader? It wasn't her fault that Will got hurt and shut her out. It wasn't like she wanted to dump him for Ken. She'd just had no other choice. In fact, if things were different, she'd be with Will right now.

But maybe things are *different,* she couldn't help thinking.

If Will was being genuinely nice to Ken, then something must have changed. Maybe now he wouldn't be so bitter and pathetic. He still had some power around school, and she could help him get even more back.

That's it. No more games, she told herself as she and the other girls headed back to the line for the next cheer. *It's time for me to forgive him. Time to finally get back together.*

After all, if Will could push aside his pride, then maybe she could too.

Andy Marsden

I'm not exactly sure what I'm supposed to be feeling here, but I'm pretty sure I should be feeling <u>something</u>. Sure, Dale is great. He's cute, nice, funny, and easy to talk to, and he's told me about some great online gaming sites. But that's it. No music swelling. No fireworks. Not even a drop of sweat on my palms. Either I'm doing this all wrong or he's just not "the one."

Now for the really tough part—how am I going to break this to Tia?

CHAPTER
Back in the Game
10

"Great. There goes the lead," Ken muttered from his spot next to Will on the bench. The Raiders had luckily missed a couple of attempts at a touchdown, but they did manage to kick a field goal to tie the score on their final play.

"Matthews, you ready to go back in?" Coach Riley asked.

Will watched the frustration drain out of Ken's face, replaced by a mask of concentration. He had to admit it, the guy was a pro.

"You sure about the out and up?" Ken asked as he fastened his helmet.

"Positive," Will replied.

"Don't let that tackle mess with your mind," Coach Riley warned. "It's a tie game, and we're down to the last few minutes, but I need someone with a cool head. Can you do that?"

"No problem," Ken promised. Then he turned toward Will. "Thanks for your advice. I've got Huxley's number now."

Will nodded. "Go kick some Raider butt."

As Ken ran onto the field with the offense, Will settled himself onto the end of the bench. His leg was hurting, but otherwise he felt better than he had in a long time.

Will stretched his injured leg out in front of him and lost himself in the game. Ken led the offense on a long drive down to the Raider thirty-five-yard line, using several short passes and running plays. Soon, though, it was third down and long with less than a minute left on the clock. Ken would definitely have to launch a pass. Will knew it. No doubt the Raiders did too.

Sure enough, Ken called the snap and dropped back for a pass—this time with solid protection from Matt and Josh. Meanwhile Todd ran ten yards downfield and cut toward the sideline with Huxley hot on his trail.

"Do it, Matthews," Will muttered. "Fake him out."

Ken pumped his arm sharply, as if it were another out pattern, and just as Will had predicted, Huxley reared up and jumped in front of Todd in anticipation of the pass. Only the ball never came. Meanwhile Todd took the opportunity to spin around and continue upfield. He was now a good twenty yards behind Huxley, running wide open. Ken pumped his arm again and this time let the ball go. It soared through the air, over Todd's shoulder and into his waiting hands. As Huxley tried vainly to catch up, Todd easily streaked the final five yards into the end zone.

"Yeah!" Will shouted, raising his right fist into the air.

Behind him the stands rumbled in celebration. Only thirty seconds left on the clock and Sweet Valley was up by six.

"Simmons!" Will jerked around to see Coach Riley stalking toward him.

"Coach?" Will answered. He swallowed hard.

Coach Riley planted himself right next to Will, then whacked him on the shoulder. "You did it," he said, a wide smile cracking his tough, leathery features. "Your pep talk with Matthews got us back in the game."

Will hunched his shoulders uncomfortably.

"Thanks for being such a good sport." He lowered his voice. "I know it's tough watching the rest of your season from the bench. But you've still got that team spirit. We all appreciate that." Giving Will a final grin and another punch on the shoulder, he turned and marched back to his assistants.

Will felt a sharp twinge of guilt. If Coach knew the whole story, instead of complimenting him he would have grabbed Will by his bum leg, whirled him around, and tossed him out of the field like a human discus. Still, it did turn out okay in the end. At least he had that to feel good about.

The Sweet Valley team kicker easily scored the extra point, widening the lead to seven. Will sat forward and watched the Raiders, who had already used their time-outs, try a couple of desperate plays in their no-huddle offense. Still the defense managed to hold them back, and before long the entire home crowd was counting down the final seconds at the top of their lungs.

". . . Three, two, one!"

Then everything seemed to explode. The players gathered on the sidelines, jumping and cheering. People in the stands ran down to the field. All around Will people were shouting and clapping and jumping around. He stood up gingerly and leaned on his crutches, trying to take it inside him and feel it, even if he couldn't join in.

To his right a knot of players were jostling Ken around, chanting his name. Will managed to catch his eye and give him a congratulatory nod. He saw Ken nod back, his face beaming with gratitude, before getting swallowed up by the throng.

Will turned to his left, where another group of players and fans were surrounding Coach Riley.

"Excuse me," Will said, trying to step past a grinning spectator.

At that moment all he wanted was to get out of there. Suddenly it seemed like he didn't belong. This was Ken's big moment, not his. And even if he'd been the one to make this happen, he just couldn't stomach a big Ken love fest right now.

Will was just about to shuffle off the field when the TV reporter he had overheard earlier pushed right in front of him, followed by a tall guy carrying a large video camera. They barely gave Will a passing glance as they trapped him up against the bench, directing all their attention at Coach Riley.

"Coach Riley!" said the reporter as he shoved his microphone under the coach's nose. "Congratulations on your advancement to the semifinals. What would you say made the difference for you in this game?"

"Well, Don. What you saw tonight was a solid team effort," Coach replied. "But I'd say the most valuable contributions came from our two quarterbacks. Ken Matthews"—he turned and gestured toward Ken's crowd—"and Will Simmons," he added, looking straight at Will.

"Looks like the entire Sweet Valley student population is out there, celebrating with the players," Kelsey remarked. Her dark blue eyes darted over to Jade. "Don't you want to go down there and congratulate them?"

In other words, get lost so you can continue to have Evan all to yourself? Jade fumed. She couldn't believe it when she'd raced up here after the game ended to be with Evan and he'd introduced her to Kelsey the bimbette, then made *no* move to leave with her.

"No," she replied. "They don't need me to shake their hands. They look pumped up enough on their own."

"What about you?" Kelsey asked Evan, poking his stomach. Jade bit the inside of her lip. "Where's your *team spirit?*" She twisted the last two words with obvious sarcasm.

Evan frowned up at her. "What do you expect me to do? Turn flips? Name my kids after Ken Matthews?"

"But you won!" Kelsey laughed. "Aren't you excited?"

"*I* didn't win," Evan corrected. "*They* won. Why do people automatically get this we're-better-than-you-are attitude after a game when all they did was sit on their butts, eating hot dogs?"

Jarvis, who Jade had been introduced to along with Kelsey, chuckled through a mouthful of nachos, and Kelsey leaned sideways as she laughed, letting the top half of her body fall toward Evan. Her long, blond hair draped across his chest.

Get a grip, Jade thought. *It wasn't that funny.*

Why couldn't Jade be alone with Evan for two whole minutes? Kelsey got to sit with him during the whole game, so why did she have to keep hanging around?

"Don't listen to him," Kelsey told Jade. "He's really cynical about big team sports."

Again Jade's blood simmered. Where did Kelsey get off, sounding so authoritative about Evan? It was like she owned the guy or something.

Jade flashed Kelsey a phony smile. "I know," she said, an edge to her voice.

Kelsey ignored her and turned back to Evan. "I've got to say, Ev. You've totally sold out since you started going to Sweet Valley."

Evan raised his eyebrows. "Sold out?" he repeated.

"Yes," she replied. "Come on, think about it. You actually attended a football game."

"Yeah, and you actually sat and watched it instead of picketing from the other side of the fence," Jarvis joined in.

Kelsey shook her head and made annoying little clicking sounds with her tongue. "You are really going soft, Plummer. Hey, you even dated a *cheerleader!* What was her name? Jessica?"

A flash of anger surged through Jade. She wouldn't have been surprised to find her breath coming out in flames. In fact, she wished it would. She'd love to be able to frizz up Kelsey's perfect mane of hair with one well-directed sneeze.

"Um . . . hello?" Jade said, waving a hand toward Kelsey. She pulled at her cheerleading sweater with the other hand. "In case you hadn't noticed, I am a *'cheerleader.'*" Jade mimicked Kelsey's breathy voice.

"Uh-oh," Jarvis teased. "Trouble."

"I was making fun of *Evan*, not cheerleaders," Kelsey explained, never entirely shifting her attention from Evan to Jade.

"Oh, right." Jade nodded slowly. "So . . . you weren't making fun of *cheerleaders*. You were making fun of people who *date* them. Totally different. My mistake."

"Hey, everyone chill, okay?" Evan cut in, sitting forward. "We're all friends here."

Friends. There was that word again.

"Stop it! Just stop it! How can you be so clueless?" Jade burst out.

"What?" Evan stared back at her, his mouth hanging open slightly.

What did it take with this guy? Would she ever get the chance to tell him how she felt? Or did it even matter? It was all getting to be too much. The hint dropping. The dates that weren't. Kelsey . . .

"Look, just forget it," she snapped. "Forget everything!" She stood and had started to head down the bleachers when Evan grabbed hold of her arm.

"What's going on, Jade?" he asked, his voice soft with worry.

"Nothing." Jade wrenched out of his grasp, afraid to meet his gaze. She felt like she was totally losing it. "You just stay here, in your own little world, with your rude little friends. I'm out of here."

She turned and raced down the wide metal steps, tripping a couple of times in her hurry. Eventually she made it to the bottom and disappeared through one of the dark exits.

That *certainly didn't turn out the way I wanted*, she thought, feeling tears of embarrassment collect in her eyes. *But hey—at least I wasn't subtle.*

"Oh my God, there's Phil Zuniga," Rebecca exclaimed, pointing to a group of spectators who had just emerged, still cheering, from the playing field. "He's, like, three inches taller than last year. And look! There's Tamara Bloomenfeld! She's as trendy as ever. Wow. I *never* see these people. This is like an El Carro reunion."

"Rebecca! Andy!"

Andy turned his head and caught sight of Tia running toward them, her long, brown hair streaming behind her and her faced flushed with excitement.

"Hey!" Rebecca exclaimed, grabbing for Tia's arms

158

and pulling her into their circle. "Congratulations on the big win."

"Yeah, it was a great game, wasn't it?" Tia asked, looking from Andy to Dale and back again.

Andy knew the enthusiasm in her voice had more to do with his big blind date than with the Gladiators' win over the Raiders. He'd seen her full of team spirit many times. But he'd hardly ever seen her stare at him so expectantly—as if he were Santa Claus, ready to hand her a giant present.

"Oh, yes. Football at its most brilliant," Andy joked. "Wouldn't you say so, Dale?"

"I agree. The best example of head bashing I've seen in a long time," Dale deadpanned.

"All right, all right. I know who the real fans are," Tia grumbled. "So where's the rest of the gang?"

"Liz and Megan are off trying to console Maria," Andy explained. "She's still pretty upset."

"Yeah," Tia said, her smile fading. "I tried to stop her when she was running onto the field." Her grin quickly returned. "So," she said, "who wants a root-beer float?"

"I do," Rebecca replied. "But"—Andy watched as she and Tia exchanged a brief, knowing glance—"is that Ted Masters over there? Is he still dressing like a lounge singer? Come on, Dale. I want you to meet this guy. He's, like, a vintage weirdo." She grabbed Dale's arm and pulled him away with her. "Meet you guys in a second," she called back over her shoulder.

Andy rolled his eyes. It was so obvious the girls had planned to pull him and Dale aside for their own little fact-gathering missions.

"So?" Tia gazed up at him, bouncing her weight from one foot to the other. "Come on, Andy, what happened?"

"Well, Tee," he began, hoping she wouldn't be too crushed. "Dale is . . . really cool." *Might as well start with the good news,* he told himself.

Tia clasped her hands together. "I knew it," she said, a gigantic grin nearly splitting her face in half.

"But . . . no sparks flew," Andy added, cringing.

Tia completely deflated, her expression sagging. "Really?" she said. "Are you sure?"

A cyclone of reactions swirled within Andy. He was relieved she wasn't punching him, guilty for having disappointed her, and amused that she was so caught up in his social life. He knew Tia just needed a distraction, but in a way, it was sort of flattering. Not too long ago she hadn't had *any* time for him. But maybe now she had a little too much. It was time for her to find a hobby.

"I'm sorry, Tee," Andy said with a shrug. "It just didn't happen. You can't really force this kind of thing, I guess."

"But I don't understand," she whined. "You guys have so much in common. Maybe you just need a few more dates?"

"No, it's not happening," Andy said firmly. He gently grabbed her cheeks and stared her straight in the eye. "It's never going to happen. It's over."

He let go of her and watched as a sad comprehension came over her features. She heaved a big sigh. "Okay. I understand," she muttered. "How does Dale feel?"

"I'm pretty sure it's the same for him," Andy replied. "But hey." He reached out and punched her lightly on the arm. "Thanks for pushing me into this. I did sort of need that. And even if there was no love connection, Dale and I will definitely be friends. And it's cool to have someone who knows exactly what I'm going through right now."

Tia smiled weakly. "I'm glad," she said.

"Besides," Andy began, shoving his hands in his pockets. He stared down at the broken asphalt under his feet. "I've realized that I really am ready to try and meet someone."

Out of the corner of his eye he could see Tia immediately perk up.

"But," he added, holding up a hand, "it should be someone *I* find. Okay?"

Tia's hopeful stare slowly dissolved into a resigned grin. "Okay," she replied.

Suddenly Andy felt a rush of sympathy for Tia as he realized how much this had meant to her. *She must be really lonely,* he thought.

"Hey, Tee? If I can start looking for someone, I know you can too. What do you say? Want to date together? Well, maybe not *together,* together, but you know what I mean."

Tia let out a small giggle. She stared down at her sneakers and lifted her shoulders. "I don't know, Andy. I don't know if I'm ready yet. But . . . thanks." Her eyes met his, and her face broke out into a very wide, very Tia smile. "Now, come on," she added, hooking her arm through his. "Let's go take Dale and Rebecca to First and Ten. We can still hang out, right? Just a bunch of *friends* getting some coffee."

Evan Plummer

See? <u>This</u> is why I hate football. It makes people confrontational for no reason. It brings out latent hostility. It feeds the us-against-them mentality.

I knew I shouldn't have come to this stupid game. I just really wanted to see Jade. So now I've totally compromised my ethics <u>and</u> somehow offended her too.

How lame can a guy get?

Maria Slater

I hate football. I hate football. I hate football. I hate football. And did I mention, I hate football?

It hurts people. It changes people. It gets people worked up for no reason.

I don't care if Walt Tibbets is in a full body cast—I'm never setting foot on these bleachers again. I'd rather stay home and paint my toenails, or wash the windows, or organize my bathroom cupboard.

How lame can a girl get?

CHAPTER 11

Dealing with All Those Feelings

Will moved carefully through the small groups of football players who were still jumping and hollering and crushing each other in rough displays of emotion. Occasionally one or two of the guys would run up and clap him on the back, thanking him for helping out the team.

It didn't hurt any less that he wasn't a part of this, that he knew his dreams of a football career were as smashed as his knee. It still felt like he was trapped in someone else's broken body. But somehow not having that consuming rage inside him—at Ken, at his doctors, at *everyone* who could walk on their own—made it seem like he might end up okay.

Right now all he wanted was to get home to bed. He didn't want to be here. But first there was something important he had to do.

A group of people parted in front of him, and Will caught sight of Matt and Josh up by the bleachers. He cautiously maneuvered around some frenzied fans and approached them.

"Hey," he said as he came up behind them.

They turned around, and Will felt a surge of relief when Matt flashed a wide grin.

"Hey!" Matt said. "Excellent game, man."

Will nodded. "Yeah."

"We couldn't have pulled it off without you," Matt added, holding up a hand.

Will propped his right arm on his crutch in order to high-five him. Then he turned his attention to Josh.

"Radinsky, man. I—I'm—" He stopped, unsure how to finish. Now that he had his head straight again, he realized how out of line he'd been with his friends. It was unfair for him to pull rank and ask them to do his dirty work for him. Matt, who lived moment to moment, seemed to have already put it all behind him. But Josh could hold a grudge. And he'd been the one who didn't want to go through with this. If only Will had listened to him.

"Hey, it's all right," Josh reassured him. "Everything's cool. Matt's right about you coming through for us."

Will met Josh's eyes and saw the respect there. Respect he'd missed more than he knew since the accident, when all his gaze ever found in people's eyes was pity.

"You guys will rule the semifinals," he said. "Even without me." He lifted a corner of his mouth in a wry grin.

Josh looked like he was about to respond but then stopped short. He cleared his throat and gestured at something behind Will.

Will turned around and saw Melissa standing a couple of feet in back of him, staring right at him. Her expression was hard to read, but she didn't seem upset.

"Hi," she said. "Can we talk?"

He spun back toward Josh and Matt, but they were already walking downfield. Slowly he turned to face Melissa again. What was she up to? She'd probably already figured out he had something to do with Ken getting sacked. Was she going to call him on it?

"Congratulations on helping out the team," she said, taking another step toward him. Her face was still a blank mask, giving him no clues about her goal. And Will knew there had to be a goal. Melissa did *not* give out compliments for free.

"What do you want, Li—Melissa?" he asked, purposely catching himself before using her old nickname. He was not in the mood for her games. Not now—when he'd finally gotten on top of things again.

She reached out and ran her hand up his arm. "That's funny," she said, her voice low. "I don't think you've ever asked me that. You always seem to know what I want."

Will pulled his arm away in disgust, searching her blue eyes for an explanation. What was going on with her? Why wasn't she standing next to Ken doll, basking in all his glory? Melissa lived for moments like that.

A sudden realization shot through him. Over Melissa's shoulder he could see Ken standing only a few yards away, talking with his dad and Coach Riley. Melissa should be right next to the guy, playing the part of the happy girlfriend. But she wasn't. In fact, she and Ken seemed to be purposely ignoring each other.

That must be it, Will thought. *Ken broke up with her, and now she wants to come running back to me. Typical.*

He took a step backward. "Forget it," he growled. "I'm not falling for this."

Melissa's eyes filled with hurt, and her lower lip began to tremble.

She obviously didn't count on that *reaction,* Will thought.

"Will, I don't know what you're talking about," she said. "I was just trying to be nice."

"I mean it," Will shot back. "Save your comments for someone who cares. I don't want anything to do with you."

Before he could see the wounded, accusing look on her face—he had that expression memorized from all their past fights—Will turned and hobbled off toward the parking lot.

As he made his way across the turf, Will felt better than he had in a long, long time. He might have

168

lost his football career, but at least he'd found his pride again. Now that he had it back, he never wanted to lose it again.

And that meant never letting his ex-girlfriend back into his life.

Jade marched past the ticket booth toward the parking lot, her vinyl gym bag banging against her hipbone with every step. All around her people were still running back and forth, yelling about the big win. But their giddy enthusiasm only made her more irritated.

"Gladiators rule!" shouted one guy as he whizzed past.

Oh, get a life, she moaned inwardly. *It's just a stupid game.*

Some cheerleader she was. Here her team had its best shot in years to make it to the state finals, and she couldn't even manage a smile. Of course, if she were out there turning cartwheels on the field right now, Evan and Kelsey could have a blast making fun of her. That is, if they weren't too busy making out.

"Jade!" someone called from behind her.

Jade whirled around to glare at whoever was picking now to bug her. If one more lunatic screeched to her about how great a game it was, she was going to shove her cheerleading uniform over their head.

But it wasn't another crazy fan—it was Evan.

Jade froze in shock as she watched him jog toward her, his hair lifting off his face to reveal those piercing blue eyes. Then, annoyed with herself, she turned and resumed her march to the parking lot. No matter what he said, she was not going to apologize for her little outburst. It had been the only direct, honest thing she'd said to him in two days.

"Jade! Wait up!" Evan shouted again. Jade could hear the pounding of his feet as he approached. He quickly ran around in front of her and began walking backward, staring her right in the eye.

Jade forced herself to gaze right past him at the rows of parked cars.

"What's wrong, Jade?" he asked while sidestepping a small shrub. "I know you're mad at me, but why? What's going on?"

Jade gave a frustrated grunt and stopped. She stared at his worried, confused, adorable face and wondered just how clueless a guy could be. After everything that had happened, he *still* had no idea how she felt about him? What was it going to take?

"You want to know what's wrong?" she asked. "Do you *really* want to know?"

Evan blinked, obviously more confused than ever. "Yes," he said firmly.

"Fine," she said, letting her hands drop to her sides. Her gym bag, megaphone, and pom-poms thudded against the concrete. "*This* is what's wrong," she snapped. Then, throwing her arms around him, she pulled him toward her and kissed him hard on the lips.

After a long, spine-tingling moment she pulled back. "You see now?" she said, trying to maintain the angry edge in her voice. But the kiss had electrified her entire body, leaving her breathless and almost dizzy.

Evan looked back at her, stunned. "Wh-What?" he stammered. "What does that mean?"

Jade glared at him. "What does it *usually* mean?"

"Wait a minute. Wait a minute." He shook his head, making his sheepdog bangs wave back and forth across his face. "But you . . . I thought . . . aren't you still hung up on Jeremy?"

"No!" Jade cried out. "I've only been dropping a million hints these past couple of days," she added. "Didn't you get that you're the one I want?"

"You're kidding." A wide grin crept over his face, replacing the puzzlement. "I figured you kept bringing him up because you were still crazy about him. You kept going on about how great he was, so I just assumed you weren't over him yet."

"You *what?*" She groaned. "But . . . but I was trying to show you how together I was. You were supposed to think I'd never be that mature if I was still hung up on Jeremy."

His brow furrowed. "But why didn't you just come out and tell me?"

"I was being subtle," she said quietly.

Evan laughed. "You know, you're pretty lousy at it."

"Hey! I wasn't *that* hard to figure out," she said, trying not to smile. "And what about you? I asked you to the game, and you made it into a group thing. Then I see you in the stands with Kelsey practically in your lap. What am *I* supposed to think?"

He met her gaze without flinching. "Wait a sec," he said. "Kelsey is just a friend—a friend who likes to flirt. In fact," he said, giving a sheepish shrug, "that's what I figured you were. I thought you and Kelsey might hit it off."

Jade stared at him in amazement for a couple of seconds, then let out a choked laugh. "That's a good one," she said.

"Yeah. I guess so," he said, his eyes taking on an amused gleam. He took a step closer to her. "You know what, though? You don't ever have to be subtle with me. For one thing, you're no good at it. And besides"—he ran his finger under her chin, making her spine shiver—"I like it when you're obvious."

"Oh, really?" Jade murmured, her entire body tingling from his touch. "Well, how's this for obvious?" She looped her hands around Evan's head and slid herself toward him. Then she kissed him again—a long, lingering kiss that made everything around her melt away.

"So . . . did you have fun?" Elizabeth asked Megan. They were sitting on a bench outside the front entrance of Sweet Valley High, waiting for Maria to come back from the rest room so they could leave. Elizabeth knew Maria just needed some time to get herself together, and she completely understood. Still, she wished the girl would hurry. Even though the game had been a major victory and the parking lot was filled with people celebrating, Elizabeth wasn't really feeling the whole partying spirit.

"Yeah," Megan replied brightly. "I really did. It's just . . . well, I feel so bad for Maria."

Elizabeth nodded. "Me too. I'm really worried about her. You know, she acts like everything's fine and she's totally okay without Ken. But inside she's still a wreck, I can tell. And I guess tonight she kind of had to face how much she still cares about him."

Megan glanced out at the parking lot. "Yeah, Maria's really not over Ken, is she?" she said.

"No," Elizabeth replied. She twisted her beaded bracelet around her wrist, staring down at her lap. "I know how hard it must be for her right now, having to deal with all those feelings."

"Liz?" Megan turned back to face her, fixing her

with an intent gaze. "Um . . . I was wondering—you know that Conner's coming back next week, right?"

Elizabeth pressed her lips together. Leave it to Megan to read her mind.

"Yeah, I heard," she mumbled, thinking of Conner's letter to Tia. "That's really great. You must be so relieved."

"Yeah," Megan replied. She paused, still watching her closely. "But how do *you* feel about it? I mean . . . do you think you guys might get back together?"

Elizabeth opened her mouth, but nothing came out. The truth was, she didn't know what to say. She didn't even know what she *wanted*. The only thing she was sure of was that she still loved Conner. It was there, inside her, just like Maria with Ken. But whether they could really start over again . . .

At least Conner was getting better. Obviously the doctors wouldn't let him go home if they didn't think he had control of the drinking. But she still had no idea what to expect or how to even prepare herself. What if he didn't want to see her?

Elizabeth's head started to throb. She propped her elbows on her lap and clasped her hands together in front of her.

"I don't know, Megan," she finally answered. "I honestly don't know what will happen when Conner comes back."

TIA RAMIREZ

10:32 P.M.

OKAY, SO ANDY DIDN'T FALL HEAD OVER HEELS. BUT JUST BECAUSE HE CAN'T USE MY HELP DOESN'T MEAN I SHOULD GIVE UP, DOES IT? HMMM. MAYBE MARIA WOULD LIKE TO MEET ONE OF MY OLD EL CARRO FRIENDS. OR MAYBE LIZ MIGHT LIKE ONE OF MY OLDER BROTHER'S FRIENDS. REBECCA MIGHT BE INTO MY COUSIN MICKEY. HE'S BEEN A LOT NICER SINCE HE GOT KICKED OUT OF MILITARY SCHOOL.

OR MAYBE, JUST MAYBE, I SHOULD GET A LIFE.

KEN MATTHEWS

10:34 P.M.

I feel great, right? I really do. Krubowski's on the cell phone to some U of Michigan big shot. The team is cheering and tossing me around. I'm all in one piece. And we're on to the semifinals next week. I should be totally psyched.

But somehow it still doesn't feel right. Something's missing. Or maybe some<u>one</u>.

MELISSA FOX
10:36 P.M.

He shot me down. I can't believe it. He really shot me down. First Ken and now Will, all in one day. This absolutely can't happen. I won't let it. The thing is, I _hate_ being alone. And one way or another, I won't be for long.

~~Dear Conner,~~

~~I hear you're heading back home next week. That's great. And it sounds like you're doing much better. That's also great. Things are pretty great here.~~

What's wrong with me? Since when do I have the vocabulary of a fourth grader?

~~Dear Conner,~~

~~I know I wasn't the best girlfriend in the world when you were having problems with the drinking, and I just want to say that I'm sorry. I'm sorry I didn't hang in there. And I'm sorry I never knew what to say. And I'm sorry~~

No! No! No! Why bring up all of that? Conner's getting better.

~~Dear Conner,~~

~~Hey! What's up? Things are pretty busy here. Work has been a little crazier than usual, but at least school isn't as stressful now that the last round of exams is over. Tonight I went to the football game, and you wouldn't believe how~~

No. Forget that too. No need to act like I'm in total denial.

~~Dear Conner,~~

~~Why did you write Tia instead of me? Do you ever think of me at all? Does what we had together still mean anything to you?~~

Yuck. Can you say, "soap-opera queen"?
Okay. One last try:

Dear Conner,
   I love you. I miss you. I'm scared of
what to say to you. And even though I
will never mail this letter, at least I
feel better for having written it down.
Maybe I'll have things more figured out
when I see you face-to-face.
                              Liz

THE NEW WINDMILL SERIES
General Editors: Anne and Ian Serraillier

35

SHANE

This is not only a superb cowboy story (which made a fine film), but also a work of literature. The story is told by the boy into whose family corral a mysterious stranger rode in the summer of '89. For all who enjoy a thrilling western.

Jack Schaefer

SHANE

Patrick lassidy

D.3

HEINEMANN EDUCATIONAL BOOKS
LONDON

Heinemann Educational Books Ltd
22 Bedford Square, London WC1B 3HH

LONDON EDINBURGH MELBOURNE AUCKLAND
HONG KONG SINGAPORE KUALA LUMPUR NEW DELHI
IBADAN NAIROBI JOHANNESBURG KINGSTON
EXETER (NH) PORT OF SPAIN

ISBN 0 435 12035 2

Shane is included in this series
by kind permission of Messrs. André Deutsch Ltd

FIRST PUBLISHED IN THE NEW WINDMILL SERIES 1957
REPRINTED 1958, 1959, 1960, 1961, 1962, 1964, 1965
RESET 1966
REPRINTED 1967, 1969, 1970, 1972, 1974, 1975,
1977, 1979, 1981

Printed in Great Britain by
Morrison & Gibb Ltd., London and Edinburgh

To Carl, for my first son, my first book

I

HE RODE into our valley in the summer of '89. I was a kid then, barely topping the backboard of father's old chuck-wagon. I was on the upper rail of our small corral, soaking in the late afternoon sun, when I saw him far down the road where it swung into the valley from the open plain beyond.

In that clear Wyoming air I could see him plainly, though he was still several miles away. There seemed nothing remarkable about him, just another stray horseman riding up the road toward the cluster of frame buildings that was our town. Then I saw a pair of cowhands, loping past him, stop and stare after him with a curious intentness.

He came steadily on, straight through the town without slackening pace, until he reached the fork a half-mile below our place. One branch turned left across the river ford and onto Luke Fletcher's big spread. The other bore ahead along the right bank where we homesteaders had pegged our claims in a row up the valley. He hesitated briefly, studying the choice, and moved again steadily on our side.

As he came near, what impressed me first was his clothes. He wore dark trousers of some serge material tucked into tall boots and held at the waist by a wide

5

belt, both of a soft black leather tooled in intricate design. A coat of the same dark material as the trousers was neatly folded and strapped to his saddle-roll. His shirt was finespun linen, rich brown in colour. The handkerchief knotted loosely around his throat was black silk. His hat was not the familiar Stetson, not the familiar grey or muddy tan. It was a plain black, soft in texture, unlike any hat I had ever seen, with a creased crown and a wide curling brim swept down in front to shield the face.

All trace of newness was long since gone from these things. The dust of distance was beaten into them. They were worn and stained and several neat patches showed on the shirt. Yet a kind of magnificence remained and with it a hint of men and manners alien to my limited boy's experience.

Then I forgot the clothes in the impact of the man himself. He was not much above medium height, almost slight in build. He would have looked frail alongside father's square, solid bulk. But even I could read the endurance in the lines of that dark figure and the quiet power in its effortless, unthinking adjustment to every movement of the tired horse.

He was clean-shaven and his face was lean and hard and burned from high forehead to firm, tapering chin. His eyes seemed hooded in the shadow of the hat's brim. He came closer, and I could see that this was because the brows were drawn in a frown of fixed and habitual alertness. Beneath them the eyes were endlessly searching from side to side and forward, checking off every item in view, missing nothing. As I noticed this, a sudden chill, I could not have told why, struck through me in the warm and open sun.

He rode easily, relaxed in the saddle, leaning his

6

weight lazily into the stirrups. Yet even in this easiness was a suggestion of tension. It was the easiness of a coiled spring, of a trap set.

He drew rein not twenty feet from me. His glance hit me, dismissed me, flicked over our place. This was not much, if you were thinking in terms of size and scope. But what there was was good. You could trust father for that. The corral, big enough for about thirty head if you crowded them in, was railed right to true sunk posts. The pasture behind, taking in nearly half of our claim, was fenced tight. The barn was small, but it was solid, and we were raising a loft at one end for the alfalfa growing green in the north forty. We had a fair-sized field in potatoes that year and father was trying a new corn he had sent all the way to Washington for and they were showing properly in weedless rows.

Behind the house, mother's kitchen garden was a brave sight. The house itself was three rooms—two really, the big kitchen where we spent most of our time indoors and the bedroom beside it. My little lean-to room was added back of the kitchen. Father was planning, when he could get around to it, to build mother the parlour she wanted.

We had wooden floors and a nice porch across the front. The house was painted too, white with green trim, rare thing in all that region, to remind her, mother said when she made father do it, of her native New England. Even rarer, the roof was shingled. I knew what that meant. I had helped father split those shingles. Few places so spruce and well worked could be found so deep in the Territory in those days.

The stranger took it all in, sitting there easily in the

saddle. I saw his eyes slow on the flowers mother had planted by the porch steps, then come to rest on our shiny new pump and the trough beside it. They shifted back to me, and again, without knowing why, I felt that sudden chill. But his voice was gentle and he spoke like a man schooled to patience.

'I'd appreciate a chance at the pump for myself and the horse.'

I was trying to frame a reply and choking on it, when I realized that he was not speaking to me but past me. Father had come up behind me and was leaning against the gate to the corral.

'Use all the water you want, stranger.'

Father and I watched him dismount in a single flowing tilt of his body and lead the horse over to the trough. He pumped it almost full and let the horse sink its nose in the cool water before he picked up the dipper for himself.

He took off his hat and slapped the dust out of it and hung it on a corner of the trough. With his hands he brushed the dust from his clothes. With a piece of rag pulled from his saddle-roll he carefully wiped his boots. He untied the handkerchief from around his neck and rolled his sleeves and dipped his arms in the trough, rubbing thoroughly and splashing water over his face. He shook his hands dry and used the handkerchief to remove the last drops from his face. Taking a comb from his shirt pocket, he smoothed back his long dark hair. All his movements were deft and sure, and with a quick precision he flipped down his sleeves, reknotted the handkerchief, and picked up his hat.

Then, holding it in his hand, he spun about and strode directly towards the house. He bent low and snapped the stem of one of mother's petunias and tucked this into the hatband. In another moment the hat was on his head, brim swept down in swift, unconscious gesture, and he was swinging gracefully into the saddle and starting toward the road.

I was fascinated. None of the men I knew were proud like that about their appearance. In that short time the kind of magnificence I had noticed had emerged into plainer view. It was in the very air of him. Everything about him showed the effects of long use and hard use, but showed too the strength of quality and competence. There was no chill on me now. Already I was imagining myself in hat and belt and boots like those.

He stopped the horse and looked down at us. He was refreshed and I would have sworn the tiny wrinkles around his eyes were what with him would be a smile. His eyes were not restless when he looked at you like this. They were still and steady and you knew the man's whole attention was concentrated on you even in the casual glance.

'Thank you,' he said in his gentle voice and was turning into the road, back to us, before father spoke in his slow, deliberate way.

'Don't be in such a hurry, stranger.'

I had to hold tight to the rail or I would have fallen backwards into the corral. At the first sound of father's voice, the man and the horse, like a single being, had wheeled to face us, the man's eyes boring at father, bright and deep in the shadow of the hat's brim. I was shivering, struck through once more. Something intangible and cold and terrifying was there in the air between us.

I stared in wonder as father and the stranger looked

at each other a long moment, measuring each other in an unspoken fraternity of adult knowledge beyond my reach. Then the warm sunlight was flooding over us, for father was smiling and he was speaking with the drawling emphasis that meant he had made up his mind.

'I said don't be in such a hurry, stranger. Food will be on the table soon and you can bed down here to-night.'

The stranger nodded quietly as if he too had made up his mind. 'That's mighty thoughtful of you,' he said and swung down and came toward us, leading his horse. Father slipped into step beside him and we all headed for the barn.

'My name's Starrett,' said father. 'Joe Starrett. This here,' waving at me, 'is Robert MacPherson Starrett. Too much name for a boy. I make it Bob.'

The stranger nodded again. 'Call me Shane,' he said. Then to me: 'Bob it is. You were watching me for quite a spell coming up the road.'

It was not a question. It was a simple statement. 'Yes . . .' I stammered. 'Yes. I was.'

'Right,' he said. 'I like that. A man who watches what's going on around him will make his mark.'

A man who watches. . . . For all his dark appearance and lean, hard look, this Shane knew what would please a boy. The glow of it held me as he took care of his horse, and I fussed around, hanging up his saddle, forking over some hay, getting in his way and my own in my eagerness. He let me slip the bridle off and the horse, bigger and more powerful than I had thought now that I was close beside it, put its head down patiently for me and stood quietly while I helped him curry away the caked dust. Only once did he stop me. That was when I reached for his saddle-roll to put it to one side. In the instant my fingers touched it, he was taking it from me and he put it on a shelf with a finality that indicated no interference.

When the three of us went up to the house, mother was waiting and four places were set at the table. 'I saw you through the window,' she said and came to shake our visitor's hand. She was a slender, lively woman with a fair complexion even our weather never seemed to affect and a mass of light brown hair she wore piled high to bring her, she used to say, closer to father's size.

'Marian,' father said, 'I'd like you to meet Mr Shane.'

'Good evening, ma'am,' said our visitor. He took her hand and bowed over it. Mother stepped back and, to my surprise, dropped in a dainty curtsy. I had never seen her do that before. She was an unpredictable woman. Father and I would have painted the house three times over and in rainbow colours to please her.

'And a good evening to you, Mr Shane. If Joe hadn't called you back, I would have done it myself. You'd never find a decent meal up the valley.'

She was proud of her cooking, was mother. That was one thing she learned back home, she would often say, that was of some use out in this raw land. As long as she could still prepare a proper dinner, she would tell father when things were not going right, she knew she was still civilized and there was hope of getting ahead. Then she would tighten her lips and whisk together her special most delicious biscuits and father would watch her bustling about and eat them to the last little crumb and stand up and wipe his eyes and stretch his big frame and stomp out to his always unfinished work like daring anything to stop him now.

We sat down to supper and a good one. Mother's eyes sparkled as our visitor kept pace with father and me. Then we all leaned back and while I listened the talk ran on almost like old friends around a familiar table. But I could sense that it was following a pattern. Father was trying, with mother helping and both of them avoiding direct questions, to get hold of facts about this Shane and he was dodging at every turn. He was aware of their purpose and not in the least annoyed by it. He was mild and courteous and spoke readily enough. But always he put them off with words that gave no real information.

He must have been riding many days, for he was full of news from towns along his back trail as far as Cheyenne and even Dodge City and others beyond I had never heard of before. But he had no news about himself. His past was fenced as tightly as our pasture. All they could learn was that he was riding through, taking each day as it came, with nothing particular in mind except maybe seeing a part of the country he had not been in before.

Afterwards mother washed the dishes and I dried and the two men sat on the porch, their voices carrying through the open door. Our visitor was guiding the conversation now and in no time at all he had father talking about his own plans. That was no trick. Father was ever one to argue his ideas whenever he could find a listener. This time he was going strong.

'Yes, Shane, the boys I used to ride with don't see

it yet. They will some day. The open range can't last forever. The fence lines are closing in. Running cattle in big lots is good business only for the top ranchers and it's really a poor business at that. Poor in terms of the resources going into it. Too much space for too little results. 'It's certain to be crowded out.'

'Well, now,' said Shane, 'that's mighty interesting. I've been hearing the same quite a lot lately and from men with pretty clear heads. Maybe there's something to it.'

'By Godfrey, there's plenty to it. Listen to me, Shane. The thing to do is pick your spot, get your land, your own land. Put in enough crops to carry you and make your money play with a small herd, not all horns and bone, but bred for meat and fenced in and fed right. I haven't been at it long, but already I've raised stock that averages three hundred pounds more than that long-legged stuff Fletcher runs on the other side of the river and it's better beef, and that's only a beginning.

'Sure, his outfit sprawls over most of this valley and it looks big. But he's got range rights on a lot more acres than he has cows and he won't even have those acres as more homesteaders move in. His way is wasteful. Too much land for what he gets out of it. He can't see that. He thinks we small fellows are nothing but damned nuisances.'

'You are,' said Shane mildly. 'From his point of view, you are.'

'Yes, I guess you're right. I'll have to admit that. Those of us here now would make it tough for him if he wanted to use the range behind us on this side of the river as he used to. Altogether we cut some pretty good slices out of it. Worse still, we block off part of the river, shut the range off from the water. He's been grumbling about that off and on ever since we've been here. He's worried that more of us will keep coming and settle on the other side too, and then he will be in a fix.'

The dishes were done and I was edging to the door. Mother nailed me as she usually did and shunted me off to bed. After she had left me in my little back room and went to join the men on the porch, I tried to catch more of the words. The voices were too low. Then I must have dozed, for with a start I realized that father and mother were again in the kitchen. By now, I gathered, our visitor was out in the barn in the bunk father had built there for the hired man who had been with us for a few weeks in the spring.

'Wasn't it peculiar,' I heard mother say, 'how he wouldn't talk about himself?'

'Peculiar?' said father. 'Well, yes. In a way.'

'Everything about him is peculiar.' Mother sounded as if she was stirred up and interested. 'I never saw a man quite like him before.'

'You wouldn't have. Not where you come from. He's a special brand we sometimes get out here in the grass country. I've come across a few. A bad one's poison. A good one's straight grain clear through.'

'How can you be so sure about him? Why, he wouldn't even tell where he was raised.'

'Born back east a ways would be my guess. And pretty far south. Tennessee maybe. But he's been around plenty.'

'I like him.' Mother's voice was serious. 'He's so nice and polite and sort of gentle. Not like most men I've met out here. But there's something about him.

Something underneath the gentleness. . . . Something
. . .' Her voice trailed away.

'Mysterious?' suggested father.

'Yes, of course. Mysterious. But more than that.
Dangerous.'

'He's dangerous all right.' Father said it in a musing
way. Then he chuckled. 'But not to us, my dear.'
And then he said what seemed to me a curious thing.
'In fact, I don't think you ever had a safer man in your
house.'

II

IN THE morning I slept late and stumbled into the kitchen to find father and our visitor working their way through piles of mother's flapjacks. She smiled at me from over by the stove. Father slapped my rump by way of greeting. Our visitor nodded at me gravely over his heaped-up plate.

'Good morning. Bob. You'd better dig in fast or I'll do away with your share too. There's magic in your mother's cooking. Eat enough of these flannel cakes and you'll grow a bigger man than your father.'

'Flannel cakes! Did you hear that, Joe?' Mother came whisking over to tousle father's hair. 'You must be right. Tennessee or some such place. I never heard them called that out here.'

Our visitor looked up at her. 'A good guess, ma'am. Mighty close to the mark. But you had a husband to help you. My folks came out of Mississippi and settled in Arkansas. Me, though—I was fiddle-footed and left home at fifteen. Haven't had anything worth being called a real flannel cake since.' He put his hands on the table edge and leaned back and the little wrinkles at the corners of his eyes were plainer and deeper. 'That is, ma'am, till now.'

Mother gave what in a girl I would have called a giggle. 'If I'm any judge of men,' she said, 'that means more.' And she whisked back to the stove.

That was how it was often in our house, kind of

16

jolly and warm with good feeling. It needed to be this morning because there was a cool greyness in the air and before I had even begun to slow on my second plate of flapjacks the wind was rushing down the valley with the rain of one of our sudden summer storms following fast.

Our visitor had finished his breakfast. He had eaten so many flapjacks that I had begun to wonder whether he really would cut into my share. Now he turned to look out the window and his lips tightened. But he pushed back from the table and started to rise. Mother's voice held him to his chair.

'You'll not be travelling in any such weather. Wait a bit and it'll clear. These rains don't last long. I've another pot of coffee on the stove.'

Father was getting his pipe going. He kept his eyes carefully on the smoke drifting upward. 'Marian's right. Only she doesn't go far enough. These rains are short. But they sure mess up the road. It's new. Hasn't settled much yet. Mighty soggy when wet. Won't be fit for travelling till it drains. You better stay over till to-morrow.'

Our visitor stared down at his empty plate as if it was the most important object in the whole room. You could see he liked the idea. Yet he seemed somehow worried about it.

'Yes,' said father. 'That's the sensible dodge. That horse of yours was pretty much beat last night. If I was a horse doctor now, I'd order a day's rest right off. Damned if I don't think the same prescription would do me good too. You stick here the day and I'll follow it. I'd like to take you around, show you what I'm doing with the place.'

He looked pleadingly at mother. She was surprised

and good reason. Father was usually so set on working every possible minute to catch up on his plans that she would have a tussle making him ease some once a week out of respect for the Sabbath. In bad weather like this he usually would fidget and stomp about the house as if he thought it was a personal insult to him, a trick to keep him from being out and doing things. And here he was talking of a whole day's rest. She was puzzled. But she played right up.

'You'd be doing us a favour, Mr Shane. We don't get many visitors from outside the valley. It'd be real nice to have you stay. And besides—' She crinkled her nose at him the way she did when she would be teasing father into some new scheme of hers. 'And besides—I've been waiting for an excuse to try a deep-dish apple pie I've heard tell of. It would just be wasted on these other two. They eat everything in sight and don't rightly know good from poor.'

He was looking up, straight at her. She shook a finger at him. 'And another thing. I'm fair bubbling with questions about what the women are wearing back in civilization. You know, hats and such. You're the kind of man would notice them. You're not getting away till you've told me.'

Shane sat back in his chair. A faint quizzical expression softened the lean ridges of his face. 'Ma'am, I'm not positive I appreciate how you've pegged me. No one else ever wrote me down an expert on ladies' millinery.' He reached out and pushed his cup across the table toward her. 'You said something about more coffee. But I draw the line on more flannel cakes. I'm plumb full. I'm starting in to conserve space for that pie.'

'You'd better!' Father was mighty pleased about

something. 'When Marian puts her mind to cooking, she makes a man forget he's got any limits to his appetite. Only don't you go giving her fancy notions of new hats so she'll be sending off to the mail-order house and throwing my money away on silly frippery. She's got a hat.'

Mother did not even notice that. She knew father was just talking. She knew that whenever she wanted anything real much and said so, father would bust himself trying to get it for her. She whisked over to the table with the coffee pot, poured a fresh round, then set it down within easy reach and sat down herself.

I thought that business about hats was only a joke she made up to help father persuade our visitor to stay. But she began almost at once, pestering him to describe the ladies he had seen in Cheyenne and other towns where the new styles might be. He sat there, easy and friendly, telling her how they were wearing wide floppy-brimmed bonnets with lots of flowers in front on top and slits in the brims for scarves to come through and be tied in bows under their chins.

Talk like that seemed foolish to me to be coming from a grown man. Yet this Shane was not bothered at all. And father listened as if he thought it was all right, only not very interesting. He watched them most of the time in a good-natured quiet, trying every so often to break in with his own talk about crops and steers and giving up and trying again and giving up again with a smiling shake of his head at those two. And the rain outside was a far distance away and meaningless because the friendly feeling in our kitchen was enough to warm all our world.

Then Shane was telling about the annual stock show at Dodge City and father was interested and excited, and it was mother who said: 'Look, the sun's shining.'

It was, so clear and sweet you wanted to run out and breathe the brilliant freshness. Father must have felt that way because he jumped up and fairly shouted, 'Come on, Shane. I'll show you what this hop-scotch climate does to my alfalfa. You can almost see the stuff growing.'

Shane was only a step behind him, but I beat them to the door. Mother followed and stood watching awhile on the porch as we three started out, picking our path around the puddles and the taller clumps of grass bright with the raindrops. We covered the whole place pretty thoroughly, father talking all the time, more enthusiastic about his plans than he had been for many weeks. He really hit his stride when we were behind the barn where we could have a good view of our little herd spreading out through the pasture. Then he stopped short. He had noticed that Shane was not paying much attention. He was quiet as could be for a moment when he saw that Shane was looking at the stump.

That was the one bad spot on our place. It stuck out like an old scarred sore in the cleared space back of the barn—a big old stump, all jagged across the top, the legacy of some great tree that must have died long before we came into the valley and finally been snapped by a heavy windstorm. It was big enough, I used to think, so that if it was smooth on top you could have served supper to a good-sized family on it.

But you could not have done that because you could not have got them close around it. The huge old roots humped out in every direction, some as big about as my waist, pushing out and twisting down into the ground like they would hold there to eternity and past.

Father had been working at it off and on, gnawing at the roots with an axe, ever since he finished poleing the corral. The going was slow, even for him. The wood was so hard that he could not sink the blade much more than a quarter inch at a time. I guess it had been an old burr oak. Not many of those grew that far up in the Territory, but the ones that did grew big and hard. Ironwood we called it.

Father had tried burning brushpiles against it. That old stump just jeered at fire. The scorching seemed to make the wood harder than ever. So he was fighting his way around root by root. He never thought he had much time to spare on it. The rare occasions he was real mad about something he would stomp out there and chew into another root.

He went over to the stump now and kicked the nearest root, a smart kick, the way he did every time he passed it. 'Yes,' he said. 'That's the millstone round my neck. That's the one fool thing about this place I haven't licked yet. But I will. There's no wood ever grew can stand up to a man that's got the strength and the will to keep hammering at it.'

He stared at the stump like it might be a person sprouting in front of him. 'You know, Shane, I've been feuding with this thing so long I've worked up a spot of affection for it. It's tough. I can admire toughness. The right kind.'

He was running on again, full of words and sort of happy to be letting them out, when he noticed again that Shane was not paying much attention,

21

was listening to some sound in the distance. Sure enough, a horse was coming up the road.

Father and I turned with him to look toward town. In a moment we saw it as it cleared the grove of trees and tall bushes about a quarter-mile away, a high-necked sorrel drawing a light buckboard wagon. The mud was splattering from its hooves, but not bad, and it was stepping free and easy. Shane glanced sideways at father.

'Not fit for travelling,' he said softly. 'Starrett, you're poor shakes as a liar.' Then his attention was on the wagon and he was tense and alert, studying the man upright on the swaying seat.

Father simply chuckled at Shane's remark. 'That's Jake Ledyard's outfit,' he said, taking the lead toward our lane. 'I thought maybe he'd get up this way this week. Hope he has that cultivator I've been wanting.'

Ledyard was a small, thin-featured man, a peddler or trader who came through every couple of months with things you could not get at the general store in town. He would pack in his stock on a mule-team freighter driven by an old, white-haired Negro who acted like he was afraid even to speak without permission. Ledyard would make deliveries in his buckboard, claiming a hard bargain always and picking up orders for articles to bring on the next trip. I did not like him, and not just because he said nice things about me he did not mean for father's benefit. He smiled too much and there was no real friendliness in it.

By the time we were beside the porch, he had swung the horse into our lane and was pulling it to a stop. He jumped down, calling greetings. Father went to meet him. Shane stayed by the porch, leaning against the end post.

'It's here,' said Ledyard. 'The beauty I told you about.' He yanked away the canvas covering from the body of the wagon and the sun was bright on a shiny new seven-pronged cultivator lying on its side on the floor boards. 'That's the best buy I've toted this haul.'

'Hm-m-m-m,' said father. 'You've hit it right. That's what I've been wanting. But when you start chattering about a best buy that always means big money. What's the tariff?'

'Well, now.' Ledyard was slow with his reply. 'It cost me more than I figured when we was talking last time. You might think it a bit steep. I don't. Not for a new beauty like that there. You'll make up the difference in no time with the work you'll save with that. Handles so easy even the boy here will be using it before long.'

'Pin it down,' said father. 'I've asked you a question.'

Ledyard was quick now. 'Tell you what, I'll shave the price, take a loss to please a good customer. I'll let you have it for a hundred and ten.'

I was startled to hear Shane's voice cutting in, quiet and even and plain. 'Let you have it? I reckon he will. There was one like that in a store in Cheyenne. List price sixty dollars.'

Ledyard shifted part way around. For the first time he looked closely at our visitor. The surface smile left his face. His voice held an ugly undertone. 'Did anyone ask you to push in on this?'

'No,' said Shane, quietly and evenly as before. 'I reckon no one did.' He was still leaning against the

23

post. He did not move and he did not say anything more. Ledyard turned to father, speaking rapidly.

'Forget what he says, Starrett. I've spotted him now. Heard of him half a dozen times along the road up here. No one knows him. No one can figure him. I think I can. Just a stray wandering through, probably chased out of some town and hunting cover. I'm surprised you'd let him hang around.'

'You might be surprised at a lot of things,' said father, beginning to bite off his words. 'Now give it to me straight on the price.'

'It's what I said. A hundred and ten. Hell, I'll be out money on the deal anyway, so I'll shave it to a hundred if that'll make you feel any better.' Ledyard hesitated, watching father. 'Maybe he did see something in Cheyenne. But he's mixed up. Must have been one of those little makes—flimsy and barely half the size. That might match his price.'

Father did not say anything. He was looking at Ledyard in a steady, unwavering way. He had not even glanced at Shane. You might have believed he had not even heard what Shane had said. But his lips were folding in to a tight line like he was thinking what was not pleasant to think. Ledyard waited and father did not say anything and the climbing anger in Ledyard broke free.

'Starrett! Are you going to stand there and let that— that tramp nobody knows about call me a liar? Are you going to take his word over mine? Look at him! Look at his clothes! He's just a cheap, tinhorn—'

Ledyard stopped, choking on whatever it was he had meant to say. He fell back a step with a sudden fear showing in his face. I knew why even as I turned

24

my head to see Shane. That same chill I had felt the day before, intangible and terrifying, was in the air again. Shane was no longer leaning against the porch post. He was standing erect, his hands clenched at his sides, his eyes boring at Ledyard, his whole body alert and alive in the leaping instant.

You felt without knowing how that each teetering second could bring a burst of indescribable deadliness. Then the tension passed, fading in the empty silence. Shane's eyes lost their sharp focus on Ledyard and it seemed to me that reflected in them was some pain deep within him.

Father had pivoted so that he could see the two of them in the one sweep. He swung back to Ledyard alone.

'Yes, Ledyard, I'm taking his word. He's my guest. He's here at my invitation. But that's not the reason.' Father straightened a little and his head went up and he gazed into the distance beyond the river. 'I can figure men for myself. I'll take his word on anything he wants to say any day of God's whole year.'

Father's head came down and his voice was flat and final. 'Sixty is the price. Add ten for a fair profit, even though you probably got it wholesale. Another ten for hauling it here. That tallies to eighty. Take that or leave that. Whatever you do, snap to it and get off my land.'

Ledyard stared down at his hands, rubbing them together as if they were cold. 'Where's your money?' he said.

Father went into the house, into the bedroom where he kept our money in a little leather bag on the closet shelf. He came back with the crumpled

25

bills. All this while Shane stood there, not moving, his face hard, his eyes following father with a strange wildness in them that I could not understand.

Ledyard helped father heave the cultivator to the ground, then jumped to the wagon seat and drove off like he was glad to get away from our place. Father and I turned from watching him into the road. We looked around for Shane and he was not in sight. Father shook his head in wonderment. 'Now where do you suppose—' he was saying, when we saw Shane coming out of the barn.

He was carrying an axe, the one father used for heavy kindling. He went directly around the corner of the building. We stared after him and we were still staring when we heard it, the clear ringing sound of steel biting into wood.

I never could have explained what that sound did to me. It struck through me as no single sound had ever done before. With it ran a warmth that erased at once and forever the feelings of sudden chill terror that our visitor had evoked in me. There were sharp hidden hardnesses in him. But these were not for us. He was dangerous as mother had said. But not to us as father too had said. And he was no longer a stranger. He was a man like father in whom a boy could believe in the simple knowing that what was beyond comprehension was still clean and solid and right.

I looked up at father to try to see what he was thinking, but he was starting toward the barn with strides so long that I had to run to stay close behind him. We went around the far corner and there was Shane squared away at the biggest uncut root of that big old stump. He was swinging the axe in steady rhythm. He was chewing into that root with bites almost as deep as father could drive.

Father halted, legs wide, hands on hips. 'Now looka-here,' he began, 'there's no call for you—'

Shane broke his rhythm just long enough to level a straight look at us. 'A man has to pay his debts,' he said and was again swinging the axe. He was really slicing into that root.

He seemed so desperate in his determination that I had to speak. 'You don't owe us anything,' I said. 'Lots of times we have folks in for meals and—'

Father's hand was on my shoulder. 'No, Bob. He doesn't mean meals.' Father was smiling, but he was having to blink several times together and I would have sworn that his eyes were misty. He stood in silence now, not moving, watching Shane.

It was something worth seeing. When father worked on that old stump, that was worth seeing too. He could handle an axe mighty well and what impressed you was the strength and will of him making it behave and fight for him against the tough old wood. This was different. What impressed you as Shane found what he was up against and settled to it was the easy way the power in him poured smoothly into each stroke. The man and the axe seemed to be partners in the work. The blade would sink into the parallel grooves almost as if it knew itself what to do and the chips from between would come out in firm and thin little blocks.

Father watched him and I watched the two of them and time passed over us, and then the axe sliced through the last strip and the root was cut. I was sure that Shane would stop. But he stepped right

27

around to the next root and squared away again and the blade sank in once more.

As it hit this second root, father winced like it had hit him. Then he stiffened and looked away from Shane and stared at the old stump. He began to fidget, throwing his weight from one foot to the other. In a short while more he was walking around inspecting the stump from different angles as if it was something he had never seen before. Finally he gave the nearest root a kick and hurried away. In a moment he was back with the other axe, the big double-bladed one that I could hardly heft from the ground.

He picked a root on the opposite side from Shane. He was not angry the way he usually was when he confronted one of those roots. There was a kind of serene and contented look on his face. He whirled that big axe as if it was only a kid's tool. The striking blade sank in maybe a whole half-inch. At the sound Shane straightened on his side. Their eyes met over the top of the stump and held and neither one of them said a word. Then they swung up their axes and both of them said plenty to that old stump.

III

IT WAS exciting at first watching them. They were
hitting a fast pace, making the chips dance. I thought
maybe each one would cut through a root now and
stop. But Shane finished his and looked over at father
working steadily away and with a grim little smile
pulling at his mouth he moved on to another root.
A few moments later father smashed through his with
a blow that sent the axe head into the ground beneath.
He wrestled with the handle to yank the head loose
and he too tackled another root without even waiting
to wipe off the dirt. This began to look like a long
session, so I started to wander away. Just as I headed
around the corner of the barn, mother came past the
corner.

She was the freshest, prettiest thing I had ever seen.
She had taken her hat and stripped the old ribbon
from it and fixed it as Shane had told her. Some of
the flowers by the house were in a small bouquet in
front. She had cut slits in the brim and the sash from
her best dress came around the crown and through the
slits and was tied in a perky bow under her chin.
She was stepping along daintily, mighty proud of
herself.

She went up close to the stump. Those two choppers
were so busy and intent that even if they were aware
she was there they did not really notice her.

'Well,' she said, 'aren't you going to look at me?'

They both stopped and they both stared at her.

'Have I got it right?' she asked Shane. 'Is this the way they do it?'

'Yes, ma'am,' he said. 'About like that. Only their brims are wider.' And he swung back to his root.

'Joe Starrett,' said mother, 'aren't you at least going to tell me whether you like me in this hat?'

'Lookahere, Marian,' said father, 'you know damned well that whether you have a hat on or whether you don't have a hat on, you're the nicest thing to me that ever happened on God's green earth. Now stop bothering us. Can't you see we're busy?' And he swung back to his root.

Mother's face was a deep pink. She pulled the bow out and the hat from her head. She held it swinging from her hand by the sash ends. Her hair was mussed and she was really mad.

'Humph,' she said. 'This is a funny kind of resting you're doing to-day.'

Father set the axe head on the ground and leaned on the handle. 'Maybe it seems funny to you, Marian. But this is the best resting I've had for about as long as I can remember.'

'Humph,' said mother again. 'You'll have to quit your resting for a while anyhow and do what I suppose you'll call work. Dinner's hot on the stove and waiting to be served.'

She flounced around and went straight back to the house. We all tagged her in and to an uncomfortable meal. Mothers always believed you should be decent and polite at mealtime, particularly with company. She was polite enough now. She was being special sweet, talking enough for the whole table of us without once saying a word about her hat lying where she had thrown it on the chair by the stove. The trouble was that she was too polite. She was trying too hard to be sweet.

As far as you could tell, though, the two men were not worried by her at all. They listened absently to her talk, chiming in when she asked them direct questions, but otherwise keeping quiet. Their minds were on that old stump and whatever it was that old stump had come to mean to them and they were in a hurry to get at it again.

After they had gone out and I had been helping mother with the dishes awhile, she began humming low under her breath and I knew she was not mad any more. She was too curious and puzzled to have room for anything else.

'What went on out there, Bob?' she asked me. 'What got into those two?'

I did not rightly know. All I could do was try to tell her about Ledyard and how our visitor had called him on the cultivator. I must have used the wrong words, because, when I told her about Ledyard talking mean and the way Shane acted, she got all flushed and excited.

'What do you say, Bob? You were afraid of him? He frightened you? Your father would never let him do that.'

'I wasn't frightened of him,' I said, struggling to make her see the difference. 'I was—well, I was just frightened. I was scared of whatever it was that might happen.'

She reached out and rumpled my hair. 'I think I understand,' she said softly. 'He's made me feel a little that way too.' She went to the window and stared toward the barn. The steady rhythm of double blows, so together they sounded almost as one, was faint yet clear in the kitchen. 'I hope Joe knows what he's doing,' she murmured to herself. Then she turned to me. 'Skip along out, Bob. I'll finish myself.'

It was no fun watching them now. They had eased down to a slow, dogged pace. Father sent me once for the hone, so they could sharpen the blades, and again for a spade so he could clear the dirt away from the lower roots, and I realized he might keep me running as long as I was handy. I slipped off by myself to see how mother's garden was doing after the rain and maybe add to the population in the box of worms I was collecting for when I would go fishing with the boys in town.

I took my time about it. I played pretty far afield. But no matter where I went, always I could hear that chopping in the distance. You could not help beginning to feel tired just to hear it, to think how they were working and staying at it.

Along the middle of the afternoon, I wandered into the barn. There was mother by the rear stall, up on a box peering through the little window above it. She hopped down as soon as she heard me and put a finger to her lips.

'I declare,' she whispered. 'In some ways those two aren't even as old as you are, Bob. Just the same—' She frowned at me in such a funny, confiding manner that I felt all warm inside. 'Don't you dare tell them I said so. But there's something splendid in the battle they're giving that old monster.' She went past me and toward the house with such a brisk air that I followed to see what she was going to do.

She whisked about the kitchen and in almost no

time at all she had a pan of biscuits in the oven. While they were baking, she took her hat and carefully sewed the old ribbon into its old place. 'Humph,' she said, more to herself than to me. 'You'd think I'd learn. This isn't Dodge City. This isn't even a whistle stop. It's Joe Starrett's farm. It's where I'm proud to be.'

Out came the biscuits. She piled as many as she could on a plate, popping one of the leftovers into her mouth and giving me the rest. She picked up the plate and marched with it out behind the barn. She stepped over the cut roots and set the plate on a fairly smooth spot on top of the stump. She looked at the two men, first one and then the other. 'You're a pair of fools,' she said. 'But there's no law against me being a fool too.' Without looking at either of them again, she marched away, her head high, back toward the house.

The two of them stared after her till she was out of sight. They turned to stare at the biscuits. Father gave a deep sigh, so deep it seemed to come all the way from his heavy work shoes. There was nothing sad or sorrowful about it. There was just something in him too big to be held tight in comfort. He let his axe fall to the ground. He leaned forward and separated the biscuits into two piles beside the plate, counting them even. One was left on the plate. He set this by itself on the stump. He took up his axe and reached it out and let it drop gently on the lone biscuit exactly in the middle. He rested the axe against the stump and took the two halves of the biscuit and put one on each pile.

He did not say a word to Shane. He pitched into one pile and Shane did into the other, and the two of them faced each other over the last uncut roots, munching at those biscuits as if eating them was the most serious business they had ever done.

Father finished his pile and dabbled his fingers on the plate for the last crumbs. He straightened and stretched his arms high and wide. He seemed to stretch and stretch until he was a tremendous tower of strength reaching up into the late afternoon sun. He swooped suddenly to grab the plate and toss it to me. Still in the same movement he seized his axe and swung it in a great arc into the root he was working on. Quick as he was, Shane was right with him, and together they were talking again to that old stump.

I took the plate in to mother. She was peeling apples in the kitchen, humming gaily to herself. 'The wood-box, Bob," she said, and went on humming. I carried in stove-lengths till the box would not hold any more. Then I slipped out before she might think of more chores.

I tried to keep myself busy down by the river skipping flat stones across the current all muddy still from the rain. I was able to for a while. But that steady chopping had a peculiar fascination. It was always pulling me toward the barn. I simply could not grasp how they could stick at it hour after hour. It made no sense to me, why they should work so when routing out that old stump was not really so important. I was wavering in front of the barn, when I noticed that the chopping was different. Only one axe was working.

I hurried around back. Shane was still swinging, cutting into the last root. Father was using the spade, was digging under one side of the stump, bringing the dirt out between the cut roots. As I watched, he laid the spade aside and put his shoulder to the stump.

He heaved against it. Sweat started to pour down his face. There was a little sucking sound and the stump moved ever so slightly.

That did it. Of a sudden I was so excited that I could hear my own blood pounding past my eardrums. I wanted to dash to that stump and push it and feel it move. Only I knew father would think I was in the way.

Shane finished the root and came to help him. Together they heaved against the stump. It angled up nearly a whole inch. You could begin to see an open space in the dirt where it was ripping loose. But as soon as they released the pressure, it fell back.

Again and again they heaved at it. Each time it would angle up a bit farther. Each time it would fall back. They had it up once about a foot and a half, and that was the limit. They could not get past it.

They stopped, breathing hard, mighty streaked now from the sweat rivulets down their faces. Father peered underneath as best he could. 'Must be a taproot,' he said. That was the one time either of them had spoken to the other, as far as I knew, the whole afternoon through. Father did not say anything more. And Shane said nothing. He just picked up his axe and looked at father and waited.

Father began to shake his head. There was some unspoken thought between them that bothered him. He looked down at his own big hands and slowly the fingers curled until they were clenched into big fists. Then his head stopped shaking and he stood taller and he drew a deep breath. He turned and backed in between two cut root ends, pressing against the stump. He pushed his feet into the ground for firm footholds. He bent his knees and slid his shoulders down the

35

stump and wrapped his big hands around the root ends. Slowly he began to straighten. Slowly that huge old stump began to rise. Up it came, inch by inch, until the side was all the way up to the limit they had reached before.

Shane stooped to peer under. He poked his axe into the opening and I heard it strike wood. But the only way he could get in position to swing the axe into the opening was to drop on his right knee and extend his left leg and thigh into the opening and lean his weight on them. Then he could bring the axe sweeping in at a low angle close to the ground.

He flashed one quick glance at father beside and behind him, eyes closed, muscles locked in that great sustained effort, and he dropped into position with the whole terrible weight of the stump poised above nearly half of his body, and sent the axe sweeping under in swift powerful strokes.

Suddenly father seemed to slip. Only he had not slipped. He had straightened even farther. The stump had leaped up a few more inches. Shane jumped out and up and tossed his axe aside. He grabbed one of the root ends and helped father ease the stump down. They both were blowing like they had run a long way. But they would not stay more than a minute before they were heaving again at the stump. It came up more easily now and the dirt was tearing loose all around it.

I ran to the house fast as I could. I dashed into the kitchen and took hold of mother's hand. 'Hurry!' I yelled. 'You've got to come!' She did not seem to want to come at first and I pulled at her. 'You've got to see it! They're getting it out!' Then she was excited as I was and was running right with me.

· · · · ·

They had the stump way up at a high angle. They were down in the hole, one on each side of it, pushing up and forward with hands flat on the under part reared before them higher than their heads. You would have thought the stump was ready to topple over clear of its ancient foundation. But there it stuck. They could not quite push it the final inches.

Mother watched them battling with it. 'Joe,' she called, 'why don't you use some sense? Hitch up the team. Horses will have it out in no time at all.'

Father braced himself to hold the stump still. He turned his head to look at her. 'Horses!' he shouted. All the pent silence of the two of them that long afternoon through was being shattered in the one wonderful shout. 'Horses! Great jumping Jehosaphat! No! We started this with manpower and, by Godfrey, we'll finish it with manpower!'

He turned his head to face the stump once more and dropped it lower between his humped shoulders. Shane, opposite him, stiffened, and together they pushed in a fresh assault. The stump quivered and swayed a little—and hung fixed at its crazy high angle.

Father grunted in exasperation. You could see the strength building up in his legs and broad shoulders and big corded arms. His side of the upturned stump rocked forward and Shane's side moved back and the whole stump trembled like it would twist down and into the hole on them at a grotesque new angle.

I wanted to shout a warning. But I could not speak, for Shane had thrown his head in a quick sideways gesture to fling his hair from falling over his face and I had caught a glimpse of his eyes. They were aflame with a concentrated cold fire. Not another separate discernible movement did he make. It was all of him, the whole man, pulsing in the one incredible surge of power. You could fairly feel the fierce energy suddenly burning in him, pouring through him in the single co-ordinated drive. His side of the stump rocked forward even with father's and the whole mass of the stump tore loose from the last hold and toppled away to sprawl in ungainly defeat beyond them.

Father climbed slowly out of the hole. He walked to the stump and placed a hand on the rounded bole and patted it like it was an old friend and he was perhaps a little sorry for it. Shane was with him, across from him, laying a hand gently on the old hard wood. They both looked up and their eyes met and held as they had so long ago in the morning hours.

The silence should have been complete. It was not because someone was shouting, a high-pitched, wordless shout. I realized that the voice was mine and I closed my mouth. The silence was clean and wholesome, and this was one of the things you could never forget whatever time might do to you in the furrowing of the years, an old stump on its side with root ends making a strange pattern against the glow of the sun sinking behind the far mountains and two men looking over it into each other's eyes.

I thought they should join hands so close on the bole of the stump. I thought they should at least say something to each other. They stood quiet and motionless. At last father turned and came toward mother. He was so tired that the weariness showed in his walk. But there was no weariness in his voice. 'Marian,' he said, 'I'm rested now. I don't believe any man since the world began was ever more rested.'

Shane too was coming toward us. He too spoke only to mother. 'Ma'am, I've learned something to-day.

Being a farmer has more to it than I ever thought. Now I'm about ready for some of that pie.'

Mother had been watching them in a wide-eyed wonder. At his last words she let out a positive wail. 'Oh-h-h—you—you—men! You made me forget about it! It's probably all burned!' And she was running for the house so fast she was tripping over her skirt.

The pie was burned all right. We could smell it when we were in front of the house and the men were scrubbing themselves at the pump-trough. Mother had the door open to let the kitchen air out. The noises from inside sounded as if she might be throwing things around. Kettles were banging and dishes were clattering. When we went in, we saw why. She had the table set and was putting supper on it and she was grabbing the things from their places and putting them down on the table with solid thumps. She would not look at one of us.

We sat down and waited for her to join us. She put her back to us and stood by the low shelf near the stove staring at her big pie tin and the burned stuff in it. Finally father spoke kind of sharply. 'Lookahere, Marian. Aren't you ever going to sit down?'

She whirled and glared at him. I thought maybe she had been crying. But there were no tears on her face. It was dry and pinched-looking and there was no colour in it. Her voice was sharp like father's. 'I was planning to have a deep-dish apple pie. Well, I will. None of your silly man foolishness is going to stop me.'

She swept up the big tin and went out the door with it. We heard her on the steps, and a few seconds later the rattle of the cover of the garbage pail. We heard her on the steps again. She came in and went to the side bench where the dishpan was and began to scrub the pie tin. The way she acted, we might not have been in the room.

Father's face was getting red. He picked up his fork to begin eating and let it drop with a little clatter. He squirmed on his chair and kept taking quick side looks at her. She finished scrubbing the tin and went to the apple barrel and filled her wooden bowl with fat round ones. She sat by the stove and started peeling them. Father fished in a pocket and pulled out his old jack-knife. He moved over to her, stepping softly. He reached out for an apple to help her.

She did not look up. But her voice caught him like she had flicked him with a whip. 'Joe Starrett, don't you dare touch a one of these apples.'

He was sheepish as he returned to his chair. Then he was downright mad. He grabbed his knife and fork and dug into the food on his plate, taking big bites and chewing vigorously. There was nothing for our visitor and me to do but follow his example. Maybe it was a good supper. I could not tell. The food was only something to put in your mouth. And when we finished, there was nothing to do but wait because mother was sitting by the stove, arms folded, staring at the wall, waiting herself for her pie to bake.

We three watched her in a quiet so tight that it hurt. We could not help it. We would try to look away and always our eyes would turn back to her. She did not appear to notice us. You might have said she had forgotten we were there.

She had not forgotten because as soon as she sensed that the pie was done, she lifted it out, cut four wide pieces, and put them on plates. The first two she set in front of the two men. The third one she set down for me. The last one she laid at her own place and she sat down in her own chair at the table. Her voice was still sharp.

'I'm sorry to keep you men waiting so long. Your pie is ready now.'

Father inspected his portion like he was afraid of it. He needed to make a real effort to take his fork and lift a piece. He chewed on it and swallowed and he flipped his eyes sidewise at mother and back again quickly to look across the table at Shane. 'That's prime pie,' he said.

Shane raised a piece on his fork. He considered it closely. He put it in his mouth and chewed on it gravely. 'Yes,' he said. The quizzical expression on his face was so plain you could not possibly miss it. 'Yes. That's the best bit of stump I ever tasted.'

What could a silly remark like that mean? I had no time to wonder, for father and mother were acting so queer. They both stared at Shane and their mouths were sagging open. Then father snapped his shut and he chuckled and chuckled till he was swaying in his chair.

'By Godfrey, Marian, he's right. You've done it, too.'

Mother stared from one to the other of them. Her pinched look faded and her cheeks were flushed and her eyes were soft and warm as they should be, and she was laughing so that the tears came. And all of us were pitching into that pie, and the one thing wrong in the whole world was that there was not enough of it.

IV

THE SUN was already well up the sky when I awakened the next morning. I had been a long time getting to sleep because my mind was full of the day's excitement and shifting moods. I could not straighten out in my mind the way the grown folks had behaved, the way things that did not really matter so much had become so important to them.

I had lain in my bed thinking of our visitor out in the bunk in the barn. It scarce seemed possible that he was the same man I had first seen, stern and chilling in his dark solitude, riding up our road. Something in father, something not of words or of actions but of the essential substance of the human spirit, had reached out and spoken to him and he had replied to it and had unlocked a part of himself to us. He was far off and unapproachable at times even when he was right there with you. Yet somehow he was closer, too, than my uncle, mother's brother, had been when he visited us the summer before.

I had been thinking, too, of the effect he had on father and mother. They were more alive, more vibrant, like they wanted to show more what they were, when they were with him. I could appreciate that because I felt the same way myself. But it puzzled me that a man so deep and vital in his own being, so ready to respond to father, should be riding a lone trail out of a closed and guarded past.

I realized with a jolt how late it was. The door to my little room was closed. Mother must have closed it so I could sleep undisturbed. I was frantic that the others might have finished breakfast and that our visitor was gone and I had missed him. I pulled on my clothes, not even bothering with buttons, and ran to the door.

They were still at the table. Father was fussing with his pipe. Mother and Shane were working on a last round of coffee. All three of them were subdued and quiet. They stared at me as I burst out of my room.

'My heavens,' said mother. 'You came in here like something was after you. What's the matter?'

'I just thought,' I blurted out, nodding at our visitor, 'that maybe he had ridden off and forgotten me.'

Shane shook his head slightly, looking straight at me. 'I wouldn't forget you, Bob.' He pulled himself up a little in his chair. He turned to mother and his voice took on a bantering tone. 'And I wouldn't forget your cooking, ma'am. If you begin having a special lot of people passing by at mealtimes, that'll be because a grateful man has been boasting of your flannel cakes all along the road.'

'Now there's an idea,' stuck in father as if he was glad to find something safe to talk about. 'We'll turn this place into a boarding house. Marian'll fill folks full of her meals and I'll fill my pockets full of their money. That hits me as a mighty convenient arrangement.'

Mother sniffed at him. But she was pleased at their talk and she was smiling as they kept on playing with the idea while she stirred me up my breakfast. She came right back at them, threatening to take father at his word and make him spend all his time peeling potatoes and washing dishes. They were enjoying themselves even though I could feel a bit of constraint behind the easy joshing. It was remarkable, too, how natural it was to have this Shane sitting there and joining in almost like he was a member of the family. There was none of the awkwardness some visitors always brought with them. You did feel you ought to be on your good behaviour with him, a mite extra careful about your manners and your speech. But not stiffly so. Just quiet and friendly about it.

He stood up at last and I knew he was going to ride away from us and I wanted desperately to stop him. Father did it for me.

'You are certainly a man for being in a hurry. Sit down, Shane. I've a question to ask you.'

Father was suddenly very serious. Shane, standing there, was as suddenly withdrawn into a distant alertness. But he dropped back into his chair.

Father looked directly at him. 'Are you running away from anything?'

Shane stared at the plate in front of him for a long moment. It seemed to me that a shade of sadness passed over him. Then he raised his eyes and looked directly at father.

'No. I'm not running away from anything. Not in the way you mean.'

'Good.' Father stooped forward and stabbed at the table with a forefinger for emphasis. 'Look, Shane. I'm not a rancher. Now you've seen my place, you know that. I'm a farmer. Something of a stockman, maybe. But really a farmer. That's what I decided to be when I quit punching cattle for another man's money. That's what I want to be and I'm proud of it. I've made a fair start. This outfit isn't as big as I hope to have it some

44

day. But there's more work here already than one man can handle if it's to be done right. The young fellow I had ran out on me after he tangled with a couple of Fletcher's boys in town one day.' Father was talking fast and he paused to draw breath.

Shane had been watching him intently. He moved his head to look out the window over the valley to the mountains marching along the horizon. 'It's always the same,' he murmured. He was sort of talking to himself. 'The old ways die hard.' He looked at mother and then at me, and as his eyes came back to father he seemed to have decided something that had been troubling him. 'So Fletcher's crowding you,' he said gently.

Father snorted. 'I don't crowd easy. But I've got a job to do here and it's too big for one man, even for me. And none of the strays that drift up this way are worth a damn.'

'Yes?' Shane said. His eyes were crinkling again, and he was one of us again and waiting.

'Will you stick here awhile and help me get things in shape for the winter?'

Shane rose to his feet. He loomed up taller across the table than I had thought him. 'I never figured to be a farmer, Starrett. I would have laughed at the notion a few days ago. All the same, you've hired yourself a hand.' He and father were looking at each other in a way that showed they were saying things words could never cover. Shane snapped it by swinging toward mother. 'And I'll rate your cooking, ma'am, wages enough.'

Father slapped his hands on his knees. 'You'll get good wages and you'll earn 'em. First off, now, why don't you drop into town and get some work clothes.

Try Sam Grafton's store. Tell him to put it on my bill.'

Shane was already at the door. 'I'll buy my own,' he said, and was gone.

Father was so pleased he could not sit still. He jumped up and whirled mother around. 'Marian, the sun's shining mighty bright at last. We've got ourselves a man.'

'But, Joe, are you sure what you're doing? What kind of work can a man like that do? Oh, I know he stood right up to you with that stump. But that was something special. He's been used to good living and plenty of money. You can tell that. He said himself he doesn't know anything about farming.'

'Neither did I when I started here. What a man knows isn't important. It's what he is that counts. I'll bet you that one was a cowpuncher when he was younger and a top hand too. Anything he does will be done right. You watch. In a week he'll be making even me hump or he'll be bossing the place.'

'Perhaps.'

'No perhapsing about it. Did you notice how he took it when I told him about Fletcher's boys and young Morley? That's what fetched him. He knows I'm in a spot and he's not the man to leave me there. Nobody'll push him around or scare him away. He's my kind of a man.'

'Why, Joe Starrett. He isn't like you at all. He's smaller and he looks different and his clothes are different and he talks different. I know he's lived different.'

'Huh?' Father was surprised. 'I wasn't talking about things like that.'

Shane came back with a pair of dungaree pants, a

flannel shirt, stout work shoes, and a good, serviceable Stetson. He disappeared into the barn and emerged a few moments later in his new clothes, leading his horse unsaddled. At the pasture gate he slipped off the halter, turned the horse in with a hearty slap, and tossed the halter to me.

'Take care of a horse, Bob, and it will take care of you. This one now has brought me better than a thousand miles in the last few weeks.' And he was striding away to join father, who was ditching the field out past the growing corn where the ground was rich but marshy and would not be worth much till it was properly drained. I watched him swinging through the rows of young corn, no longer a dark stranger but part of the place, a farmer like father and me.

Only he was not a farmer and never really could be. It was not three days before you saw that he could stay right beside father in any kind of work. Show him what needed to be done and he could do it, and like as not would figure out a better way of getting it done. He never shirked the meanest task. He was ever ready to take the hard end of any chore. Yet you always felt in some indefinable fashion that he was a man apart.

There were times when he would stop and look off at the mountains and then down at himself and any tool he happened to have in his hands as if in wry amusement at what he was doing. You had no impression that he thought himself too good for the work or did not like it. He was just different. He was shaped in some firm forging of past circumstance for other things.

For all his slim build he was plenty rugged. His slenderness could fool you at first. But when you saw him close in action, you saw that he was solid, compact, that there was no waste weight on his frame just as there was no waste effort in his smooth, flowing motion. What he lacked alongside father in size and strength, he made up in quickness of movement, in instinctive co-ordination of mind and muscle, and in that sudden fierce energy that had burned in him when the old stump tried to topple back on him. Mostly this last slept in him, not needed while he went easily through the day's routine. But when a call came, it could flame forward with a driving intensity that never failed to frighten me.

I would be frightened, as I had tried to explain to mother, not at Shane himself, but at the suggestion it always gave me of things in the human equation beyond my comprehension. At such times there would be a concentration in him, a singleness of dedication to the instant need, that seemed to me at once wonderful and disturbing. And then he would be again the quiet, steady man who shared with father my boy's allegiance.

I was beginning to feel my oats about then, proud of myself for being able to lick Ollie Johnson at the next place down the road. Fighting, boy style, was much in my mind.

Once, when father and I were alone, I asked him: 'Could you beat Shane? In a fight, I mean.'

'Son, that's a tough question. If I had to, I might do it. But, by Godfrey, I'd hate to try it. Some men just plain have dynamite inside them, and he's one. I'll tell you, though. I've never met a man I'd rather have more on my side in any kind of trouble.'

I could understand that and it satisfied me. But there were things about Shane I could not understand.

When he came in to the first meal after he agreed to stay on with us, he went to the chair that had always been father's and stood beside it waiting for the rest of us to take the other places. Mother was surprised and somewhat annoyed. She started to say something. Father quieted her with a warning glance. He walked to the chair across from Shane and sat down like this was the right and natural spot for him and afterwards he and Shane always used these same places.

I could not see any reason for the shift until the first time one of our homestead neighbours knocked on the door while we were eating and came straight on in as most of them usually did. Then I suddenly realized that Shane was sitting opposite the door where he could directly confront anyone coming through it. I could see that was the way he wanted it to be. But I could not understand why he wanted it that way.

In the evenings after supper when he was talking lazily with us, he would never sit by a window. Out on the porch he would always face the road. He liked to have a wall behind him and not just to lean against. No matter where he was, away from the table, before sitting down he would swing his chair into position, back to the nearest wall, not making any show, simply putting it there and bending into it in one easy motion. He did not even seem to be aware that this was unusual. It was part of his fixed alertness. He always wanted to know everything happening around him.

This alertness could be noted, too, in the watch he kept, without appearing to make any special effort, on every approach to our place. He knew first when anyone was moving along the road and he would stop whatever he was doing to study carefully any passing rider.

We often had company in the evenings, for the other homesteaders regarded father as their leader and would drop in to discuss their affairs with him. They were interesting men in their own fashions, a various assortment. But Shane was not anxious to meet people. He would share little in their talk. With us he spoke freely enough. We were, in some subtle way, his folks. Though we had taken him in, you had the feeling that he had adopted us. But with others he was reserved; courteous and soft-spoken, yet withdrawn beyond a line of his own making.

These things puzzled me and not me alone. The people in town and those who rode or drove in pretty regularly were all curious about him. It was a wonder how quickly everyone in the valley, and even on the ranches out in the open country, knew that he was working with father.

They were not sure they liked having him in their neighbourhood. Ledyard had told some tall tale about what happened at our place that made them stare sharply at Shane whenever they had a chance. But they must have had their own measure of Ledyard, for they did not take his story too straight. They just could not really make up their minds about Shane and it seemed to worry them.

More than once, when I was with Ollie Johnson on the way to our favourite fishing hole the other side of town, I heard men arguing about him in front of Mr Grafton's store. 'He's like one of these here slow-burning fuses,' I heard an old mule-skinner say one day. 'Quiet and no sputtering. So quiet you forget it's burning. Then it sets off one hell of a blow-off of trouble when it touches powder. That's him. And there's been trouble brewing in this valley for a long spell now. Maybe it'll be good when it comes. Maybe it'll be bad. You just can't tell." And that puzzled me too.

What puzzled me most, though, was something it took me nearly two weeks to appreciate. And yet it was the most striking thing of all. Shane carried no gun.

In those days guns were as familiar all through the Territory as boots and saddles. They were not used much in the valley except for occasional hunting. But they were always in evidence. Most men did not feel fully dressed without one.

We homesteaders went in mostly for rifles and shot-guns when we had any shooting to do. A pistol slapping on the hip was a nuisance for a farmer. Still every man had his cartridge belt and holstered Colt to be worn when he was not working or loafing around the house. Father buckled his on whenever he rode off on any trip, even just into town, as much out of habit, I guess, as anything else.

But this Shane never carried a gun. And that was a peculiar thing because he had a gun.

I saw it once. I saw it when I was alone in the barn one day and I spotted his saddle-roll lying on his bunk. Usually he kept it carefully put away underneath. He must have forgotten it this time, for it was there in the open by the pillow. I reached to sort of feel it—and I felt the gun inside. No one was near, so I un-fastened the straps and unrolled the blankets. There it was, the most beautiful-looking weapon I ever saw. Beautiful and deadly-looking.

The holster and filled cartridge belt were of the same soft black leather as the boots tucked under the bunk, tooled in the same intricate design. I knew enough to know that the gun was a single-action Colt, the same model as the Regular Army issue that was the favourite of all men in those days, and that oldtimers used to say was the finest pistol ever made.

This was the same model. But this was no Army gun. It was black, almost blue black, with the darkness not in any enamel but in the metal itself. The grip was clear on the outer curve, shaped to the fingers on the inner curve, and two ivory plates were set into it with exquisite skill, one on each side.

The smooth invitation of it tempted your grasp. I took hold and pulled the gun out of the holster. It came so easily that I could hardly believe it was there in my hand. Heavy like father's, it was somehow much easier to handle. You held it up to aiming level and it seemed to balance itself into your hand.

It was clean and polished and oiled. The empty cylinder, when I released the catch and flicked it, spun swiftly and noiselessly. I was surprised to see that the front sight was gone, the barrel smooth right down to the end, and that the hammer had been filed to a sharp point.

Why should a man do that to a gun? Why should a man with a gun like that refuse to wear it and show it off? And then, staring at that dark and deadly efficiency, I was again suddenly chilled, and I quickly put everything back exactly as before and hurried out into the sun.

The first chance I tried to tell father about it. 'Father,' I said, all excited, 'do you know what Shane has rolled up in his blankets?'

'Probably a gun.'

'But—but how did you know? Have you seen it?'

'No. That's what he would have.'

52

I was all mixed up. 'Well, why doesn't he ever carry it? Do you suppose maybe it's because he doesn't know how to use it very well?'

Father chuckled like I had made a joke. 'Son, I wouldn't be surprised if he could take that gun and shoot the buttons off your shirt with you awearing it and all you'd feel would be a breeze.'

'Gosh agorry! Why does he keep it hidden in the barn then?'

'I don't know. Not exactly.'

'Why don't you ask him?'

Father looked straight at me, very serious. 'That's one question I'll never ask him. And don't you ever say anything to him about it. There are some things you don't ask a man. Not if you respect him. He's entitled to stake his claim to what he considers private to himself alone. But you can take my word for it, Bob, that when a man like Shane doesn't want to tote a gun you can bet your shirt, buttons and all, he's got a mighty good reason.'

That was that. I was still mixed up. But whenever father gave you his word on something, there was nothing more to be said. He never did that except when he knew he was right. I started to wander off.

'Bob.'

'Yes, father.'

'Listen to me, son. Don't get to liking Shane too much.'

'Why not? Is there anything wrong with him?' . .

'No-o-o-o. There's nothing wrong about Shane. Nothing you could put that way. There's more right about him than most any man you're ever likely to meet. But—' Father was throwing around for what to say. 'But he's fiddle-footed. Remember. He said so himself. He'll be moving on one of these days and then you'll be all upset if you get to liking him too much.'

That was not what father really meant. But that was what he wanted me to think. So I did not ask any more questions.

V

THE WEEKS went rocking past, and soon it did not seem possible that there ever had been a time when Shane was not with us. He and father worked together more like partners than boss and hired man. The amount they could get through in a day was a marvel. The ditching father had reckoned would take him most of the summer was done in less than a month. The loft was finished and the first cutting of alfalfa stowed away.

We would have enough fodder to carry a few more young steers through the winter for fattening next summer, so father rode out of the valley and all the way to the ranch where he worked once and came back herding a half-dozen more. He was gone two days. He came back to find that Shane, while he was gone, had knocked out the end of the corral and posted a new section making it half again as big.

'Now we can really get going next year,' Shane said as father sat on his horse staring at the corral like he could not quite believe what he saw. 'We ought to get enough hay off that new field to help us carry forty head.'

'Oho!' said father. 'So we can get going. And we ought to get enough hay.' He was pleased as could be because he was scowling at Shane the way he did at me when he was tickled silly over something I had done and did not want to let on that he was. He jumped off his horse and hurried up to the house where mother was standing on the porch.

'Marian,' he demanded right off, waving at the corral, 'whose idea was that?'

'Well-l-l,' she said, 'Shane suggested it.' Then she added slyly, 'But I told him to go ahead.'

'That's right.' Shane had come up beside him. 'She rode me like she had spurs to get it done by to-day. Kind of a present. It's your wedding anniversary.'

'Well, I'll be damned,' said father. 'So it is.' He stared foolishly at one and then the other of them. With Shane there watching, he hopped on the porch and gave mother a kiss. I was embarrassed for him and I turned away—and hopped about a foot myself.

'Hey! Those steers are running away!'

The grown folks had forgotten about them. All six were wandering up the road, straggling and separating. Shane, that soft-spoken man, let out a whoop you might have heard halfway to town and ran to father's horse, putting his hands on the saddle and vaulting into it. He fairly lifted the horse into a gallop in one leap and that old cowpony of father's lit out after those steers like this was fun. By the time father reached the corral gate, Shane had the runaways in a compact bunch and padding back at a trot. He dropped them through the gateway neat as pie.

He was tall and straight in the saddle the few seconds it took father to close the gate. He and the horse were blowing a bit and both of them were perky and proud.

'It's been ten years,' he said, 'since I did anything like that.'

Father grinned at him. 'Shane, if I didn't know better, I'd say you were a faker. There's still a lot of kid in you.'

The first real smile I had seen yet flashed across Shane's face. 'Maybe. Maybe there is at that.'

I think that was the happiest summer of my life.

The only shadow over our valley, the recurrent trouble between Fletcher and us homesteaders, seemed to have faded away. Fletcher himself was gone most of those months. He had gone to Fort Bennett in Dakota and even on East to Washington, so we heard, trying to get a contract to supply beef to the Indian agent at Standing Rock, the big Sioux reservation over beyond the Black Hills. Except for his foreman, Morgan, and several surly older men, his hands were young, easy-going cowboys who made a lot of noise in town once in a while but rarely did any harm and even then only in high spirits. We liked them—when Fletcher was not there driving them into harassing us in constant shrewd ways. Now, with him away, they kept to the other side of the river and did not bother us. Sometimes, riding in sight on the other bank, they might even wave to us in their rollicking fashion.

Until Shane came, they had been my heroes. Father, of course, was special all to himself. There could never be anyone quite to match him. I wanted to be like him, just as he was. But first I wanted, as he had done, to ride the range, to have my own string of ponies and take part in an all-brand round-up and in a big cattle drive and dash into strange towns with just such a rollicking crew and with a season's pay jingling in my pockets.

Now I was not so sure. I wanted more and more to be like Shane, like the man I imagined he was in the past fenced off so securely. I had to imagine most of it. He would never speak of it, not in any way at all.

Even his name remained mysterious. Just Shane. Nothing else. We never knew whether that was his first name or last name or, indeed, any name that came from his family. 'Call me Shane,' he said, and that was all he ever said. But I conjured up all manner of adventures for him, not tied to any particular time or place, seeing him as a slim and dark and dashing figure coolly passing through perils that would overcome a lesser man.

I would listen in what was closely akin to worship while my two men, father and Shane, argued long and amiably about the cattle business. They would wrangle over methods of feeding and bringing steers up to top weight. But they were agreed that controlled breeding was better than open range running and that improvement of stock was needed even if that meant spending big money on imported bulls. And they would speculate about the chances of a railroad spur ever reaching the valley, so you could ship direct without thinning good meat off your cattle driving them to market.

It was plain that Shane was beginning to enjoy living with us and working the place. Little by little the tension in him was fading out. He was still alert and watchful, instinct with that unfailing awareness of everything about him. I came to realize that this was inherent in him, not learned or acquired, simply a part of his natural being. But the sharp extra edge of conscious alertness, almost of expectancy of some unknown trouble always waiting, was wearing away.

Yet why was he sometimes so strange and stricken in his own secret bitterness? Like the time I was playing with a gun Mr Grafton gave me, an old frontier model Colt with a cracked barrel someone had turned in at the store.

I had rigged a holster out of a torn chunk of oilcloth and a belt of rope. I was stalking around near the barn, whirling every few steps to pick off a skulking Indian, when I saw Shane watching me from the barn door. I stopped short, thinking of that beautiful gun under his bunk and afraid he would make fun of me and my sorry old broken pistol. Instead he looked gravely at me.

'How many you knocked over so far, Bob?'

Could I ever repay the man? My gun was a shining new weapon, my hand steady as a rock as I drew a bead on another one.

'That makes seven.'

'Indians or timber wolves?'

'Indians. Big ones.'

'Better leave a few for the other scouts,' he said gently. 'It wouldn't do to make them jealous. And look here, Bob. You're not doing that quite right.'

He sat down on an upturned crate and beckoned me over. 'Your holster's too low. Don't let it drag full arm's length. Have it just below the hip, so the grip is about halfway between your wrist and elbow when the arm's hanging limp. You can take the gun then as your hand's coming up and there's still room to clear the holster without having to lift the gun too high.'

'Gosh agorry! Is that the way the real gunfighters do?'

A queer light flickered in his eyes and was gone. 'No. Not all of them. Most have their own tricks. One likes a shoulder holster; another packs his gun in his pants belt. Some carry two guns, but that's a show-off stunt and a waste of weight. One's enough, if you know how to use it. I've even seen a man have a tight holster with an open end and fastened on a little swivel to the belt. He didn't have to pull the gun then. Just swung up the barrel and blazed away from the hip. That's mighty fast for close work and a big target. But it's not certain past ten or fifteen paces and no good at all for putting your shot right where you want it. The way I'm telling you is as good as any and better than most. And another thing—'

He reached and took the gun. Suddenly, as for the first time, I was aware of his hands. They were broad and strong, but not heavy and fleshy like father's. The fingers were long and square on the ends. It was funny how, touching the gun, the hands seemed to have an intelligence all their own, a sure movement that needed no guidance of thought.

His right hand closed around the grip and you knew at once it was doing what it had been created for. He hefted the old gun, letting it lie loosely in the hand. Then the fingers tightened and the thumb toyed with the hammer, testing the play of it.

While I gaped at him, he tossed it swiftly in the air and caught it in his left hand and in the instant of catching, it nestled snugly into this hand too. He tossed it again, high this time, and spinning end over end, and as it came down, his right hand flicked forward and took it. The forefinger slipped through the trigger guard and the gun spun, coming up into firing position in the one unbroken motion. With him that old pistol seemed alive, not an inanimate and rusting metal object but an extension of the man himself.

'If it's speed you're after, Bob, don't split the move into parts. Don't pull, cock, aim, and fire. Slip back the hammer as you bring the gun up and squeeze the trigger the second it's up level.'

'How do you aim it, then? How do you get a sight on it?'

'No need to. Learn to hold it so the barrel's right in line with the fingers if they were out straight. You won't have to waste time bringing it high to take a sight. Just point it, low and quick and easy, like pointing a finger.'

Like pointing a finger. As the words came, he was doing it. The old gun was bearing on some target over by the corral and the hammer was clicking at the empty cylinder. Then the hand around the gun whitened and the fingers slowly opened and the gun fell to the ground. The hand sank to his side, stiff and awkward. He raised his head and the mouth was a bitter gash in his face. His eyes were fastened on the mountains climbing in the distance.

'Shane! Shane! What's the matter?'

He did not hear me. He was back somewhere along the dark trail of the past.

He took a deep breath, and I could see the effort run through him as he dragged himself into the present and a realization of a boy staring at him. He beckoned to me to pick up the gun. When I did he leaned forward and spoke earnestly.

'Listen, Bob. A gun is just a tool. No better and no worse than any other tool, a shovel—or an axe or a saddle or a stove or anything. Think of it always that way. A gun is as good—and as bad—as the man who carries it. Remember that.'

He stood up and strode off into the fields and I knew he wanted to be alone. I remembered what he said all right, tucked away unforgettably in my mind. But in those days I remembered more the way he handled the gun and the advice he gave me about using it. I would practise with it and think of the time when I could have one that would really shoot.

And then the summer was over. School began again and the days were growing shorter and the first cutting edge of cold was creeping down from the mountains.

VI

MORE than the summer was over. The season of
friendship in our valley was fading with the sun's
warmth. Fletcher was back and he had his contract.
He was talking in town that he would need the
whole range again. The homesteaders would have to
go.

He was a reasonable man, he was saying in his
smooth way, and he would pay a fair price for any
improvements they had put in. But we knew what Luke
Fletcher would call a fair price. And we had no inten-
tion of leaving. The land was ours by right of settlement,
guaranteed by the government. Only we knew, too,
how far away the government was from our valley way
up there in the Territory.

The nearest marshal was a good hundred miles away.
We did not even have a sheriff in our town. There
never had been any reason for one. When folks had
any lawing to do, they would head for Sheridan, nearly
a full day's ride away. Our town was small, not even
organized as a town. It was growing, but it was still not
much more than a roadside settlement.

The first people there were three or four miners who
had come prospecting after the blow-up of the Big
Horn Mining Association about twenty years before,
and had found gold traces leading to a moderate vein
in the jutting rocks that partially closed off the valley
where it edged into the plain. You could not have

called it a strike, for others that followed were soon disappointed. Those first few, however, had done fairly well and had brought in their families and a number of helpers.

Then a stage and freighting line had picked the site for a relay post. That meant a place where you could get drinks as well as horses, and before long the cowboys from the ranches out on the plain and Fletcher's spread in the valley were drifting in of an evening. With us homesteaders coming now, one or two almost every season, the town was taking shape. Already there were several stores, a harness and blacksmith shop, and nearly a dozen houses. Just the year before, the men had put together a one-room schoolhouse.

Sam Grafton's place was the biggest. He had a general store with several rooms for living quarters back of it in one half of his rambling building, a saloon with a long bar and tables for cards and the like in the other half. Upstairs he had some rooms he rented to stray drummers or anyone else stranded overnight. He acted as our postmaster, an elderly man, a close bargainer but honest in all his dealings. Sometimes he served as a sort of magistrate in minor disputes. His wife was dead. His daughter Jane kept house for him and was our schoolteacher when school was in session.

Even if we had had a sheriff, he would have been Fletcher's man. Fletcher was the power in the valley in those days. We homesteaders had been around only a few years and the other people still thought of us as there by his sufferance. He had been running cattle through the whole valley at the time the miners arrived, having bought or bulldozed out the few small ranchers there ahead of him. A series of bad years

working up to the dry summer and terrible winter of
'86 had cut his herds about the time the first of the
homesteaders moved in and he had not objected too
much. But now there were seven of us in all and the
number rising each year.

It was a certain thing, father used to say, that the
town would grow and swing our way. Mr Grafton
knew that too, I guess, but he was a careful man who
never let thoughts about the future interfere with
present business. The others were the kind to veer with
the prevailing wind. Fletcher was the big man in the
valley, so they looked up to him and tolerated us.
Led to it, they probably would have helped him run
us out. With him out of the way, they would just as
willingly accept us. And Fletcher was back, with a
contract in his pocket, wanting his full range again.

There was a hurried counsel in our house soon as the
news was around. Our neighbour toward town, Lew
Johnson, who heard it in Grafton's store, spread the
word and arrived first. He was followed by Henry
Shipstead, who had the place next to him, the closest
to town. These two had been the original homesteaders,
staking out their hundred and eighties two years before
the drought and riding out Fletcher's annoyance until
the cut in his herds gave him other worries. They were
solid, dependable men, old-line farmers who had come
West from Iowa.

You could not say quite as much for the rest, straggling in at intervals. James Lewis and Ed Howells were
two middle-aged cowhands who had grown dissatisfied
and tagged father into the valley, coming pretty much
on his example. Lacking his energy and drive, they had
not done too well and could be easily discouraged.

Frank Torrey from farther up the valley was a nervous, fidgety man with a querulous wife and a string of dirty kids growing longer every year. He was always talking about pulling up stakes and heading for California. But he had a stubborn streak in him, and he was always saying, too, that he'd be damned if he'd make tracks just because some big-hatted rancher wanted him to.

Ernie Wright, who had the last stand up the valley butting out into the range still used by Fletcher, was probably the weakest of the lot. Not in any physical way. He was a husky, likable man, so dark-complected that there were rumours he was part Indian. He was always singing and telling tall stories. But he would be off hunting when he should be working and he had a quick temper that would trap him into doing fool things without taking thought.

He was as serious as the rest of them that night. Mr Grafton had said that this time Fletcher meant business. His contract called for all the beef he could drive in the next five years and he was determined to push the chance to the limit.

'But what can he do?' asked Frank Torrey. 'The land's ours as long as we live on it and we get title in three years. Some of you fellows have already proved up.'

'He won't really make trouble,' chimed in James Lewis. 'Fletcher's never been the shooting kind. He's a good talker, but talk can't hurt us.' Several of the others nodded. Johnson and Shipstead did not seem to be so sure. Father had not said anything yet and they all looked at him.

'Jim's right,' he admitted. 'Fletcher hasn't ever let his boys get careless thataway. Not yet anyhow. That

66

ain't saying he wouldn't, if there wasn't any other way. There's a hard streak in him. But he won't get real tough for a while. I don't figure he'll start moving cattle in now till spring. My guess is he'll try putting pressure on us this fall and winter, see if he can wear us down. He'll probably start right here. He doesn't like any of us. But he doesn't like me most.'

'That's true.' Ed Howells was expressing the un-spoken verdict that father was their leader. 'How do you figure he'll go about it?'

'My guess on that,' father said—drawling now and smiling a grim little smile like he knew he was holding a good hole card in a tight game—'my guess on that is that he'll begin by trying to convince Shane here that it isn't healthy to be working with me.'

'You mean the way he—' began Ernie Wright.

'Yes.' Father cut him short. 'I mean the way he did with young Morley.'

I was peeping around the door of my little room. I saw Shane sitting off to one side, listening quietly as he had been right along. He didn't seem the least bit surprised. He did not seem the least bit interested in finding out what had happened to young Morley. I knew what had. I had seen Morley come back from town, bruised and a beaten man, and gather his things and curse father for hiring him and ride away without once looking back.

Yet Shane sat there quietly as if what had happened to Morley had nothing to do with him. He simply did not care what it was. And then I understood why. It was because he was not Morley. He was Shane.

Father was right. In some strange fashion the feeling was abroad that Shane was a marked man. Attention was on him as a sort of symbol. By taking him on father had accepted in a way a challenge from the big ranch across the river. What had happened to Morley had been a warning and father had deliberately answered it. The long unpleasantness was sharpened now after the summer lull. The issue in our valley was plain and would in time have to be pushed to a showdown. If Shane could be driven out, there would be a break in the homestead ranks, a defeat going beyond the loss of a man into the realm of prestige and morale. It could be the crack in the dam that weakens the whole structure and finally lets through the flood.

The people in town were more curious than ever, not now so much about Shane's past as about what he might do if Fletcher tried any move against him. They would stop me and ask me questions when I was hurrying to and from school. I knew that father would not want me to say anything and I pretended that I did not know what they were talking about. But I used to watch Shane closely myself and wonder how all the slow-climbing tenseness in our valley could be so focused on one man and he seem to be so indifferent to it.

For of course he was aware of it. He never missed anything. Yet he went about his work as usual, smiling frequently now at me, bantering mother at mealtimes in his courteous manner, arguing amiably as before with father on plans for next year. The only thing that was different was that there appeared to be a lot of new activity across the river. It was surprising how often Fletcher's cowboys were finding jobs to do within view of our place.

Then one afternoon, when we were stowing away the second and last cutting of hay, one fork of the big tongs we were using to haul it up to the loft broke loose. 'Have to get it welded in town,' father said in disgust and began to hitch up the team.

Shane stared over the river where a cowboy was riding lazily back and forth by a bunch of cattle. 'I'll take it in,' he said.

Father looked at Shane and he looked across the way and he grinned. 'All right. It's as good a time as any.' He slapped down the final buckle and started for the house. 'Just a minute and I'll be ready.'

'Take it easy, Joe.' Shane's voice was gentle, but it stopped father in his tracks. 'I said I'll take it in.'

Father whirled to face him. 'Damn it all, man. Do you think I'd let you go alone? Suppose they—' He bit down on his own words. He wiped a hand slowly across his face and he said what I had never heard him say to any man. 'I'm sorry,' he said. 'I should have known better.' He stood there silently watching as Shane gathered up the reins and jumped to the wagon seat.

I was afraid father would stop me, so I waited till Shane was driving out of the lane. I ducked behind the barn, around the end of the corral, and hopped into the wagon going past. As I did, I saw the cowboy across the river spin his horse and ride rapidly off in the direction of the ranch-house.

Shane saw it, too, and it seemed to give him a grim amusement. He reached backwards and hauled me over the seat and sat me beside him.

'You Starretts like to mix into things.' For a moment I thought he might send me back. Instead he grinned at me. 'I'll buy you a jack-knife when we hit town.'

He did, a dandy big one with two blades and a cork-screw. After we left the tongs with the blacksmith and found the welding would take nearly an hour, I squatted on the steps on the long porch across the front of Grafton's building, busy whittling, while Shane stepped into the saloon side and ordered a drink. Will Atkey, Grafton's thin, sad-faced clerk and bartender, was behind the bar and several other men were loafing at one of the tables.

It was only a few moments before two cowboys came galloping down the road. They slowed to a walk about fifty yards off and with a show of nonchalance ambled the rest of the way to Grafton's, dismounting and looping their reins over the rail in front. One of them I had seen often, a young fellow everyone called Chris, who had worked for Fletcher several years and was known for a gay manner and reckless courage. The other was new to me, a sallow, pinch-cheek man, not much older, who looked like he had crowded a lot of hard living into his years. He must have been one of the new hands Fletcher had been bringing into the valley since he got his contract.

They paid no attention to me. They stepped softly up on the porch and to the window of the saloon part of the building. As they peered through, Chris nodded and jerked his head toward the inside. The new man stiffened. He leaned closer for a better look. Abruptly he turned clear about and came right down past me and went over to his horse.

Chris was startled and hurried after him. They were both so intent they did not realize I was there. The new man was lifting the reins back over his horse's head when Chris caught his arm.

'What the hell?'

'I'm leaving.'

'Huh? I don't get it.'

'I'm leaving. Now. For good.'

'Hey, listen. Do you know that guy?'

'I didn't say that. There ain't nobody can claim I said that. I'm leaving, that's all. You can tell Fletcher. This is a hell of a country up here anyhow.'

Chris was getting mad. 'I might have known,' he said. 'Scared, eh. Yellow.'

Colour rushed into the new man's sallow face. But he climbed on his horse and swung out from the rail. 'You can call it that,' he said flatly and started down the road, out of town, out of the valley.

Chris was standing still by the rail, shaking his head in wonderment. 'Hell,' he said to himself, 'I'll brace him myself.' He stalked up on the porch, into the saloon.

I dashed into the store side, over to the opening between the two big rooms. I crouched on a box just inside the store where I could hear everything and see most of the other room. It was long and fairly wide. The bar curved out from the opening and ran all the way along the inner wall to the back wall, which closed off a room Grafton used as an office. There was a row of windows on the far side, too high for anyone to look in from outside. A small stairway behind them led up to a sort of balcony across the back with doors opening into several little rooms.

Shane was leaning easily with one arm on the bar, his drink in his other hand, when Chris came to perhaps six feet away and called for a whisky bottle and a glass. Chris pretended he did not notice Shane at first and bobbed his head in greeting to the men at the table. They were a pair of mule-skinners who made regular trips into the valley freighting in goods for Grafton and the other shops. I could have sworn that Shane, studying Chris in his effortless way, was somehow disappointed.

Chris waited until he had his whisky and had gulped a stiff shot. Then he deliberately looked Shane over like he had just spotted him.

'Hello, farmer,' he said. He said it as if he did not like farmers.

Shane regarded him with grave attention. 'Speaking to me?' he asked mildly and finished his drink.

'Hell, there ain't nobody else standing there. Here, have a drink of this.' Chris shoved his bottle along the bar. Shane poured himself a generous slug and raised it to his lips.

'I'll be damned,' flipped Chris. 'So you drink whisky.'

Shane tossed off the rest in his glass and set it down. 'I've had better,' he said, as friendly as could be. 'But this will do.'

Chris slapped his leather chaps with a loud smack. He turned to take in the other men. 'Did you hear that? This farmer drinks whisky! I didn't think these plough-pushing dirt-grubbers drank anything stronger than soda pop!'

'Some of us do,' said Shane, friendly as before. Then he was no longer friendly and his voice was like winter frost. 'You've had your fun and it's mighty young fun. Now run home and tell Fletcher to send a grown-up man next time.' He turned away and sang out to Will Atkey. 'Do you have any soda pop? I'd like a bottle.'

Will hesitated, looked kind of funny, and scuttled past me into the store room. He came back right away with a bottle of the pop Grafton kept there for us school kids. Chris was standing quiet, not so much mad, I would have said, as puzzled. It was as though they

72

were playing some queer game and he was not sure of the next move. He sucked on his lower lip for a while. Then he snapped his mouth and began to look elaborately around the room, sniffing loudly.

'Hey, Will!' he called. 'What's been happening in here? It smells. That ain't no clean cattleman smell. That's plain dirty barnyard.' He stared at Shane. 'You farmer. What are you and Starrett raising out there? Pigs.'

Shane was just taking hold of the bottle Will had fetched him. His hand closed on it and the knuckles showed white. He moved slowly, almost unwillingly, to face Chris. Every line of his body was as taut as stretched whipcord, was alive and somehow rich with an immense eagerness. There was that fierce concentration in him, filling him, blazing in his eyes. In that moment there was nothing in the room for him but that mocking man only a few feet away.

The big room was so quiet the stillness fairly hurt. Chris stepped back involuntarily, one pace, two, then pulled up erect. And still nothing happened. The lean muscles along the sides of Shane's jaw were ridged like rock.

Then the breath, pent in him, broke the stillness with a soft sound as it left his lungs. He looked away from Chris, past him, over the tops of the swinging doors beyond, over the roof of the shed across the road, on into the distance where the mountains loomed in their own unending loneliness. Quietly he walked, the bottle forgotten in his hand, so close by Chris as almost to brush him yet apparently not even seeing him, through the doors and was gone.

I heard a sigh of relief near me. Mr Grafton had come up from somewhere behind me. He was watching

Chris with a strange, ironic quirk at his mouth corners. Chris was trying not to look pleased with himself. But he swaggered as he went to the doors and peered over them.

'You saw it, Will,' he called over his shoulder. 'He walked out on me.' Chris pushed up his hat and rolled back on his heels and laughed. 'With a bottle of soda pop too!' He was still laughing as he went out and we heard him ride away.

'That boy's a fool,' Mr Grafton muttered.

Will Atkey came sidling over to Mr Grafton. 'I never pegged Shane for a play like that,' he said.

'He was afraid, Will.'

'Yeah. That's what was so funny. I would've guessed he could take Chris.'

Mr Grafton looked at Will as he did often, like he was a little sorry for him. 'No, Will. He wasn't afraid of Chris. He was afraid of himself.' Mr Grafton was thoughtful and perhaps sad too. 'There's trouble ahead, Will. The worst trouble we've ever had.'

He noticed me, realizing my presence. 'Better skip along, Bob, and find your friend. Do you think he got that bottle for himself?'

True enough, Shane had it waiting for me at the blacksmith shop. Cherry pop, the kind I favoured most. But I could not enjoy it much. Shane was so silent and stern. He had slipped back into the dark mood that was on him when he first came riding up our road. I did not dare say anything. Only once did he speak to me, and I knew he did not expect me to understand or to answer.

'Why should a man be smashed because he has courage and does what he's told? Life's a dirty business,

74

Bob. I could like that boy.' And he turned inward again to his own thoughts and stayed the same until we had loaded the tongs in the wagon and were well started home. Then the closer we came, the more cheerful he was. By the time we swung in toward the barn, he was the way I wanted him again, crinkling his eyes at me and gravely joshing me about the Indians I would scalp with my new knife.

Father popped out the barn door so quick you could tell he had been itching for us to return. He was busting with curiosity, but he would not come straight out with a question to Shane. He tackled me instead.

'See any of your cowboy heroes in town?'

Shane cut in ahead of me. 'One of Fletcher's crew chased us in to pay his respects.'

'No,' I said, proud of my information. 'There was two of them.'

'Two?' Shane said it. Father was the one who was not surprised. 'What did the other one do?'

'He went up on the porch and looked in the window where you were and came right back down and rode off.'

'Back to the ranch?.

'The other way. He said he was leaving for good.'

Father and Shane looked at each other. Father was smiling. 'One down and you didn't even know it. What did you do to the other?'

'Nothing. He passed a few remarks about farmers. I went back to the blacksmith shop.'

Father repeated it, spacing the words like there might be meanings between them. 'You—went—back—to the—blacksmith—shop.'

I was worried that he must be thinking what Will Atkey did. Then I knew nothing like that had even entered his head. He switched to me. 'Who was it?'

'It was Chris.'

Father was smiling again. He had not been there but he had the whole thing clear. 'Fletcher was right to send two. Young ones like Chris need to hunt in pairs or they might get hurt.' He chuckled in a sort of wry amusement. 'Chris must have been considerable surprised when the other fellow skipped. And more when you walked out. It was too bad the other one didn't stick around.'

'Yes,' Shane said, 'it was.'

The way he said it sobered father. 'I hadn't thought of that. Chris is just cocky enough to take it wrong. That can make things plenty unpleasant.'

'Yes,' said Shane again, 'it can.'

VII

It was just as father and Shane had said. The story Chris told was common knowledge all through the valley before the sun set the next day and the story grew in the telling. Fletcher had an advantage now and he was quick to push it. He and his foreman, Morgan, a broad slab of a man with flattened face and head small in proportion to great sloping shoulders, were shrewd at things like this and they kept their men primed to rowel us homesteaders at every chance.

They took to using the upper ford, up above Ernie Wright's stand, and riding down the road past our places every time they had an excuse for going to town. They would go by slowly, looking everything over with insolent interest and passing remarks for our benefit.

The same week, maybe three days later, a covey of them came riding by while father was putting a new hinge on the corral gate. They acted like they were too busy staring over our land to see him there close.

'Wonder where Starrett keeps the critters,' said one of them. 'I don't see a pig in sight.'

'But I can smell 'em!' shouted another one. With that they all began to laugh and whoop and holler and went tearing off, kicking up a lot of dust and leaving father with a tightness around his mouth that was not there before.

They were impartial with attentions like that. They would hand them out anywhere along the line an opportunity offered. But they liked best to catch father within earshot and burn him with their sarcasm.

It was crude. It was coarse. I thought it silly for grown men to act that way. But it was effective. Shane, as self-sufficient as the mountains, could ignore it. Father, while it galled him, could keep it from getting him. The other homesteaders, though, could not help being irritated and showing they felt insulted. It roughed their nerves and made them angry and restless. They did not know Shane as father and I did. They were not sure there might not be some truth in the big talk Chris was making.

Things became so bad they could not go into Grafton's store without someone singing out for soda pop. And wherever they went, the conversation nearby always snuck around somehow to pigs. You could sense the contempt building up in town, in people who used to be neutral, not taking sides.

The effect showed, too, in the attitude our neighbours now had toward Shane. They were constrained when they called to see father and Shane was there. They resented that he was linked to them. And as a result their opinion of father was changing.

That was what finally drove Shane. He did not mind what they thought of him. Since his session with Chris he seemed to have won a kind of inner peace. He was as alert and watchful as ever, but there was a serenity in him that had erased entirely the old tension. I think he did not care what anyone anywhere thought of him. Except us, his folks. And he knew that with us he was one of us, unchangeable and always.

But he did care what they thought of father. He was standing silently on the porch the night Ernie Wright and Henry Shipstead were arguing with father in the kitchen.

'I can't stomach much more,' Ernie Wright was saying. 'You know the trouble I've had with those blasted cowboys cutting my fence. To-day a couple of them rode over and helped me repair a piece. Helped me, damn them! Waited till we were through, then said Fletcher didn't want any of my pigs getting loose and mixing with his cattle. My pigs! There ain't a pig in this whole valley and they know it. I'm sick of the word.'

Father made it worse by chuckling. Grim, maybe, yet still a chuckle. 'Sounds like one of Morgan's ideas. He's smart. Mean, but—'

Henry Shipstead would not let him finish. 'This is nothing to laugh at, Joe. You least of all. Damn it, man, I'm beginning to doubt your judgment. None of us can keep our heads up around here any more. Just a while ago I was in Grafton's and Chris was there blowing high about your Shane must be thirsty because he's so scared he hasn't been in town lately for his soda pop.'

Both of them were hammering at father now. He was sitting back, saying nothing, his face clouding.

'You can't dodge it, Joe.' This was Wright. 'Your man's responsible. You can try explaining all right, but you can't change the facts. Chris braced him for a fight and he ducked out—and left us stuck with those stinking pigs.'

'You know as well as I do what Fletcher's doing,' growled Henry Shipstead. 'He's pushing us with this and he won't let up till one of us gets enough and makes a fool play and starts something so he can move in and finish it.'

'Fool play or not,' said Ernie Wright. 'I've had all I can take. The next time one of those—'

Father stopped him with a hand up for silence. 'Listen. What's that?'

It was a horse, picking up speed and tearing down our lane into the road. Father was at the door in a single jump, peering out.

The others were close behind him. 'Shane?'

Father nodded. He was muttering under his breath. As I watched from the doorway of my little room, I could see that his eyes were bright and dancing. He was calling Shane names, cursing him, softly, fluently. He came back to his chair and grinned at the other two. 'That's Shane,' he told them and the words meant more than they seemed to say, 'All we can do now is wait.'

They were a silent crew waiting. Mother got up from her sewing in the bedroom where she had been listening as she always did and came into the kitchen and made up a pot of coffee and they all sat there sipping at the hot stuff and waiting.

It could not have been much more than twenty minutes before we heard the horse again, coming swiftly and slewing around to make the lane without slowing. There were quick steps on the porch and Shane stood in the doorway. He was breathing strongly and his face was hard. His mouth was a thin line in the bleakness of his face and his eyes were deep and dark. He looked at Shipstead and Wright and he made no effort to hide the disgust in his voice.

'Your pigs are dead and buried.'

As his gaze shifted to father, his face softened. But the voice was still bitter. 'There's another one down. Chris won't be bothering anybody for quite a spell.'

He turned and disappeared and we could hear him leading the horse into the barn.

In the quiet following, hoofbeats like an echo sounded in the distance. They swelled louder and this second horse galloped into our lane and pulled to a stop. Ed Howells jumped to the porch and hurried in.

'Where's Shane?'

'Out in the barn,' father said.

'Did he tell you what happened?'

'Not much,' father said mildly. 'Something about burying pigs.'

Ed Howells slumped into a chair. He seemed a bit dazed. The words came out of him slowly at first as he tried to make the others grasp just how he felt. 'I never saw anything like it,' he said, and he told about it.

He had been in Grafton's store buying a few things, not caring about going into the saloon because Chris and Red Marlin, another of Fletcher's cowboys, had hands in the evening poker game, when he noticed how still the place was. He went over to sneak a look and there was Shane just moving to the bar, cool and easy as if the room was empty and he the only one in it. Neither Chris nor Red Marlin was saying a word, though you might have thought this was a good chance for them to cut loose with some of their raw sarcasm. One look at Shane was enough to tell why. He was cool and easy, right enough. But there was a curious kind of smooth flow to his movements that made you realize without being conscious of thinking about it that being quiet was a mighty sensible way to be at the moment.

'Two bottles of soda pop,' he called to Will Atkey. He leaned his back to the bar and looked the poker game over with what seemed a friendly interest while Will fetched the bottles from the store. Not another person even twitched a muscle. They were all watching him and wondering what the play was. He took the two bottles and walked to the table and set them down, reaching over to put one in front of Chris.

'The last time I was in here you bought me a drink. Now it's my turn.'

The words sort of lingered in the stillness. He got the impression, Ed Howells said, that Shane meant just what the words said. He wanted to buy Chris a drink. He wanted Chris to take that bottle and grin at him and drink with him.

You could have heard a bug crawl, I guess, while Chris carefully laid down the cards in his right hand and stretched it to the bottle. He lifted it in a sudden jerk and flung it across the table at Shane.

So fast Shane moved, Ed Howells said, that the bottle was still in the air when he had dodged, lunged forward, grabbed Chris by the shirtfront and hauled him right out of his chair and over the table. As Chris struggled to get his feet under him, Shane let go the shirt and slapped him, sharp and stinging, three times, the hand flicking back and forth so quick you could hardly see it, the slaps sounding like pistol shots.

Shane stepped back and Chris stood swaying a little and shaking his head to clear it. He was a game one and mad down to his boots. He plunged in, fists smashing, and Shane let him come, slipping inside the flailing arms and jolting a powerful blow low into his stomach. As Chris gasped and his head came down, Shane brought his right hand up, open, and with the heel of it caught Chris full on the mouth, snapping his head back and raking up over the nose and eyes.

82

The force of it knocked Chris off balance and he staggered badly. His lips were crushed. Blood was dripping over them from his battered nose. His eyes were red and watery and he was having trouble seeing with them. His face, Ed Howells said, and shook a little as he said it, looked like a horse had stomped it. But he drove in again, swinging wildly.

Shane ducked under, caught one of the flying wrists, twisted the arm to lock it and keep it from bending, and swung his shoulder into the armpit. He yanked hard on the wrist and Chris went up and over him. As the body hurtled over, Shane kept hold of the arm and wrenched it sideways and let the weight bear on it and you could hear the bone crack as Chris crashed to the floor.

A long sobbing sigh came from Chris and that died away and there was not a sound in the room. Shane never looked at the crumpled figure. He was straight and deadly and still. Every line of him was alive and eager. But he stood motionless. Only his eyes shifted to search the faces of the others at the table. They stopped on Red Marlin and Red seemed to dwindle lower in his chair.

'Perhaps,' Shane said softly, and the very softness of his voice sent shivers through Ed Howells, 'perhaps you have something to say about soda pop or pigs.'

Red Marlin sat quiet like he was trying not even to breathe. Tiny drops of sweat appeared on his forehead. He was frightened, maybe for the first time in his life, and the others knew it and he knew they knew and he did not care. And none of them blamed him at all.

Then, as they watched, the fire in Shane smouldered down and out. He seemed to withdraw back within himself. He forgot them all and turned toward Chris unconscious on the floor, and a sort of sadness, Ed Howells said, crept over him and held him. He bent and scooped the sprawling figure up in his arms and carried it to one of the other tables. Gently he set it down, the legs falling limp over the edge. He crossed to the bar and took the rag Will used to wipe it and returned to the table and tenderly cleared the blood from the face. He felt carefully along the broken arm and nodded to himself at what he felt.

All this while no one said a word. Not a one of them would have interfered with that man for a year's top wages. He spoke and his voice rang across the room at Red Marlin. 'You'd better tote him home and get that arm fixed. Take right good care of him. He has the makings of a good man.' Then he forgot them all again and looked at Chris and went on speaking as if to that limp figure that could not hear him. 'There's only one thing really wrong with you. You're young. That's the one thing time can always cure.'

The thought hurt him and he strode to the swinging doors and through them into the night. That was what Ed Howells told. 'The whole business,' he finished, 'didn't take five minutes. It was maybe thirty seconds from the time he grabbed hold of Chris till Chris was out cold on the floor. In my opinion that Shane is the most dangerous man I've ever seen. I'm glad he's working for Joe here and not for Fletcher.'

Father levelled a triumphant look at Henry Shipstead. 'So I've made a mistake, have I?'

Before anyone else could push in a word, mother was speaking. I was surprised, because she was upset and her voice was a little shrill. 'I wouldn't be too sure about that, Joe Starrett. I think you've made a bad mistake.'

'Marian, what's got into you?'

'Look what you've done just because you got him to stay on here and get mixed up in this trouble with Fletcher!'

Father was edging toward being peeved himself. 'Women never do understand these things. Lookahere, Marian. Chris will be all right. He's young and he's healthy. Soon as that arm is mended, he'll be in as good shape as he ever was.'

'Oh, Joe, can't you see what I'm talking about? I don't mean what you've done to Chris. I mean what you've done to Shane.'

VIII

THIS time mother was right. Shane was changed. He tried to keep things as they had been with us and on the surface nothing was different. But he had lost the serenity that had seeped into him through the summer. He would no longer sit around and talk with us as much as he had. He was restless with some far hidden desperation.

At times, when it rode him worst, he would wander alone about our place, and this was the one thing that seemed to soothe him. I used to see him, when he thought no one was watching, run his hands along the rails of the corral he had fastened, test with a tug the posts he had set, pace out past the barn looking up at the bulging loft and stride out where the tall corn was standing in big shocks to dig his hands in the loose soil and lift some of it and let it run through his fingers.

He would lean on the pasture fence and study our little herd like it meant more to him than lazy steers to be fattened for market. Sometimes he would whistle softly, and his horse, filled out now so you could see the quality of him and moving with a quiet sureness and power that made you think of Shane himself, would trot to the fence and nuzzle at him.

Often he would disappear from the house in the early evening after supper. More than once, the dishes done, when I managed to slip past mother, I found him far back in the pasture alone with the horse. He would be standing there, one arm on the smooth arch of the horse's neck, the fingers gently rubbing around the ears, and he would be looking out over our land where the last light of the sun, now out of sight, would be flaring up the far side of the mountains, capping them with a deep glow and leaving a mystic gloaming in the valley.

Some of the assurance that was in him when he came was gone now. He seemed to feel that he needed to justify himself even to me, to a boy tagging his heels.

'Could you teach me,' I asked him, 'to throw somebody the way you threw Chris?'

He waited so long I thought he would not answer. 'A man doesn't learn things like that,' he said at last. 'You know them and that's all.' Then he was talking rapidly to me, as close to pleading as he could ever come. 'I tried. You can see that, can't you, Bob? I let him ride me and I gave him his chance. A man can keep his self-respect without having to cram it down another man's throat. Surely you can see that, Bob?'

I could not see it. What he was trying to explain to me was beyond my comprehension then. And I could think of nothing to say.

'I left it up to him. He didn't have to jump me that second time. He could have called it off without crawling. He could have if he was man enough. Can't you see that, Bob?'

And still I could not. But I said I could. He was so earnest and he wanted me to so badly. It was a long, long time before I did see it and then I was a man myself and Shane was not there for me to tell. . . .

I was not sure whether father and mother were aware of the change in him. They did not talk about it, not while I was around anyway. But one afternoon I over-heard something that showed mother knew.

I had hurried home from school and put on my old clothes and started out to see what father and Shane were doing in the cornfield, when I thought of a trick that had worked several times. Mother was firm set against eating between meals. That was a silly notion. I had my mind set on the cookies she kept in a tin box on a shelf by the stove. She was settled on the porch with a batch of potatoes to peel, so I slipped up to the back of the house, through the window of my little room, and tiptoed into the kitchen. Just as I was carefully putting a chair under the shelf, I heard her call to Shane.

He must have come to the barn on some errand, for he was there by the porch in only a moment. I peeped out the front window and saw him standing close in, his hat in his hand, his face tilted up slightly to look at her leaning forward in her chair.

'I've been wanting to talk to you when Joe wasn't around.'

'Yes, Marian.' He called her that the same as father did, familiar yet respectful, just as he always regarded her with a tenderness in his eyes he had for no one else.

'You've been worrying, haven't you, about what may happen in this Fletcher business? You thought it would just be a case of not letting him scare you away and of helping us through a hard time. You didn't know it would come to what it had. And now you're worried about what you might do if there's any more fighting.'

'You're a discerning woman. Marian.'

'You've been worrying about something else too.'

'You're a mighty discerning woman, Marian.'

88

'And you've been thinking that maybe you'll be moving on.'

'And how did you know that?'

'Because it's what you ought to do. For your own sake. But I'm asking you not to.' Mother was intense and serious, as lovely there with the light striking through her hair as I had ever seen her. 'Don't go, Shane. Joe needs you. More than ever now. More than he would ever say.'

'And you?' Shane's lips barely moved and I was not sure of the words.

Mother hesitated. Then her head went up. 'Yes. It's only fair to say it. I need you too.'

'So-o-o,' he said softly, the word lingering on his lips. He considered her gravely. 'Do you know what you're asking, Marian?'

'I know. And I know that you're the man to stand up to it. In some ways it would be easier for me, too, if you rode out of this valley and never came back. But we can't let Joe down. I'm counting on you not ever to make me do that. Because you've got to stay, Shane, no matter how hard it is for us. Joe can't keep this place without you. He can't buck Fletcher alone.'

Shane was silent, and it seemed to me that he was troubled and hard pressed in his mind. Mother was talking straight to him, slow and feeling for the words, and her voice was beginning to tremble.

'It would just about kill Joe to lose this place. He's too old to start in again somewhere else. Oh, we would get along and might even do real well. After all, he's Joe Starrett. He's all man and he can do what has to be done. But he promised me this place when we were married. He had it in his mind for all the first years. He did two men's work to get the extra money for the things we would need. When Bob was big enough to walk and help some and he could leave us, he came on here and filed his claim and built this house with his own hands, and when he brought us here it was home. Nothing else would ever be the same.'

Shane drew a deep breath and let it ease out slowly. He smiled at her and yet, somehow, as I watched him, my heart ached for him. 'Joe should be proud of a wife like you. Don't fret any more, Marian. You'll not lose this place.'

Mother dropped back in her chair. Her face, the side I could see from the window, was radiant. Then, womanlike, she was talking against herself. 'But that Fletcher is a mean and tricky man. Are you sure it will work out all right?'

Shane was already starting toward the barn. He stopped and turned to look at her again. 'I said you won't lose this place.' You knew he was right because of the way he said it and because he said it.

IX

ANOTHER period of peace had settled over our valley. Since the night Shane rode into town, Fletcher's cowboys had quit using the road past the homesteads. They were not annoying us at all and only once in a while was there a rider in view across the river. They had a good excuse to let us be. They were busy fixing the ranch buildings and poleing a big new corral in preparation for the spring drive of new cattle Fletcher was planning.

Just the same, I noticed that father was as watchful as Shane now. The two of them worked always together. They did not split any more to do separate jobs in different parts of the farm. They worked together, rode into town together when anything was needed. And father took to wearing his gun all the time, even in the fields. He strapped it on after breakfast the first morning following the fight with Chris, and I saw him catch Shane's eye with a questioning glance as he buckled the belt. But Shane shook his head and father nodded, accepting the decision, and they went out together without saying a word.

Those were beautiful fall days, clear and stirring, with the coolness in the air just enough to set one atingling, not yet mounting to the bitter cold that soon would come sweeping down out of the mountains. It did not seem possible that in such a harvest season, giving a lift to the spirit to match the well-being of the body, violence could flare so suddenly and swiftly.

Saturday evenings all of us would pile into the light work wagon, father and mother on the seat, Shane and I swinging legs at the rear, and go into town. It was the break in routine we looked forward to all week.

There was always a bustle in Grafton's store with people we knew coming and going. Mother would lay in her supplies for the week ahead, taking a long time about it and chatting with the womenfolk. She and the wives of the other homesteaders were great ones for swapping recipes and this was their bartering ground. Father would give Mr Grafton his order for what he wanted and go direct for the mail. He was always getting catalogues of farm equipment and pamphlets from Washington. He would flip through their pages and skim through any letters, then settle on a barrel and spread out his newspaper. But like as not he would soon be bogged down in an argument with almost any man handy about the best crops for the Territory and it would be Shane who would really work his way into the newspaper.

I used to explore the store, filling myself with crackers from the open barrel at the end of the main counter, playing hide and seek with Mr Grafton's big and knowing old cat that was a whiz of a mouser. Many a time, turning up boxes, I chased out fat furry ones for her to pounce on. If mother was in the right mood, I would have a bag of candy in my pocket.

This time we had a special reason for staying longer than usual, a reason I did not like. Our schoolteacher, Jane Grafton, had made me take a note home to mother asking her to stop in for a talk. About me. I never was too smart at formal schooling to begin with. Being all excited over the doings at the big ranch and what they might mean to us had not helped any. Miss Grafton, I guess, just sort of endured me under the best of conditions. But what tipped her into being downright annoyed and writing to mother was the weather. No one could expect a boy with any spirit in him to be shut up in a schoolroom in weather like we had been having. Twice that week I had persuaded Ollie Johnson to sneak away with me after the lunch hour to see if the fish were still biting in our favourite pool below town.

Mother finished the last item on her list, looked around at me, sighed a little, and stiffened her shoulders. I knew she was going to the living quarters behind the store and talk to Miss Grafton. I squirmed and pretended I did not notice her. Only a few people were left in the store, though the saloon in the adjoining big room was doing fair business. She went over to where father was leafing through a catalogue and tapped him.

'Come along, Joe. You should hear this, too. I declare, that boy is getting too big for me to handle.'

Father glanced quickly over the store and paused, listening to the voices from the next room. We had not seen any of Fletcher's men all evening and he seemed satisfied. He looked at Shane, who was folding the newspaper.

'This won't take long. We'll be out in a moment.'

As they passed through the door at the rear of the store, Shane strolled to the saloon opening. He took in the whole room in his easy, alert way and stepped inside. I followed. But I was supposed not ever to go in there, so I stopped at the entrance. Shane was at the bar, joshing Will Atkey with a grave face that he didn't think he'd have soda pop to-night. It was a scattered group in the room, most of them from around town and familiar to me by sight at least. Those close to Shane moved a little away, eyeing him curiously. He did not appear to notice.

He picked up his drink and savoured it, one elbow on the bar, not shoving himself forward into the room's companionship and not withdrawing either, just ready to be friendly if anyone wanted that and unfriendly if anyone wanted that too.

I was letting my eyes wander about, trying to tag names to faces, when I saw that one of the swinging doors was partly open and Red Marlin was peeking in. Shane saw it too. But he could not see that more men were out on the porch, for they were close by the building wall and on the store side. I could sense them through the window near me, hulking shapes in the darkness. I was so frightened I could scarcely move.

But I had to. I had to go against mother's rule. I scrambled into the saloon and to Shane and I gasped: 'Shane! There's a lot of them out front!'

I was too late. Red Marlin was inside and the others were hurrying in and fanning out to close off the store opening. Morgan was one of them, his flat face sour and determined, his huge shoulders almost filling the doorway as he came through. Behind him was the cowboy they called Curly because of his shock of unruly hair. He was stupid and slow-moving, but he was thick and powerful and he had worked in harness with Chris for several years. Two others followed them, new men to me, with the tough experienced look of old herd hands.

94

There was still the back office with its outside door opening on a side stoop and the rear alley. My knees were shaking and I tugged at Shane and tried to say something about it. He stopped me with a sharp gesture. His face was clear, his eyes bright. He was somehow happy, not in the pleased and laughing way, but happy that the waiting was over and what had been ahead was here and seen and realized and he was ready for it. He put one hand on my head and rocked it gently, the fingers feeling through my hair.

'Bobby boy, would you have me run away?'

Love for that man raced through me and the warmth ran down and stiffened my legs and I was so proud of being there with him that I could not keep the tears from my eyes. I could see the rightness of it and I was ready to do as he told me when he said: 'Get out of here, Bob. This isn't going to be pretty.'

But I would go no farther than my perch just inside the store where I could watch most of the big room. I was so bound in the moment that I did not even think of running for father.

Morgan was in the lead now with his men spread out behind him. He came about half way to Shane and stopped. The room was quiet except for the shuffling of feet as the men by the bar and the nearest tables hastened over to the far wall and some of them ducked out the front doors. Neither Shane nor Morgan gave any attention to them. They had attention only for each other. They did not look aside even when Mr Grafton, who could smell trouble in his place from any distance, stalked in from the store, planting his feet down firmly, and pushed past Will Atkey behind the bar. He had a resigned expression on his face and he reached under the counter, his hands reappearing with a short-barrelled shotgun. He laid it before him on the bar and he said in a dry, disgusted voice: 'There will be no gunplay, gentlemen. And all damages will be paid for.'

Morgan nodded curtly, not taking his eyes from Shane. He came closer and stopped again little more than an arm's length away. His head was thrust forward. His big fists were clenched at his sides.

'No one messes up one of my boys and gets away with it. We're riding you out of this valley on a rail, Shane. We're going to rough you a bit and ride you out and you'll stay out.'

'So you have it planned,' Shane said softly. Even as he was speaking, he was moving. He flowed into action so swift you could hardly believe what was happening. He scooped up his half-filled glass from the bar, whipped it and its contents into Morgan's face, and when Morgan's hands came up reaching or striking for him, he grasped the wrists and flung himself backwards, dragging Morgan with him. His body rolled to meet the floor and his legs doubled and his feet, catching Morgan just below the belt, sent him flying on and over to fall flat in a grotesque spraddle and slide along the boards in a tangle of chairs and a table.

The other four were on Shane in a rush. As they came he whirled to his hands and knees and leaped up and behind the nearest table, tipping it in a strong heave among them. They scattered, dodging, and he stepped, fast and light, around the end and drove into the tail man, one of the new men, now nearest to him. He took the blows at him straight on to get in close and I saw his knee surge up and into the man's groin.

A high scream was literally torn from the man and he collapsed to the floor and dragged himself toward the doors.

Morgan was on his feet, wavering, rubbing a hand across his face, staring hard as if trying to focus again on the room about him. The other three were battering at Shane, seeking to box him between them. They were piling blows into him, crowding in. Through that blur of movement he was weaving, quick and confident. It was incredible, but they could not hurt him. You could see the blows hit, hear the solid chunk of knuckles on flesh. But they had no effect. They seemed only to feed that fierce energy. He moved like a flame among them. He would burst out of the mêlée and whirl and plunge back, the one man actually pressing the three. He had picked the second new man and was driving always directly at him.

Curly, slow and clumsy, grunting in exasperation, grabbed at Shane to grapple with him and hold down his arms. Shane dropped one shoulder and as Curly hugged tighter brought it up under his jaw with a jolt that knocked him loose and away.

They were wary now and none too eager to let him get close to any one of them. Then Red Marlin came at him from one side, forcing him to turn that way, and at the same time the second new man did a strange thing. He jumped high in the air, like a jack rabbit in a spy hop, and lashed out viciously with one boot at Shane's head. Shane saw it coming, but could not avoid it, so he rolled his head with the kick, taking it along the side. It shook him badly. But it did not block the instant response. His hands shot up and seized the foot and the man crashed down to land on the small of his back. As he hit, Shane twisted the whole leg and threw his weight on it. The man buckled on the floor like a snake when you hit it and groaned sharply and hitched himself away, the leg dragging, the fight gone out of him.

But the swing to bend down on the leg had put Shane's back to Curly and the big man was ploughing at him. Curly's arms clamped around him, pinning his arms to his body. Red Marlin leaped to help and the two of them had Shane caught tight between them.

'Hold him!' That was Morgan, coming forward with the hate plain in his eyes. Even then, Shane would have broke away. He stomped one heavy work shoe, heel edged and with all the strength he could get in quick leverage, on Curly's near foot. As Curly winced and pulled it back and was unsteady, Shane strained with his whole body in a powerful arch and you could see their arms slipping and loosening. Morgan, circling in, saw it too. He swept a bottle off the bar and brought it smashing down from behind on Shane's head.

Shane slumped and would have fallen if they had not been holding him. Then, as Morgan stepped around in front of him and watched, the vitality pumped through him and his head came up.

'Hold him!' Morgan said again. He deliberately flung a huge fist to Shane's face. Shane tried to jerk aside and the fist missed the jaw, tearing along the cheek, the heavy ring on one finger slicing deep. Morgan pulled back for another blow. He never made it.

Nothing, I would have said, could have drawn my attention from those men. But I heard a kind of choking sob beside me and it was queer and yet familiar and it turned me instantly.

Father was there in the entranceway!

He was big and terrible and he was looking across the overturned table and scattered chairs at Shane, at the dark purplish bruise along the side of Shane's head and the blood running down his cheek. I had never seen father like this. He was past anger. He was filled with a fury that was shaking him almost beyond endurance.

I never thought he could move so fast. He was on them before they even knew he was in the room. He hurtled into Morgan with ruthless force, sending that huge man reeling across the room. He reached out one broad hand and grabbed Curly by the shoulder and you could see the fingers sink into the flesh. He took hold of Curly's belt with the other hand and ripped him loose from Shane and his own shirt shredded down the back and the great muscles there knotted and bulged as he lifted Curly right up over his head and hurled the threshing body from him. Curly spun through the air, his limbs waving wildly, and crashed on the top of a table way over by the wall. It cracked under him, collapsing in splintered pieces, and the man and the wreckage smacked against the wall. Curly tried to rise, pushing himself with hands on the floor, and fell back and was still.

Shane must have exploded into action the second father yanked Curly away, for now there was another noise. It was Red Marlin, his face contorted, flung against the bar and catching at it to keep himself from falling. He staggered and caught his balance and ran for the front doorway. His flight was frantic, headlong. He tore through the swinging doors without slowing to push them. They flapped with a swishing sound and my eyes shifted quickly to Shane, for he was laughing.

He was standing there, straight and superb, the blood on his face bright like a badge, and he was laughing.

It was a soft laugh, soft and gentle, not in amusement at Red Marlin or any single thing, but in the joy of being alive and released from long discipline and answering the urge in mind and body. The lithe power in him, so different from father's sheer strength, was singing in every fibre of him.

Morgan was in the rear corner, his face clouded and uncertain. Father, his fury eased by the mighty effort of throwing Curly, had looked around to watch Red Marlin's run and now was starting towards Morgan. Shane's voice stopped him.

'Wait, Joe. The man's mine.' He was at father's side and he put a hand on father's arm. 'You'd better get them out of here.' He nodded in my direction and I noticed with surprise that mother was near and watching. She must have followed father and have been there all this while. Her lips were parted. Her eyes were glowing, looking at the whole room, not at anyone or anything in particular, but at the whole room.

Father was disappointed. 'Morgan's more my size,' he said, grumbling fashion. He was not worried about Shane. He was thinking of an excuse to take Morgan himself. But he went no further. He looked at the men over by the wall. 'This is Shane's play. If a one of you tries to interfere, he'll have me to reckon with.' His tone showed that he was not mad at them, that he was not even really warning them. He was simply making the play plain. Then he came to us and looked down at mother. 'You wait out at the wagon, Marian. Morgan's had this coming to him for quite a long time now and it's not for a woman to see.'

Mother shook her head without moving her eyes now from Shane. 'No, Joe. He's one of us. I'll see this through.' And the three of us stayed there together and that was right, for he was Shane.

He advanced toward Morgan, as flowing and graceful as the old mouser in the store. He had forgotten us and the battered men on the floor and those withdrawn by the wall and Mr Grafton and Will Atkey crouched behind the bar. His whole being was concentrated on the big man before him.

Morgan was taller, half again as broad, with a long reputation as a bullying fighter in the valley. But he did not like this and he was desperate. He knew better than to wait. He rushed at Shane to overwhelm the smaller man with his weight. Shane faded from in front of him and as Morgan went past hooked a sharp blow to his stomach and another to the side of his jaw. They were short and quick, flicking in so fast they were just a blur of movement. Yet each time at the instant of impact Morgan's big frame shook and halted in its rush for a fraction of a second before the momentum carried him forward. Again and again he rushed, driving his big fists ahead. Always Shane slipped away, sending in those swift hard punches.

Breathing heavily, Morgan stopped, grasping the futility of straight fighting. He plunged at Shane now, arms wide, trying to get hold of him and wrestle him down. Shane was ready and let him come without dodging, disregarding the arms stretching to encircle him. He brought up his right hand, open, just as Ed

Howells had told us, and the force of Morgan's own lunge as the hand met his mouth and raked upwards snapped back his head and sent him staggering.

Morgan's face was puffy and red-mottled. He bellowed some insane sound and swung up a chair. Holding it in front of him, legs forward, he rushed again at Shane, who sidestepped neatly. Morgan was expecting this and halted suddenly, swinging the chair in a swift arc to strike Shane with it full on the side. The chair shattered and Shane faltered, and then, queerly for a man usually so sure on his feet, he seemed to slip and fall to the floor.

Forgetting all caution, Morgan dived at him—and Shane's legs bent and he caught Morgan on his heavy work shoes and sent him flying back and against the bar with a crash that shook the whole length of it.

Shane was up and leaping at Morgan as if there had been springs under him there on the floor. His left hand, palm out, smacked against Morgan's forehead, pushing the head back, and his right fist drove straight to Morgan's throat. You could see the agony twist the man's face and the fear widen his eyes. And Shane, using his right fist now like a club and lining his whole body behind it, struck him on the neck below and back of the ear. It made a sickening, dull sound and Morgan's eyes rolled white and he went limp all over, sagging slowly and forward to the floor.

X

IN THE hush that followed Morgan's fall, the big bar-room was so quiet again that the rustle of Will Atkey straightening from below the bar level was loud and clear and Will stopped moving, embarrassed and a little frightened.

Shane looked neither at him nor at any of the other men staring from the wall. He looked only at us, at father and mother and me, and it seemed to me that it hurt him to see us there.

He breathed deeply and his chest filled and he held it, held it long and achingly, and released it slowly and sighing. Suddenly you were impressed by the fact that he was quiet, that he was still. You saw how battered and bloody he was. In the moments before you saw only the splendour of movement, the flowing brute beauty of line and power in action. The man, you felt, was tireless and indestructible. Now that he was still and the fire in him banked and subsided, you saw, and in the seeing remembered, that he had taken bitter punishment.

His shirt collar was dark and sodden. Blood was soaking into it, and this came only in part from the cut on his cheek. More was oozing from the matted hair where Morgan's bottle had hit. Unconsciously he put up one hand and it came away smeared and sticky. He regarded it grimly and wiped it clean on his shirt. He swayed slightly and when he started toward us, his feet dragged and he almost fell forward.

One of the townsmen, Mr Weir, a friendly man who kept the stage post, pushed out from the wall, clucking sympathy, as though to help him. Shane pulled himself erect. His eyes blazed refusal. Straight and superb, not a tremor in him, he came to us and you knew that the spirit in him would sustain him thus alone for the farthest distance and forever.

But there was no need. The one man in our valley, the one man, I believe, in all the world whose help he would take, not to whom he would turn but whose help · he would take, was there and ready. Father stepped to meet him and put out a big arm reaching for his shoulders. 'All right, Joe,' Shane said, so softly I doubt whether the others in the room heard. His eyes closed and he leaned against father's arm, his body relaxing and his head dropping sideways. Father bent and fitted his other arm under Shane's knees and picked him up like he did me when I stayed up too late and got all drowsy and had to be carried to bed.

Father held Shane in his arms and looked over him at Mr Grafton. 'I'd consider it a favour, Sam, if you'd figure the damage and put it on my bill.'

For a man strict about bills and keen for a bargain, Mr Grafton surprised me. 'I'm marking this to Fletcher's account. I'm seeing that he pays.'

Mr Weir surprised me even more. He spoke promptly and he was emphatic about it. 'Listen to me, Starrett. It's about time this town worked up a little pride. Maybe it's time, too, we got to be more neighbourly with you homesteaders. I'll take a collection to cover this. I've been ashamed of myself ever since it started to-night, standing here and letting five of them jump that man of yours.'

Father was pleased. But he knew what he wanted to do. 'That's mighty nice of you, Weir. But this ain't your fight. I wouldn't worry, was I you, about keeping out of it.' He looked down at Shane and the pride was plain busting out of him. 'Matter of fact, I'd say the odds to-night, without me butting in, too, was mighty close to even.' He looked again at Mr Grafton. 'Fletcher ain't getting in on this with a nickel, I'm paying.' He tossed back his head. 'No, by Godfrey! We're paying. Me and Shane.'

He went to the swinging doors, turning sideways to push them open. Mother took my hand and we followed. She always knew when to talk and when not to talk, and she said no word while we watched father lift Shane to the wagon seat, climb beside him, hoist him to sitting position with one arm around him and take the reins in the other hand. Will Atkey trotted out with our things and stowed them away. Mother and I perched on the back of the wagon, father chirruped to the team, and we were started home.

There was not a sound for quite a stretch except the clop of hoofs and the little creakings of the wheels. Then I heard a chuckle up front. It was Shane. The cool air was reviving him and he was sitting straight, swaying with the wagon's motion.

'What did you do with the thick one, Joe? I was busy with the redhead.'

'Oh, I just kind of tucked him out of the way.' Father wanted to let it go at that. Not mother.

'He picked him up like—like a bag of potatoes and threw him clear across the room.' She did not say it to

Shane, not to any person. She said it to the night, to the sweet darkness around us, and her eyes were shining in the starlight.

We turned in at our place and father shooed the rest of us into the house while he unhitched the team. In the kitchen mother set some water to heat on the stove and chased me to bed. Her back was barely to me after she tucked me in before I was peering around the door jamb. She got several clean rags, took the water from the stove, and went to work on Shane's head. She was tender as could be, crooning like to herself under her breath the while. It pained him plenty as the warm water soaked into the gash under the matted hair and as she washed the clotted blood from his cheek. But it seemed to pain her more, for her hand shook at the worst moments, and she was the one who flinched while he sat there quietly and smiled reassuringly at her.

Father came in and sat by the stove, watching them. He pulled out his pipe and made a very careful business of packing it and lighting it.

She finished. Shane would not let her try a bandage. 'This air is the best medicine,' he said. She had to be content with cleaning the cuts thoroughly and making certain all bleeding had stopped. Then it was father's turn.

'Get that shirt off, Joe. It's torn all down the back. Let me see what I can do with it.' Before he could rise, she had changed her mind. 'No. We'll keep it just like it is. To remember to-night by. You were magnificent, Joe, tearing that man away and—'

'Shucks,' said father. 'I was just peeved. Him holding Shane so Morgan could pound him.'

'And you, Shane.' Mother was in the middle of the kitchen, looking from one to the other. 'You were magnificent, too. Morgan was so big and horrible and yet he didn't have even a chance. You were so cool and quick and—and dangerous and—'

'A woman shouldn't have to see things like that.' Shane interrupted her, and he meant it. But she was talking right ahead.

'You think I shouldn't because it's brutal, and nasty and not just fighting to see who is better at it, but mean and vicious and to win by any way, but to win. Of course it is. But you didn't start it. You didn't want to do it. Not until they made you anyway. You did it because you had to.'

Her voice was climbing and she was looking back and forth and losing control of herself. 'Did ever a woman have two such men?' And she turned from them and reached out blindly for a chair and sank into it and dropped her face into her hands and the tears came.

The two men stared at her and then at each other in that adult knowledge beyond my understanding. Shane rose and stepped over by mother. He put a hand gently on her head and I felt again his fingers in my hair and the affection flooding through me. He walked quietly out the door and into the night.

Father drew on his pipe. It was out and absently he lit it. He rose and went to the door and out on the porch. I could see him there dimly in the darkness, gazing across the river.

Gradually mother's sobs died down. She raised her head and wiped away the tears.

'Joe.'

He turned and started in and waited then by the door. She stood up. She stretched her hands toward him and he was there and had her in his arms.

'Do you think I don't know, Marian?'

'But you don't. Not really. You can't. Because I don't know myself.'

Father was staring over her head at the kitchen walls not seeing anything there. 'Don't fret yourself, Marian. I'm man enough to know a better when his trail meets mine. Whatever happens will be all right.'

'Oh, Joe . . . Joe! Kiss me. Hold me tight and don't ever let go.'

XI

WHAT happened in our kitchen that night was beyond me in those days. But it did not worry me because father had said it would be all right, and how could anyone, knowing him, doubt that he would make it so.

And we were not bothered by Fletcher's men any more at all. There might not have been a big ranch on the other side of the river, sprawling up the valley and over on our side above Ernie Wright's place, for all you could tell from our house. They left us strictly alone and were hardly ever seen now even in town. Fletcher himself, I heard from kids at school, was gone again. He went on the stage to Cheyenne and maybe farther, and nobody seemed to know why he went.

Yet father and Shane were more wary than they had been before. They stayed even closer together and they spent no more time than they had to in the fields. There was no more talking on the porch in the evenings, though the nights were so cool and lovely they called you to be out and under the winking stars. We kept to the house, and father insisted on having the lamps well shaded and he polished his rifle and hung it, ready loaded, on a couple of nails by the kitchen door.

All this caution failed to make sense to me. So at dinner about a week later I asked: 'Is there something new that's wrong? That stuff about Fletcher is finished, isn't it?'

'Finished?' said Shane, looking at me over his coffee cup. 'Bobby boy, it's only begun.'

'That's right, said father. 'Fletcher's gone too far to back out now. It's a case of now or never with him. If he can make us run, he'll be setting pretty for a long stretch. If he can't, it'll be only a matter o' time before he's shoved smack out of this valley. There's three or four of the men who looked through here last year ready right now to sharpen stakes and move in as soon they think it's safe. I'll bet Fletcher feels he got aholt of a bear by the tail and it'd be nice to be able to let go.'

'Why doesn't he do something, then?' I asked. 'Seems to me mighty quiet around here lately.'

'Seems to you, eh?' said father. 'Seems to me you're mighty young to be doing much seemsing. Don't you worry, son. Fletcher is fixing to do something. The grass that grows under his feet won't feed any cow. I'd be easier in my mind if I knew what he's up to.'

'You see, Bob'—Shane was speaking to me the way I liked, as if maybe I was a man and could understand all he said—'by talking big and playing it rough, Fletcher has made this a straight win or lose deal. it's the same as if he'd kicked loose a stone that starts a rockslide and all he can do is hope to ride it down and hit bottom safe. Maybe he doesn't realize that yet. I think he does. And don't let things being quiet fool you. When there's noise, you know where to look and what's happening. When things are quiet, you've got to be most careful.'

Mother sighed. She was looking at Shane's cheek where the cut was healing into a scar like a thin line running back from near the mouth corner. 'I suppose you two are right. But does there have to be any more fighting?'

'Like the other night?' asked father. 'No, Marian. I don't think so. Fletcher knows better now.'

'He knows better,' Shane said, 'because he knows it won't work. If he's the man I think he is, he's known that since the first time he sicced Chris on me. I doubt that was his move the other night. That was Morgan's. Fletcher'll be watching for some way that has more finesse—and will be more final.'

'Hm-m-m,' said father a little surprised. 'Some legal trick, eh?'

'Could be. If he can find one. If not—' Shane shrugged and gazed out the window. 'There are other ways. You can't call a man like Fletcher on things like that. Depends on how far he's willing to go. But whatever he does, once he's ready, he'll do it speedy and sure.'

'Hm-m-m,' said father, again. 'Now you put it that-away, I see you're right. That's Fletcher's way. Bet you've bumped against someone like him before.' When Shane did not answer, just kept staring out the window, he went on. 'Wish I could be as patient about it as you. I don't like this waiting.'

But we did not have to wait long. It was the next day, a Friday, when we were finishing supper, that Lew Johnson and Henry Shipstead brought us the news. Fletcher was back and he had not come back alone. There was another man with him.

Lew Johnson saw them as they got off the stage. He had a good chance to look the stranger over while they waited in front of the post for horses to be brought in from the ranch. Since it was beginning to get dark, he had not been able to make out the stranger's face too well. The light striking through the post window, however, was enough for him to see what kind of man he was.

He was tall, rather broad in the shoulders and slim in the waist. He carried himself with a sort of swagger. He had a moustache that he favoured and his eyes, when Johnson saw them reflecting the light from the window, were cold and had a glitter that bothered Johnson.

This stranger was something of a dude about his clothes. Still, that did not mean anything. When he turned, the coat he wore matching his pants flapped open and Johnson could see what had been half-hidden before. He was carrying two guns, big capable forty-fives, in holsters hung fairly low and forward. Those holsters were pegged down at the tips with thin straps fastened around the man's legs. Johnson said he saw the tiny buckles when the light flashed on them.

Wilson was the man's name. That was what Fletcher called him when a cowboy rode up leading a couple of horses. A funny other name. Stark. Stark Wilson. And that was not all.

Lew Johnson was worried and went into Grafton's to find Will Atkey, who always knew more than anyone else about people apt to be coming along the road because he was constantly picking up information from the talk of men drifting in to the bar. Will would not believe it at first when Johnson told him the name. What would he be doing up here, Will kept saying. Then Will blurted out that this Wilson was a bad one, a killer. He was a gun-fighter said to be just as good with either hand and as fast on the draw as the best of them. He came to Cheyenne from Kansas, Will claimed he had heard, with a reputation for killing three men there and nobody knew how many more down in the south-west territories where he used to be.

Lew Johnson was rattling on, adding details as he could think of them. Henry Shipstead was slumped in a chair by the stove. Father was frowning at his pipe, absently fishing in a pocket for a match. It was Shane who shut off Johnson with a suddenness that startled the rest of us. His voice was sharp and clear and it seemed to crackle in the air. You could feel him taking charge of that room and all of us in it.

'When did they hit town?'

'Last night.'

'And you waited till now to tell it!' There was disgust in Shane's voice. 'You're a farmer all right, Johnson. That's all you ever will be.' He whirled on father. 'Quick, Joe. Which one has the hottest head? Which one's the easiest to prod into being a fool? Torrey is it? Or Wright?'

'Ernie Wright,' father said slowly.

'Get moving, Johnson. Get out there on your horse and make it to Wright's in a hurry. Bring him here. Pick up Torry, too. But get Wright first.'

'He'll have to go into town for that,' Henry Shipstead said heavily. 'We passed them both down the road riding in.'

Shane jumped to his feet. Lew Johnson was shuffling reluctantly toward the door. Shane brushed him aside. He strode to the door himself, yanked it open, started out. He stopped, leaning forward and listening.

'Hell, man,' Henry Shipstead was grumbling, 'what's your hurry? We told them about Wilson. They'll stop here on their way back.' His voice ceased. All of us could hear it now, a horse pounding up the road at full gallop.

Shane turned back into the room. 'There's your answer,' he said bitterly. He swung the nearest chair to the wall and sat down. The fire blazing in him a moment before was gone. He was withdrawn into his own thoughts, and they were dark and not pleasant.

We heard the horse sliding to a stop out front. The sound was so plain you could fairly see the forelegs bracing and the hooves digging into the ground. Frank Torrey burst into the doorway. His hat was gone, his hair blowing wild. His chest heaved like he had been running as hard as the horse. He put his hands on the doorposts to hold himself steady and his voice was a hoarse whisper, though he was trying to shout across the room at father.

'Ernie's shot! They've killed him!'

The words jerked us to our feet and we stood staring. All but Shane. He did not move. You might have thought he was not even interested in what Torrey had said.

Father was the one who took hold of the scene. 'Come in, Frank,' he said quietly. 'I take it we're too late to help Ernie now. Sit down and talk and don't leave anything out.' He led Frank Torrey to a chair and pushed him into it. He closed the door and returned to his own chair. He looked older and tired.

It took Frank Torrey quite a while to pull himself together and tell his story straight. He was frightened. The fear was bedded deep in him and he was ashamed of himself for it.

He and Ernie Wright, he told us, had been to the

stage office asking for a parcel Ernie was expecting. They dropped into Grafton's for a freshener before starting back. Since things had been so quiet lately, they were not thinking of any trouble even though Fletcher and the new man, Stark Wilson, were in the poker game at the big table. But Fletcher and Wilson must have been watching for a chance like that. They chucked in their hands and came over to the bar.

Fletcher was nice and polite as could be, nodding to Torrey and singling out Ernie for talk. He said he was sorry about it, but he really needed the land Ernie had filed on. It was the right place to put up winter wind-shelters for the new herd he was bringing in soon. He knew Ernie had not proved up on it yet. Just the same, he was willing to pay a fair price.

'I'll give you three hundred dollars,' he said, 'and that's more than the lumber in your buildings will be worth to me.'

Ernie had more than that of his money in the place already. He had turned Fletcher down three or four times before. He was mad, the way he always was when Fletcher started his smooth talk.

'No,' he said shortly. 'I'm not selling. Not now or ever.'

Fletcher shrugged like he had done all he could and slipped a quick nod at Stark Wilson. This Wilson was half-smiling at Ernie. But his eyes, Frank Torrey said, had nothing like a smile in them.

'I'd change my mind if I were you,' he said to Ernie. 'That is, if you have a mind to change.'

'Keep out of this,' snapped Ernie. 'It's none of your business.'

'I see you haven't heard,' Wilson said softly. 'I'm

Mr Fletcher's new business agent. I'm handling his business affairs for him. His business with stubborn jackasses like you.' Then he said what showed Fletcher had coaxed him to it. 'You're a damn fool, Wright. But what can you expect from a breed?'

'That's a lie!' shouted Ernie. 'My mother wasn't no Indian!'

'Why, you crossbred squatter,' Wilson said, quick and sharp, 'are you telling me I'm wrong?'

'I'm telling you you're a God-damned liar!'

The silence that shut down over the saloon was so complete, Frank Torrey told us, that he could hear the ticking of the old alarm clock on the shelf behind the bar. Even Ernie, in the second his voice stopped, saw what he had done. But he was mad clear through and he glared at Wilson, his eyes reckless.

'So-o-o-o,' said Wilson, satisfied now and stretching out the word with ominous softness. He flipped back his coat on the right side in front and the holster there was free with the gun grip ready for his hand.

'You'll back that, Wright. Or you'll crawl out of here on your belly.'

Ernie moved out a step from the bar, his arms stiff at his sides. The anger in him held him erect as he beat down the terror tearing at him. He knew what this meant, but he met it straight. His hand was firm on his gun and pulling up when Wilson's first bullet hit him and staggered him. The second spun him halfway around and a faint froth appeared on his lips and all expression died from his face and he sagged to the floor.

While Frank Torrey was talking, Jim Lewis and a few minutes later Ed Howells had come in. Bad news travels fast and they seemed to know something was wrong. Perhaps they had heard that frantic galloping, the sound carrying far in the still night air. They were all in our kitchen now and they were more shaken and sober than I had ever seen them.

I was pressed close to mother, grateful for her arms around me. I noticed that she had little attention for the other men. She was watching Shane, bitter and silent across the room.

'So that's it,' father said grimly. 'We'll have to face it. We sell and at his price or he slips the leash on his hired killer. Did Wilson make a move toward you, Frank?'

'He looked at me.' Simply recalling that made Torrey shiver through. 'He looked at me and he said, "Too bad, isn't it, mister, that Wright didn't change his mind?"'

'Then what?'

'I got out of there quick as I could and came here.'

Jim Lewis had been fidgeting on his seat, more nervous every minute. Now he jumped up, almost shouting. 'But damn it, Joe! A man can't just go around shooting people!'

'Shut up, Jim,' growled Henry Shipstead. 'Don't you see the set-up? Wilson badgered Ernie into getting himself in a spot where he had to go for his gun. Wilson can claim he shot in self-defence. He'll try the same thing on each of us.'

'That's right, Jim,' put in Lew Johnson. 'Even if we tried to get a marshal in here, he couldn't hold Wilson. It was an even break and the faster man won is the way most people will figure it and plenty of them saw it. A marshal couldn't get here in time anyway.'

'But we've got to stop it!' Lewis was really shouting now. 'What chance have any of us got against Wilson? We're not gunmen. We're just a bunch of old cowhands and farmers. Call it anything you want. I call it murder.'

'Yes!'

The word sliced through the room. Shane was up and his face was hard with the rock ridges running along his jaw. 'Yes. It's murder. Trick it out as self-defence or with fancy words about an even break for a fair draw and it's still murder.' He looked at father and the pain was deep in his eyes. But there was only contempt in his voice as he turned to the others.

'You five can crawl back in your burrows. You don't have to worry—yet. If the time comes, you can always sell and run. Fletcher won't bother with the likes of you now. He's going the limit and he knows the game. He picked Wright to make the play plain. That's done. Now he'll head straight for the one real man in this valley, the man who's held you here and will go on trying to hold you and keep for you what's yours as long as there's life in him. He's standing between you and Fletcher and Wilson this minute and you ought to be thankful that once in a while this country turns out a man like Joe Starrett.'

And a man like Shane. . . . Were those words only in my mind or did I hear mother whisper them? She was looking at him and then at father and she was both frightened and proud at once. Father was fumbling with his pipe, packing it and making a fuss with it like it needed his whole attention.

The others stirred uneasily. They were reassured by what Shane said and yet shamed that they should be. And they did not like the way he said it.

'You seem to know a lot about that kind of dirty business,' Ed Howells said, with maybe an edge of malice to his voice.

'I do.'

Shane let the words lie there, plain and short and ugly. His face was stern and behind the hard front of his features was a sadness that fought to break through. But he stared levelly at Howells and it was the other man who dropped his eyes and turned away.

Father had his pipe going. 'Maybe it's a lucky break for the rest of us,' he said mildly, 'that Shane here has been around a bit. He can call the cards for us plain. Ernie might still be alive, Johnson, if you had had the sense to tell us about Wilson right off. It's a good thing Ernie wasn't a family man.' He turned to Shane. 'How do you rate Fletcher now he's shown his hand?'

You could see that the chance to do something, even just to talk at the problem pressing us, eased the bitterness in Shane.

'He'll move in on Wright's place first thing to-morrow. He'll have a lot of men busy on this side of the river from now on, probably push some cattle around behind the homesteads, to keep the pressure plain on all of you. How quick he'll try you, Joe, depends on how he reads you. If he thinks you might crack, he'll wait and let knowing what happened to Wright work on you. If he really knows you, he'll not wait more than a day or two to make sure you've had time to think it over and then he'll grab the first chance to throw Wilson at you. He'll want it, like with Wright, in a public place where there'll be plenty of witnesses. If you don't give him a chance, he'll try to make one.'

'Hm-m-m,' father said soberly. 'I was sure you'd give it to me straight and that rings right.' He pulled on his pipe for a moment. 'I reckon, boys, this will be a matter of waiting for the next few days. There's no immediate danger right off anyway. Grafton will take care of Ernie's body to-night. We can meet in town in the morning to fix him a funeral. After that, we'd better stay out of town and stick close home as much as possible. I'd suggest you all study on this and drop in again to-morrow night. Maybe we can figure out something. I'd like to see how the town's taking it before I make up my mind on anything.'

They were ready to leave it at that. They were ready to leave it to father. They were decent men and good neighbours. But not a one of them, were the decision his, would have stood up to Fletcher now. They would stay as long as father was there. With him gone, Fletcher would have things his way. That was how they felt as they muttered their good-nights and bunched out to scatter up and down the road.

Father stood in the doorway and watched them go. When he came back to his chair, he walked slowly and he seemed haggard and worn. 'Somebody will have to go to Ernie's place to-morrow,' he said, 'and gather up his things. He's got relatives somewhere in Iowa.'

'No.' There was finality in Shane's tone. 'You'll not go near the place. Fletcher might be counting on that. Grafton can do it.'

'But Ernie was my friend,' father said simply.

'Ernie's past friendship. Your debt is to the living.'

Father looked at Shane and this brought him

again into the immediate moment and cheered him. He nodded assent and turned to mother, who was hurrying to argue with him.

'Don't you see, Joe? If you can stay away from any place where you might meet Fletcher and—and that Wilson, things will work out. He can't keep a man like Wilson in this little valley forever.'

She was talking rapidly and I knew why. She was not really trying to convince father as much as she was trying to convince herself. Father knew it, too.

'No, Marian. A man can't crawl into a hole somewhere and hide like a rabbit. Not if he has any pride.'

'All right, then. But can't you keep quiet and not let him ride you and drive you into any fight?'

'That won't work either.' Father was grim, but he was better and facing up to it. 'A man can stand for a lot of pushing if he has too. Specially when he has his reasons.' His glance shifted briefly to me. 'But there are some things a man can't take. Not if he's to go on living with himself.'

I was startled as Shane suddenly sucked in his breath with a long breaking intake. He was battling something within him, that old hidden desperation, and his eyes were dark and tormented against the paleness of his face. He seemed unable to look at us. He strode to the door and went out. We heard his footsteps fading toward the barn.

I was startled now at father. His breath, too, was coming in long, broken sweeps. He was up and pacing back and forth. When he swung on mother and his voice battered at her, almost fierce in its intensity, I realized that he knew about the change in Shane and that the knowing had been cankering in him all the past weeks.

'That's the one thing I can't stand, Marian. What we're doing to him. What happens to me doesn't matter too much. I talk big and I don't belittle myself. But my weight in any kind of a scale won't match his and I know it. If I understood him then as I do now, I'd never have got him to stay on here. But I didn't figure Fletcher would go this far. Shane won his fight before ever he came riding into this valley. It's been tough enough on him already. Should we let him lose just because of us? Fletcher can have his way. We'll sell out and move on.'

I was not thinking. I was only feeling. For some strange reason I was feeling Shane's fingers in my hair, gently rocking my head. I could not help what I was saying, shouting across the room. 'Father! Shane wouldn't run away! He wouldn't run away from any-thing!'

Father stopped pacing, his eyes narrowed in surprise. He stared at me without really seeing me. He was listening to mother.

'Bob's right, Joe. We can't let Shane down.' It was queer, hearing her say the same thing to father she had said to Shane, the same thing with only the name different. 'He'd never forgive us if we ran away from this. That's what we'd be doing. This isn't just a case of bucking Fletcher any more. It isn't just a case of keeping a piece of ground Fletcher wants for his range. We've got to be the kind of people Shane thinks we are. Bob's right. He wouldn't run away from anything like that. And that's the reason we can't.'

'Lookahere, Marian, you don't think I want to

do any running? No. You know me better than that. It'd go against everything in me. But what's my fool pride and this place and any plans we've had alongside of a man like that?'

'I know, Joe. But you don't see far enough.' They were both talking earnestly, not breaking in, hearing each other out, and sort of groping to put their meaning plain. 'I can't really explain it, Joe. But I just know that we're bound up in something bigger than any one of us, and that running away is the one thing that would be worse than whatever might happen to us. There wouldn't be anything real ahead for us, any of us, maybe even for Bob, all the rest of our lives.'

'Humph,' said father. 'Torrey could do it. And Johnson. All the rest of them. And it wouldn't bother them too much.'

'Joe! Joe Starrett! Are you trying to make me mad? I'm not talking about them. I'm talking about us.'

'Hm-m-m,' said father softly, musing like to himself. 'The salt would be done. There just wouldn't be any flavour. There wouldn't be much meaning left.'

'Oh, Joe! Joe! That's what I've been trying to say. And I know this will work out some way. I don't know how. But it will, if we face it and stand up to it and have faith in each other. It'll work out. Because it's got to.'

'That's a woman's reason, Marian. But you're part right anyway. We'll play this game through. It'll need careful watching and close figuring. But maybe we can wait Fletcher out and make him overplay his hand. The town won't take much to this Wilson deal. Men like that fellow Weir have minds of their own.'

Father was more cheerful now that he was beginning to get his thoughts straightened out. He and mother talked low in the kitchen for a long time after they sent me to bed, and I lay in my little room and saw through the window the stars wheeling distantly in the far outer darkness until I fell asleep at last.

XII

THE MORNING sun brightened our house and everything in the world outside. We had a good breakfast, father and Shane taking their time because they had routed out early to get the chores done and were waiting to go to town. They saddled up presently and rode off, and I moped in front of the house, not able to settle to any kind of playing.

After she bustled through the dishes, mother saw me standing and staring down the road and called me to the porch. She got our tattered old parchesi board and she kept me humping to beat her. She was a grand one for games like that. She would be as excited as a kid, squealing at the big numbers and doubles and counting proudly out loud as she moved her markers ahead.

When I had won three games running, she put the board away and brought out two fat apples and my favourite of the books she had from the time she taught school. Munching on her apple, she read to me and before I knew it the shadows were mighty short and she had to skip in to get dinner and father and Shane were riding up to the barn.

They came in while she was putting the food on the table. We sat down and it was almost like a holiday, not just because it was not a work day, but because the grown folks were talking lightly, were determined not to let this Fletcher business spoil our good times.

Father was pleased at what had happened in town.

'Yes, sir,' he was saying as we were finishing dinner. 'Ernie had a right good funeral. He would have appreciated it. Grafton made a nice speech and, by Godfrey, I believe he meant it. That fellow Weir had his clerk put together a really fine coffin. Wouldn't take a cent for it. And Sims over at the mine is knocking out a good stone. He wouldn't take a cent either. I was surprised at the crowd, too. Not a good word for Fletcher among them. And there must have been thirty people there.'

'Thirty-four,' said Shane. 'I counted 'em. They weren't just paying their respects to Wright, Marian. That wouldn't have brought in some of those I checked. They were showing their opinion of a certain man named Starrett, who made a pretty fair speech himself. This husband of yours is becoming quite a respected citizen in these parts. Soon as the town gets grown up and organized, he's likely to start going places. Give him time and he'll be mayor.'

Mother caught her breath with a little sob. 'Give . . . him . . . time,' she said slowly. She looked at Shane and there was panic in her eyes. The lightness was gone and before anyone could say more, we heard the horses turning into our yard.

I dashed to the window to peer out. It struck me strange that Shane, usually so alert, was not there ahead of me. Instead he pushed back his chair and spoke gently, still sitting in it. 'That will be Fletcher, Joe. He's heard how the town is taking this and knows he has to move fast. You take it easy. He's playing against time now, but he won't push anything here.'

Father nodded at Shane and went to the door. He

had taken off his gunbelt when he came in and now passed it to lift the rifle from its nails on the wall. Holding it in his right hand, barrel down, he opened the door and stepped out on the porch, clear to the front edge. Shane followed quietly and leaned in the doorway, relaxed and watchful. Mother was beside me at the window, staring out, crumpling her apron in her hand.

There were four of them, Fletcher and Wilson in the lead, two cowboys tagging. They had pulled up about twenty feet from the porch. This was the first time I had seen Fletcher for nearly a year. He was a tall man who must once have been a handsome figure in the fine clothes he always wore and with his arrogant air and his finely chiselled face set off by his short-cropped black beard and brilliant eyes. Now a heaviness was setting in about his features and a fatty softness was beginning to show in his body. His face had a shrewd cast and a kind of reckless determination was on him that I did not remember ever noticing before.

Stark Wilson, for all the dude look Frank Torrey had mentioned, seemed lean and fit. He was sitting idly in his saddle, but the pose did not fool you. He was wearing no coat and the two guns were swinging free. He was sure of himself, serene and deadly. The curl of his lip beneath his moustache was a combination of confidence in himself and contempt for us.

Fletcher was smiling and affable. He was certain he held the cards and was going to deal them as he wanted. 'Sorry to bother you, Starrett, so soon after that unfortunate affair last night. I wish it could have been avoided. I really do. Shooting is so unnecessary in these things, if only people would show sense.

But Wright never should have called Mr Wilson here a liar. That was a mistake.'

'It was,' father said curtly. 'But then Ernie always did believe in telling the truth.' I could see Wilson stiffen and his lips tighten. Father did not look at him. 'Speak your piece, Fletcher, and get off my land.'

Fletcher was still smiling. 'There's no call for us to quarrel, Starrett. What's done is done. Let's hope there's no need for anything like it to be done again. You've worked cattle on a big ranch and you can understand my position. I'll be wanting all the range I can get from now on. Even without that, I can't let a bunch of nesters keep coming in here and choke me off from my water rights.'

'We've been over that before,' father said. 'You know where I stand. If you have more to say, speak up and be done with it.'

'All right, Starrett. Here's my proposition. I like the way you do things. You've got some queer notions about the cattle business, but when you tackle a job, you take hold and do it thoroughly. You and that man of yours are a combination I could use. I want you on my side of the fence. I'm getting rid of Morgan and I want you to take over as foreman. From what I hear your man would make one hell of a driving trail boss. The spot's his. Since you've proved up on this place, I'll buy it from you. If you want to go on living here, that can be arranged. If you want to play around with that little herd of yours, that can be arranged too. But I want you working for me.'

Father was surprised. He had not expected anything quite like this. He spoke softly to Shane behind him. He did not turn or look away from Fletcher, but his voice carried clearly.

'Can I call the turn for you, Shane?'

'Yes, Joe.' Shane's voice was just as soft, but it, too, carried clearly and there was a little note of pride in it.

Father stood taller there on the edge of the porch. He stared straight at Fletcher. 'And the others,' he said slowly. 'Johnson, Shipstead, and the rest. What about them?'

'They'll have to go.'

Father did not hesitate. 'No.'

'I'll give you a thousand dollars for this place as it stands and that's my top offer.'

'No.'

The fury in Fletcher broke over his face and he started to turn in the saddle toward Wilson. He caught himself and forced again that shrewd smile. 'There's no percentage in being hasty, Starrett. I'll boost the ante to twelve hundred. That's a lot better than what might happen if you stick to being stubborn. I'll not take an answer now. I'll give you till to-night to think it over. I'll be waiting at Grafton's to hear you talk sense.'

He swung his horse and started away. The two cowboys turned to join him by the road. Wilson did not follow at once. He leaned forward in his saddle and drove a sneering look at father.

'Yes, Starrett. Think it over. You wouldn't like someone else to be enjoying this place of yours—and that woman there in the window.'

He was lifting his reins with one hand to pull his horse around and suddenly he dropped them and froze to attention. It must have been what he saw in father's face. We could not see it, mother and I, because father's back was to us. But we could see his hand tightening on the rifle at his side.

'Don't, Joe!'

Shane was beside father. He slipped past, moving smooth and steady, down the steps and over to one side to come at Wilson on his right hand and stop not six feet from him. Wilson was puzzled and his right hand twitched and then was still as Shane stopped and as he saw that Shane carried no gun.

Shane looked up at him and Shane's voice flicked in a whiplash of contempt. 'You talk like a man because of that flashy hardware you're wearing. Strip it away and you'd shrivel down to boy size.'

The very daring of it held Wilson motionless for an instant and father's voice cut into it. 'Shane! Stop it!'

The blackness faded from Wilson's face. He smiled grimly at Shane. 'You do need someone to look after you.' He whirled his horse and put it to a run to join Fletcher and the others in the road.

It was only then that I realized mother was gripping my shoulders so that they hurt. She dropped on a chair and held me to her. We could hear father and Shane on the porch.

'He'd have drilled you, Joe, before you could have brought the gun up and pumped in a shell.'

'But you, you crazy fool!' Father was covering his feelings with a show of exasperation. 'You'd have made him plug you just so I'd have a chance to get him.'

Mother jumped up. She pushed me aside. She flared at them from the doorway. 'And both of you would have acted like fools just because he said that about me. I'll have you two know that if it's got to be done, I can take being insulted just as much as you can.'

Peering around her, I saw them gaping at her in astonishment. 'But, Marian,' father objected mildly, coming to her. 'What better reason could a man have?'

'Yes,' said Shane gently. 'What better reason?' He was not looking just at mother. He was looking at the two of them.

XIII

I DO not know how long they would have stood there on the porch in the warmth of that moment. I shattered it by asking what seemed to me a simple question until after I had asked it and the significance hit me.

'Father, what are you going to tell Fletcher tonight?'

There was no answer. There was no need for one. I guess I was growing up. I knew what he would tell Fletcher. I knew what he would say. I knew, too, that because he was father he would have to go to Grafton's and say it. And I understood why they could no longer bear to look at one another, and the breeze blowing in from the sun-washed fields was suddenly so chill and cheerless.

They did not look at each other. They did not say a word to each other. Yet somehow I realized that they were closer together in the stillness there on the porch than they had ever been. They knew themselves and each of them knew that the other grasped the situation whole. They knew that Fletcher had dealt himself a winning hand, had caught father in the one play that he could not avoid because he would not avoid it. They knew that talk is meaningless when a common knowledge is already there. The silence bound them as no words ever could.

Father sat on the top porch step. He took out his

pipe and drew on it as the match flamed and fixed his eyes on the horizon, on the mountains far across the river. Shane took the chair I had used for the games with mother. He swung it to the house wall and bent into it in that familiar unconscious gesture and he, too, looked into the distance. Mother turned into the kitchen and went about clearing the table as if she was not really aware of what she was doing. I helped her with the dishes and the old joy of sharing with her in the work was gone and there was no sound in the kitchen except the drip of the water and the chink of dish on dish.

When we were done, she went to father. She sat beside him on the step, her hand on the wood between them, and his covered hers and the moments merged in the slow, dwindling procession of time.

Loneliness gripped me. I wandered through the house, finding nothing there to do, and out on the porch and past those three and to the barn. I searched around and found an old shovel handle and started to whittle me a play sabre with my knife. I had been thinking of this for days. Now the idea held no interest. The wood curls dropped to the barn floor, and after a while I let the shovel handle drop among them. Everything that had happened before seemed far off, almost like another existence. All that mattered was the length of the shadows creeping across the yard as the sun drove down the afternoon sky.

I took a hoe and went into mother's garden where the ground was caked around the turnips, the only things left unharvested. But there was scant work in me. I kept at it for a couple of rows, then the hoe dropped and I let it lie. I went to the front of the house, and there they were sitting, just as before.

I sat on the step below father and mother, between them, and their legs on each side of me made it seem better. I felt father's hand on my head.

'This is kind of tough on you, Bob.' He could talk to me because I was only a kid. He was really talking to himself.

'I can't see the full finish. But I can see this. Wilson down and there'll be an end to it. Fletcher'll be done. The town will see to that. I can't beat Wilson on the draw. But there's strength enough in this clumsy body of mine to keep me on my feet till I get him, too.' Mother stirred and was still, and his voice went on. 'Things could be worse. It helps a man to know that if anything happens to him, his family will be in better hands than his own.'

There was a sharp sound behind us on the porch. Shane had risen so swiftly that his chair had knocked against the wall. His hands were clenched tightly and his arms were quivering. His face was pale with the effort shaking him. He was desperate with an inner torment, his eyes tortured by thoughts that he could not escape, and the marks were obvious on him and he did not care. He strode to the steps, down past us and around the corner of the house.

Mother was up and after him, running headlong. She stopped abruptly at the house corner, clutching at the wood, panting and irresolute. Slowly she came back, her hands outstretched as if to keep from falling. She sank again on the step, close against father, and he gathered her to him with one great arm.

The silence spread and filled the whole valley and the shadows crept across the yard. They touched the road and began to merge in the deeper shading that meant the sun was dipping below the mountains far behind the house. Mother straightened, and as she stood up, father rose, too. He took hold of her two arms and held her in front of him. 'I'm counting on you, Marian, to help him win again. You can do it, if anyone can.' He smiled a strange little sad smile and he loomed up there above me the biggest man in all the world. 'No supper for me now, Marian. A cup of your coffee is all I want.' They passed through the doorway together.

Where was Shane? I hurried toward the barn. I was almost to it when I saw him out by the pasture. He was staring over it and the grazing steers at the great lonely mountains tipped with the gold of the sun now rushing down behind them. As I watched, he stretched his arms up, the fingers reaching to their utmost limits, grasping and grasping, it seemed, at the glory glowing in the sky.

He whirled and came straight back, striding with long, steady steps, his head held high. There was some subtle, new, unchangeable certainty in him. He came close and I saw that his face was quiet and untroubled and that little lights danced in his eyes.

'Skip into the house, Bobby boy. Put on a smile. Everything is going to be all right.' He was past me, without slowing, swinging into the barn.

But I could not go into the house. And I did not dare follow him, not after he had told me to go. A wild excitement was building up in me while I waited by the porch, watching the barn door.

The minutes ticked past and the twilight deepened and a patch of light sprang from the house as the lamp in the kitchen was lit. And still I waited. Then he was coming swiftly toward me and I stared and stared and broke and ran into the house with the blood pounding in my head.

'Father! Father! Shane's got his gun!'

He was close back of me. Father and mother barely had time to look up from the table before he was framed in the doorway. He was dressed as he was that first day when he rode into our lives, in that dark and worn magnificence from the black hat with its wide curling brim to the soft black boots. But what caught your eye was the single flash of white, the outer ivory plate on the grip of the gun, showing sharp and distinct against the dark material of the trousers. The tooled cartridge belt nestled around him, riding above the hip on the left, sweeping down on the right to hold the holster snug along the thigh, just as he had said, the gun handle about halfway between the wrist and elbow of his right arm hanging there relaxed and ready.

Belt and holster and gun. . . . These were not things he was wearing or carrying. They were part of him, part of the man, of the full sum of the integrate force that was Shane. You could see now that for the first time this man who had been living with us, who was one of us, was complete, was himself in the final effect of his being.

Now that he was no longer in his crude work clothes, he seemed again slender, almost slight, as he did that first day. The change was more than that. What had been seeming iron was again steel. The slenderness was that of a tempered blade and a razor edge was there. Slim and dark in the doorway, he seemed somehow to fill the whole frame.

This was not our Shane. And yet it was. I remembered Ed Howells saying that this was the most dangerous man he had ever seen. I remembered in the same rush that father had said he was the safest man we ever had in our house. I realized that both were right and that this, this at last, was Shane.

He was in the room now and he was speaking to them both in that bantering tone he used to have only for mother. 'A fine pair of parents you are. Haven't even fed Bob yet. Stack him full of a good supper. Yourselves, too. I have a little business to tend to in town.'

Father was looking fixedly at him. The sudden hope that had sprung in his face had as quickly gone. 'No, Shane. It won't do. Even your thinking of it is the finest thing any man ever did for me. But I won't let you. It's my stand. Fletcher's making his play against me. There's no dodging. It's my business.'

'There's where you're wrong, Joe,' Shane said gently. 'This is my business. My kind of business. I've had fun being a farmer. You've shown me new meaning in the word, and I'm proud that for a while maybe I qualified. But there are a few things a farmer can't handle.'

The strain of the long afternoon was telling on father. He pushed up from the table. 'Damn it, Shane, be sensible. Don't make it harder for me. You can't do this.'

Shane stepped near, to the side of the table, facing father across a corner. 'Easy does it, Joe. I'm making this my business.'

'No. I won't let you. Suppose you do put Wilson out of the way. That won't finish anything. It'll only even the score and swing things back worse than ever. Think what it'll mean to you. And where will it leave me? I couldn't hold my head up around here any more. They'd say I ducked and they'd be right. You can't do it and that's that.'

'No!' Shane's voice was even more gentle, but it had a quiet, inflexible quality that had never been there before. 'There's no man living can tell me what I can't do. Not even you, Joe. You forget there is still a way.'

He was talking to hold father's attention. As he spoke the gun was in his hand and before father could move he swung it, swift and sharp, so the barrel lined flush along the side of father's head, back of the temple, above the ear. Strength was in the blow and it thudded dully on the bone and father folded over the table and as it tipped with his weight slid toward the floor. Shane's arm was under him before he hit and Shane pivoted father's loose body up and into his chair and righted the table while the coffee cups rattled on the floor boards. Father's head lolled back and Shane caught it and eased it and the big shoulders forward till they rested on the table, the face down and cradled in the limp arms.

Shane stood erect and looked across the table at mother. She had not moved since he appeared in the doorway, not even when father fell and the table teetered under her hands on its edge. She was watching Shane, her throat curving in a lovely proud line, her eyes wide with a sweet warmth shining in them.

Darkness had shut down over the valley as they looked at each other across the table and the only light now was from the lamp swinging ever so slightly above them, circling them with its steady glow. They were alone in a moment that was all their own. Yet, when they spoke, it was of father.

'I was afraid,' Shane murmured, 'that he would

138

take it that way. He couldn't do otherwise and be Joe Starrett.'

'I know.'

'He'll rest easy and come out maybe a little groggy but all right. Tell him, Marian. Tell him no man need be ashamed of being beat by Shane.'

The name sounded queer like that, the man speaking of himself. It was the closest he ever came to boasting. And when you understood that there was not the least hint of a boast. He was stating a fact, simple and ele-mental as the power that dwelled in him.

'I know,' she said again. 'I don't need to tell him. He knows, too.' She was rising, earnest and intent. 'But there is something else I must know. We have battered down words that might have been spoken between us and that was as it should be. But I have a right to know now. I am part of this, too. And what I do depends on what you tell me now. Are you doing this just for me?'

Shane hesitated for a long, long moment. 'No, Marian.' His gaze seemed to widen and encompass us all, mother and the still figure of father and me huddled on a chair by the window, and somehow the room and the house and the whole place. Then he was looking only at mother and she was all that he could see.

'No, Marian. Could I separate you in my mind and afterwards be a man?'

He pulled his eyes from her and stared into the night beyond the open door. His face hardened, his thoughts leaping to what lay ahead in town. So quiet and easy you were scarce aware that he was moving, he was gone into the outer darkness.

XIV

NOTHING could have kept me there in the house that night. My mind held nothing but the driving desire to follow Shane. I waited, hardly daring to breathe, while mother watched him go. I waited until she turned to father, bending over him, then I slipped around the door-post to the porch. I thought for a moment she had noticed me, but I could not be sure and she did not call to me. I went softly down the steps and into the freedom of the night.

Shane was nowhere in sight. I stayed in the darker shadows, looking about, and at last I saw him emerging once more from the barn. The moon was rising low over the mountains, a clean, bright crescent. Its light was enough for me to see him plainly in outline. He was carrying his saddle and a sudden pain stabbed through me as I saw that with it was his saddle-roll. He went toward the pasture gate, not slow, not fast, just firm and steady. There was a catlike certainty in his every movement, a silent, inevitable deadliness. I heard him, there by the gate, give his low whistle and the horse came out of the shadows at the far end of the pasture, its hooves making no noise in the deep grass, a dark and powerful shape etched in the moonlight drifting across the field straight to the man.

I knew what I would have to do. I crept along the corral fence, keeping tight to it, until I reached the road. As soon as I was around the corner of the corral with it and the barn between me and the pasture, I started to run as rapidly as I could toward town, my feet plumping softly in the thick dust of the road. I walked this every school day and it had never seemed long before. Now the distance stretched ahead, lengthening in my mind as if to mock me.

I could not let him see me. I kept looking back over my shoulder as I ran. When I saw him swinging into the road, I was well past Johnson's, almost past Shipstead's, striking into the last open stretch to the edge of town. I scurried to the side of the road and behind a clump of bullberry bushes. Panting to get my breath, I crouched there and waited for him to pass. The hoofbeats swelled in my ears, mingled with the pounding beat of my own blood. In my imagination he was galloping furiously and I was positive he was already rushing past me. But when I parted the bushes and pushed forward to peer out, he was moving at a moderate pace and was only almost abreast of me.

He was tall and terrible there in the road, looming up gigantic in the mystic half-light. He was the man I saw that first day, a stranger, dark and forbidding, forging his lone way out of an unknown past in the utter loneliness of his own immovable and instinctive defiance. He was the symbol of all the dim, formless imaginings of danger and terror in the untested realm of human potentialities beyond my understanding. The impact of the menace that marked him was like a physical blow.

I could not help it. I cried out and stumbled and fell. He was off his horse and over me before I could right myself, picking me up, his grasp strong and reassuring. I looked at him, tearful and afraid, and the fear faded from me. He was no stranger. That was some trick of the shadows. He was Shane. He was shaking me gently and smiling at me.

'Bobby boy, this is no time for you to be out. Skip along home and help your mother. I told you everything would be all right.'

He let go of me and turned slowly, gazing out across the far sweep of the valley silvered in the moon's glow. 'Look at it, Bob. Hold it in your mind like this. It's a lovely land, Bob. A good place to be a boy and grow straight inside as a man should.'

My gaze followed his, and I saw our valley as though for the first time and the emotion in me was more than I could stand. I choked and reached out for him and he was not there.

He was rising into the saddle and the two shapes, the man and the horse, became one and moved down the road toward the yellow squares that were the patches of light from the windows of Grafton's building a quarter of a mile away. I wavered a moment, but the call was too strong. I started after him, running frantic in the middle of the road.

Whether he heard me or not, he kept right on. There were several men on the long porch of the building by the saloon doors. Red Marlin's hair made him easy to spot. They were scanning the road intently. As Shane hit the panel of light from the near big front window, the store window, they stiffened to attention. Red Marlin, a startled expression on his face, dived quickly through the doors.

Shane stopped, not by the rail but by the steps on the store side. When he dismounted, he did not slip the reins over the horse's head as the cowboys always did. He left them looped over the pommel of the saddle and the horse seemed to know what this meant. It stood motionless, close by the steps, head up, waiting, ready for whatever swift need.

Shane went along the porch and halted briefly, fronting the two men still there.

'Where's Fletcher?'

They looked at each other and at Shane. One of them started to speak. 'He doesn't want—' Shane's voice stopped him. It slapped at them, low and with an edge that cut right into your mind. 'Where's Fletcher?'

One of them jerked a hand toward the doors and then, as they moved to shift out of his way, his voice caught them.

'Get inside. Go clear to the bar before you turn.'

They stared at him and stirred uneasily and swung together to push through the doors. As the doors came back, Shane grabbed them, one with each hand, and pulled them out and wide open and he disappeared between them.

Clumsy and tripping in my haste, I scrambled up the steps and into the store. Sam Grafton and Mr Weir were the only persons there and they both hurrying to the entrance to the saloon, so intent that they failed to notice me. They stopped in the opening. I crept behind them to my familiar perch on my box where I could see past them.

The big room was crowded. Almost everyone who could be seen regularly around town was there, everyone but our homestead neighbours. There were many others who were new to me. They were lined up elbow to elbow nearly the entire length of the bar. The tables were full and more men were lounging along the far wall. The big round poker table at the back between the stairway to the little balcony and the door to Grafton's office was littered with glasses and chips. It seemed strange, for all the men standing, that there should be an empty chair at the far curve of the table. Someone must have been in that chair, because chips were at the place and a half-smoked cigar, a wisp of smoke curling up from it, was by them on the table.

Red Marlin was leaning against the back wall, behind the chair. As I looked, he saw the smoke and appeared to start a little. With a careful show of casualness he slid into the chair and picked up the cigar.

A haze of thinning smoke was by the ceiling over them all, floating in involved streamers around the hanging lamps. This was Grafton's saloon in the flush of a banner evening's business. But something was wrong, was missing. The hum of activity, the whirr of voices, that should have risen from the scene, been part of it, was stilled in a hush more impressive than any noise could be. The attention of everyone in the room, like a single sense, was centred on that dark figure just inside the swinging doors, back to them and touching them.

This was the Shane of the adventures I had dreamed for him, cool and competent, facing that room full of men in the simple solitude of his own invincible completeness.

His eyes searched the room. They halted on a man sitting at a small table in the front corner with his hat on low over his forehead. With a thump of surprise I recognized it was Stark Wilson and he was studying Shane with a puzzled look on his face. Shane's eyes swept on, checking off each person. They stopped again on a figure over by the wall and the beginnings of a smile showed in them and he nodded almost imperceptibly. It was Chris, tall and lanky, his arm in a sling, and as he caught the nod he flushed a little and shifted his weight from one foot to the other. Then he straightened his shoulders and over his face came a slow smile, warm and friendly, the smile of a man who knows his own mind at last.

But Shane's eyes were already moving on. They narrowed as they rested on Red Marlin. Then they jumped to Will Atkey trying to make himself small behind the bar.

'Where's Fletcher?'

Will fumbled with the cloth in his hands. 'I—I don't know. He was here awhile ago.' Frightened at the sound of his own voice in the stillness, Will dropped the cloth, started to stoop for it, and checked himself, putting his hands to the inside rim of the bar to hold himself steady.

Shane tilted his head slightly so his eyes could clear his hat brim. He was scanning the balcony across the rear of the room. It was empty and the doors there were closed. He stepped forward, disregarding the men by the bar, and walked quietly past them the long length of the room. He went through the doorway to Grafton's office and into the semi-darkness beyond.

And still the hush held. Then he was in the office doorway again and his eyes bored toward Red Marlin.

'Where's Fletcher?'

The silence was taut and unendurable. It had to break. The sound was that of Stark Wilson coming to his feet in the far front corner. His voice, lazy and insolent, floated down the room.

'Where's Starrett?'

While the words yet seemed to hang in the air,

Shane was moving toward the front of the room. But Wilson was moving, too. He was crossing toward the swinging doors and he took his stand just to the left of them, a few feet out from the wall. The position gave him command of the wide aisle running back between the bar and the tables and Shane coming forward in it.

Shane stopped about three quarters of the way forward, about five yards from Wilson. He cocked his head for one quick sidewise glance again at the balcony and then he was looking only at Wilson. He did not like the set-up. Wilson had the front wall and he was left in the open of the room. He understood the fact, assessed it, accepted it.

They faced each other in the aisle and the men along the bar jostled one another in their hurry to get to the opposite side of the room. A reckless arrogance was on Wilson, certain of himself and his control of the situation. He was not one to miss the significance of the slim deadliness that was Shane. But even now, I think, he did not believe that anyone in our valley would deliberately stand up to him.

'Where's Starrett?' he said once more, still mocking Shane but making it this time a real question.

The words went past Shane as if they had not been spoken. 'I had a few things to say to Fletcher,' he said gently. 'That can wait. You're a pushing man, Wilson, so I reckon I had better accommodate you.'

Wilson's face sobered and his eyes glinted coldly. 'I've no quarrel with you,' he said flatly, 'even if you are Starrett's man. Walk out of here without any fuss and I'll let you go. It's Starrett I want.'

'What you want, Wilson, and what you'll get are two different things. Your killing days are done.'

Wilson had it now. You could see him grasp the

146

meaning. This quiet man was pushing him just as he had pushed Ernie Wright. As he measured Shane, it was not to his liking. Something that was not fear but a kind of wondering and baffled reluctance showed in his face. And then there was no escape, for that gentle voice was pegging him to the immediate and implacable moment.

'I'm waiting, Wilson. Do I have to crowd you into slapping leather?'

Time stopped and there was nothing in all the world but two men looking into eternity in each other's eyes. And the room rocked in the sudden blur of action indistinct in its incredible swiftness and the roar of their guns was a single sustained blast. And Shane stood, solid on his feet as a rooted oak, and Wilson swayed, his right arm hanging useless, blood beginning to show in a small stream from under the sleeve over the hand, the gun slipping from the numbing fingers.

He backed against the wall, a bitter disbelief twisting his features. His left arm hooked and the second gun was showing and Shane's bullet smashed into his chest and his knees buckled, sliding him slowly down the wall till the lifeless weight of the body toppled it sideways to the floor.

Shane gazed across the space between and he seemed to have forgotten all else as he let his gun ease into the holster. 'I gave him his chance,' he murmured out of the depths of a great sadness. But the words had no meaning for me, because I noticed on the dark brown of his shirt, low and just above the belt to one side of the buckle, the darker spot gradually widening. Then others noticed, too, and there was a stir in the air and the room was coming to life.

Voices were starting, but no one focused on them.

They were snapped short by the roar of a shot from the rear of the room. A wind seemed to whip Shane's shirt at the shoulder and the glass of the front window beyond shattered near the bottom.

Then I saw it.

It was mine alone. The others were turning to stare at the back of the room. My eyes were fixed on Shane and I saw it. I saw the whole man move, all of him, in the single flashing instant. I saw the head lead and the body swing and the driving power of the legs beneath. I saw the arm leap and the hand take the gun in the lightning sweep. I saw the barrel line up like—like a finger pointing—and the flame spurt even as the man himself was still in motion.

And there on the balcony Fletcher, impaled in the act of aiming for a second shot, rocked on his heels and fell back into the open doorway behind him. He clawed at the jambs and pulled himself forward. He staggered to the rail and tried to raise the gun. But the strength was draining out of him and he collapsed over the rail, jarring it loose and falling with it.

Across the stunned and barren silence of the room Shane's voice seemed to come from a great distance. 'I expect that finishes it,' he said. Unconsciously, without looking down, he broke out the cylinder of his gun and reloaded it. The stain on his shirt was bigger now, spreading fanlike above the belt, but he did not appear to know or care. Only his movements were slow, retarded by an unutterable weariness. The hands were sure and steady, but they moved slowly and the gun dropped into the holster of its own weight.

148

He backed with dragging steps toward the swinging doors until his shoulders touched them. The light in his eyes was unsteady like the flickering of a candle guttering toward darkness. And then, as he stood there, a strange thing happened.

How could one describe it, the change that came over him? Out of the mysterious resources of his will the vitality came. It came creeping, a tide of strength that crept through him and fought and shook off the weakness. It shone in his eyes and they were alive again and alert. It welled up in him, sending that familiar power surging through him again until it was singing again in every vibrant line of him.

He faced that room full of men and read them all with the one sweeping glance and spoke to them in that gentle voice with that quiet, inflexible quality.

'I'll be riding on now. And there's not a one of you that will follow.'

He turned his back on them in the indifference of absolute knowledge they would do as he said. Straight and superb, he was silhouetted against the doors and the patch of night above them. The next moment they were closing with a soft swish of sound.

The room was crowded with action now. Men were clustering around the bodies of Wilson and Fletcher, pressing to the bar, talking excitedly. Not a one of them, though, approached too close to the doors. There was a cleared space by the doorway as if someone had drawn a line marking it off.

I did not care what they were doing or what they were saying. I had to get to Shane. I had to get to him in time. I had to know, and he was the only one who could ever tell me.

I dashed out the store door and I was in time. He was on his horse, already starting away from the steps.

'Shane,' I whispered desperately, loud as I dared without the men inside hearing me. 'Oh, Shane!'

He heard me and reined around and I hurried to him, standing by a stirrup and looking up.

'Bobby! Bobby boy! What are you doing here?'

'I've been here all along,' I blurted out. 'You've got to tell me. Was that Wilson—'

He knew what was troubling me. He always knew. 'Wilson,' he said, 'was mighty fast. As fast as I've ever seen.'

'I don't care,' I said, the tears starting. 'I don't care if he was the fastest that ever was. He'd never have been able to shoot you, would he? You'd have got him straight, wouldn't you—if you had been in practice?'

He hesitated a moment. He gazed down at me and into me and he knew. He knew what goes on in a boy's mind and what can help him stay clean inside through the muddled, dirtied years of growing up.

'Sure. Sure, Bob. He'd never even have cleared the holster.'

He started to bend down toward me, his hand reaching for my head. But the pain struck him like a whiplash and the hand jumped to his shirt front by the belt, pressing hard, and he reeled a little in the saddle.

The ache in me was more than I could bear. I stared dumbly at him, and because I was just a boy and helpless I turned away and hid my face against the firm, warm flank of the horse.

'Bob.'

'Yes, Shane.'

'A man is what he is, Bob, and there's no breaking

150

the mould. I tried that and I've lost. But I reckon it was in the cards from the moment I saw a freckled kid on a rail up the road there and a real man behind him, the kind that could back him for the chance another kid never had.'

'But—but, Shane, you—'

'There's no going back from a killing, Bob. Right or wrong, the brand sticks and there's no going back. It's up to you now. Go home to your mother and father. Grow strong and straight and take care of them. Both of them.'

'Yes, Shane.'

'There's only one thing more I can do for them now.'

I felt the horse move away from me. Shane was looking down the road and on to the open plain and the horse was obeying the silent command of the reins. He was riding away and I knew that no word or thought could hold him. The big horse, patient and powerful, was already settling into the steady pace that had brought him into our valley, and the two, the man and the horse, were a single dark shape in the road as they passed beyond the reach of the light from the windows.

I strained my eyes after him, and then in the moonlight I could make out the inalienable outline of his figure receding into the distance. Lost in my loneliness, I watched him go, out of town, far down the road where it curved out to the level country beyond the valley. There were men on the porch behind me, but I was aware only of that dark shape growing small and indistinct along the far reach of the road. A cloud passed over the moon and he merged into the general shadow and I could not see him and the cloud passed on and the road was a plain thin ribbon to the horizon and he was gone.

I stumbled back to fall on the steps, my head in my arms to hide the tears. The voices of the men around me were meaningless noises in a bleak and empty world. It was Mr Weir who took me home.

XV

FATHER and mother were in the kitchen, almost as I had left them. Mother had hitched her chair close to father's. He was sitting up, his face tired and haggard, the ugly red mark standing out plain along the side of his head. They did not come to meet us. They sat still and watched us move into the doorway.

They did not even scold me. Mother reached and pulled me to her and let me crawl into her lap as I had not done for three years or more. Father just stared at Mr Weir. He could not trust himself to speak first.

'Your troubles are over, Starrett.'

Father nodded. 'You've come to tell me,' he said wearily, 'that he killed Wilson before they got him. I know. He was Shane.'

'Wilson,' said Mr. Weir. 'And Fletcher.'

Father started. 'Fletcher, too? By Godfrey, yes. He would do it right.' Then father sighed and ran a finger along the bruise on his head. 'He let me know this was one thing he wanted to handle by himself. I can tell you, Weir, waiting here is the hardest job I ever had.'

Mr Weir looked at the bruise. 'I thought so. Listen, Starrett. There's not a man in town doesn't know you didn't stay here of your own will. And there's damn few that aren't glad it was Shane came into the saloon to-night.'

The words broke from me. 'You should have seen

him, father. He was—he was—' I could not find it at first. 'He was—beautiful, father. And Wilson wouldn't even have hit him if he'd been in practice. He told me so.'

'He told you!' The table was banging over as father drove to his feet. He grabbed Mr Weir by the coat front. 'My God, man! Why didn't you tell me? He's alive?'

'Yes,' said Mr Weir. 'He's alive all right. Wilson got to him. But no bullet can kill that man.' A puzzled, faraway sort of look flitted across Mr Weir's face. 'Sometimes I wonder whether anything ever could.'

Father was shaking him. 'Where is he?'

'He's gone,' said Mr Weir. 'He's gone, alone and unfollowed as he wanted it. Out of the valley and no one knows where.'

Father's hands dropped. He slumped again into his chair. He picked up his pipe and it broke in his fingers. He let the pieces fall and stared at them on the floor. He was still staring at them when new footsteps sounded on the porch and a man pushed into our kitchen.

It was Chris. His right arm was tight in the sling, his eyes unnaturally bright and the colour high in his face. In his left hand he was carrying a bottle, a bottle of red cherry soda pop. He came straight in and righted the table with the hand holding the bottle. He smacked the bottle on the top boards and seemed startled at the noise he made. He was embarrassed and he was having trouble with his voice. But he spoke up firmly.

'I brought that for Bob. I'm a damned poor substitute, Starrett. But as soon as this arm's healed, I'm asking you to let me work for you.'

Father's face twisted and his lips moved, but no

words came. Mother was the one who said it. 'Shane would like that, Chris.'

And still father said nothing. What Chris and Mr Weir saw as they looked at him must have shown them that nothing they could do or say would help at all. They turned and went out together, walking with long, quick steps.

Mother and I sat there watching father. There was nothing we could do either. This was something he had to wrestle alone. He was so still that he seemed even to have stopped breathing. Then a sudden restlessness hit him and he was up and pacing aimlessly about. He glared at the walls as if they stifled him and strode out the door into the yard. We heard his steps around the house and heading into the fields and then we could hear nothing.

I do not know how long we sat there. I know that the wick in the lamp burned low and sputtered awhile and went out and the darkness was a relief and a comfort. At last mother rose, still holding me, the big boy bulk of me, in her arms. I was surprised at the strength in her. She was holding me tightly to her and she carried me into my little room and helped me undress in the dim shadows of the moonlight through the window. She tucked me in and sat on the edge of the bed, and then, only then, she whispered to me: 'Now, Bob. Tell me everything. Just as you saw it happen.'

I told her, and when I was done, all she said in a soft little murmur was 'Thank you.' She looked out the window and murmured the words again and they were not for me and she was still looking out over the land to the great grey mountains when finally I fell asleep.

She must have been there the whole night through, for when I woke with a start, the first streaks of dawn were showing through the window and the bed was warm where she had been. The movement of her leaving must have wakened me. I crept out of bed and peeked into the kitchen. She was standing in the open outside doorway.

I fumbled into my clothes and tiptoed through the kitchen to her. She took my hand and I clung to hers and it was right that we should be together and that together we should go find father.

We found him out by the corral, by the far end where Shane had added to it. The sun was beginning to rise through the cleft in the mountains across the river, not the brilliant glory of midday but the fresh and renewed reddish brilliance of early morning. Father's arms were folded on the top rail, his head bowed on them. When he turned to face us, he leaned back against the rail as if he needed the support. His eyes were rimmed and a little wild.

'Marian, I'm sick of the sight of this valley and all that's in it. If I tried to stay here now, my heart wouldn't be in it any more. I know it's hard on you and the boy, but we'll have to pull up stakes and move on. Montana, maybe. I've heard there's good land for the claiming up that way.'

Mother heard him through. She had let go my hand and stood erect, so angry that her eyes snapped and her chin quivered. But she heard him through.

'Joe! Joe Starrett!' Her voice fairly crackled and was rich with emotion that was more than anger. 'So you'd run out on Shane just when he's really here to stay!'

'But, Marian. You don't understand. He's gone.'

'He's not gone. He's here, in this place, in this place he gave us. He's all around us and in us, and he always will be.'

She ran to the tall corner post, to the one Shane had set. She beat at it with her hands. 'Here, Joe. Quick. Take hold. Pull it down.'

Father stared at her in amazement. But he did as she said. No one could have denied her in that moment. He took hold of the post and pulled at it. He shook his head and braced his feet and strained at it with all his strength. The big muscles of his shoulders and back knotted and bulged till I thought this shirt, too, would shred. Creakings ran along the rails and the post moved ever so slightly and the ground at the base showed little cracks fanning out. But the rails held and the post stood.

Father turned from it, beads of sweat breaking on his face, a light creeping up his drawn cheeks.

'See, Joe. See what I mean. We have roots here now that we can never tear loose.'

And the morning was in father's face, shining in his eyes, giving him new colour and hope and understanding.

XVI

I GUESS that is all there is to tell. The folks in town and the kids at school liked to talk about Shane, to spin tales and speculate about him. I never did. Those nights at Grafton's became legends in the valley and countless details were added as they grew and spread just as the town, too, grew and spread up the river banks. But I never bothered, no matter how strange the tales became in the constant retelling. He belonged to me, to father and mother and me, and nothing could ever spoil that.

For mother was right. He was there. He was there in our place and in us. Whenever I needed him, he was there. I could close my eyes and he would be with me and I would see him plain and hear again that gentle voice.

I would think of him in each of the moments that revealed him to me. I would think of him most vividly in that single flashing instant when he whirled to shoot Fletcher on the balcony at Grafton's saloon. I would see again the power and grace of a co-ordinate force beautiful beyond comprehension. I would see the man and the weapon wedded in the one indivisible deadliness. I would see the man and the tool, a good man and a good tool, doing what had to be done.

And always my mind would go back at the last to that moment when I saw him from the bushes by the roadside just on the edge of town. I would see him there in the road, tall and terrible in the moonlight, going down to kill or be killed, and stopping to help a stumbling boy and to look out over the land, the lovely land, where that boy had a chance to live out his boyhood and grow straight inside as a man should.

And when I would hear the men in town talking among themselves and trying to pin him down to a definite past, I would smile quietly to myself. For a time they inclined to the notion, spurred by the talk of a passing stranger, that he was a certain Shannon who was famous as a gunman and gambler way down in Arkansas and Texas and dropped from sight without anyone knowing why or where. When that notion dwindled, others followed, pieced together in turn from scraps of information gleaned from stray travellers. But when they talked like that, I simply smiled because I knew he could have been none of these.

He was the man who rode into our little valley out of the heart of the great glowing West and when his work was done rode back whence he had come and he was Shane.

Main chas ~~actors~~

Joe Starrett
    marian
    Bob
    Shane
    Fletcher
        Wilson
        Red marvin
            Chris
            morgan
            Ernie Wright
                Grafton

1 Shane riding in Bo verse
3 Shane working + Starry.ng
3 fight with chris.
4 fight with Redmason +
                    morgan.
5 Wilson comes to town
6 Wilson + Starrett shot
2 shane reaves town.

TITLES IN THE NEW WINDMILL SERIES

Chinua Achebe: *Things Fall Apart*
Louisa M. Alcott: *Little Women*
Elizabeth Allen: *Deitz and Denny*
Margery Allingham: *The Tiger in the Smoke*
Michael Anthony: *The Year in San Fernando*
Enid Bagnold: *National Velvet*
Stan Barstow: *Joby*
H. Mortimer Batten: *The Singing Forest*
Nina Bawden: *On the Run; The Witch's Daughter; A Handful of Thieves; Carrie's War; Rebel on a Rock*
Rex Benedict: *Last Stand at Goodbye Gulch*
Phyllis Bentley: *The Adventures of Tom Leigh*
Paul Berna: *Flood Warning*
Pierre Boulle: *The Bridge on the River Kwai*
E. R. Braithwaite: *To Sir, With Love*
D. K. Broster: *The Flight of the Heron; The Gleam in the North*
F. Hodgson Burnett: *The Secret Garden*
Helen Bush: *Mary Anning's Treasures*
A. Calder-Marshall: *The Man from Devil's Island*
John Caldwell: *Desperate Voyage*
Albert Camus: *The Outsider*
Victor Canning: *The Runaways; Flight of the Grey Goose*
Erskine Childers: *The Riddle of the Sands*
John Christopher: *The Guardians; The Lotus Caves*
Richard Church: *The Cave; Over the Bridge; The White Doe*
Colette: *My Mother's House*
Alexander Cordell: *The Traitor Within*
Margaret Craven: *I Heard the Owl Call my Name*
Roald Dahl: *Danny, Champion of the World; The Wonderful Story of Henry Sugar*
Meindert deJong: *The Wheel on the School*
Peter Dickinson: *The Gift; Annerton Pit*
Eleanor Doorly: *The Radium Woman; The Microbe Man; The Insect Man*
Gerald Durrell: *Three Singles to Adventure; The Drunken Forest; Encounters with Animals*
Elizabeth Enright: *Thimble Summer; The Saturdays*
C. S. Forester: *The General*
Eve Garnett: *The Family from One End Street; Further Adventures of the Family from One End Street; Holiday at the Dew Drop Inn*
G. M. Glaskin: *A Waltz through the Hills*
Rumer Godden: *Black Narcissus*
Angus Graham: *The Golden Grindstone*
Graham Greene: *The Third Man* and *The Fallen Idol*
Grey Owl: *Sajo and her Beaver People*
John Griffin: *Skulker Wheat and Other Stories*
G. and W. Grossmith: *The Diary of a Nobody*
René Guillot: *Kpo the Leopard*
Esther Hautzig: *The Endless Steppe*
Jan De Hartog: *The Lost Sea*
Erik Haugaard: *The Little Fishes*
Bessie Head: *When Rain Clouds Gather*
Ernest Hemingway: *The Old Man and the Sea*
John Hersey: *A Single Pebble*
Georgette Heyer: *Regency Buck*

Alfred Hitchcock: *Sinister Spies*
C. Walter Hodges: *The Overland Launch*
Geoffrey Household: *Rogue Male; A Rough Shoot; Prisoner of the Indies; Escape into Daylight*
Fred Hoyle: *The Black Cloud*
Irene Hunt: *Across Five Aprils*
Henry James: *Washington Square*
Josephine Kamm: *Young Mother; Out of Step; Where Do We Go From Here?; The Starting Point*
Erich Kästner: *Emil and the Detectives; Lottie and Lisa*
Clive King: *Me and My Million*
John Knowles: *A Separate Peace*
D. H. Lawrence: *Sea and Sardinia; The Fox* and *The Virgin and the Gipsy; Selected Tales*
Marghanita Laski: *Little Boy Lost*
Harper Lee: *To Kill a Mockingbird*
Laurie Lee: *As I Walked Out One Mid-Summer Morning*
Ursula Le Guin: *A Wizard of Earthsea; The Tombs of Atuan; The Farthest Shore; A Very Long Way from Anywhere Else*
Doris Lessing: *The Grass is Singing*
C. Day Lewis: *The Otterbury Incident*
Lorna Lewis: *Leonardo the Inventor*
Martin Lindsay: *The Epic of Captain Scott*
David Line: *Run for Your Life; Mike and Me*
Kathleen Lines: *The House of the Nightmare; The Haunted and the Haunters*
Joan Lingard: *Across the Barricades; Into Exile; The Clearance*
Penelope Lively: *The Ghost of Thomas Kempe*
Jack London: *The Call of the Wild; White Fang*
Carson McCullers: *The Member of the Wedding*
Lee McGiffen: *On the Trail to Sacramento*
Wolf Mankowitz: *A Kid for Two Farthings*
Olivia Manning: *The Play Room*
Jan Mark: *Thunder and Lightnings*
James Vance Marshall: *A River Ran Out of Eden; Walkabout; My Boy John that Went to Sea*
David Martin: *The Cabby's Daughter*
J. P. Martin: *Uncle*
John Masefield: *The Bird of Dawning; The Midnight Folk; The Box of Delights*
W. Somerset Maugham: *The Kite and Other Stories*
Guy de Maupassant: *Prisoners of War and Other Stories*
Laurence Meynell: *Builder and Dreamer*
Yvonne Mitchell: *Cathy Away Home*
Honoré Morrow: *The Splendid Journey*
Bill Naughton: *The Goalkeeper's Revenge; A Dog Called Nelson; My Pal Spadger*
E. Nesbit: *The Railway Children; The Story of the Treasure Seekers*
E. Neville: *It's Like this, Cat*
Wilfrid Noyce: *South Col*
Robert C. O'Brien: *Mrs Frisby and the Rats of NIMH; Z for Zachariah*
Scott O'Dell: *Island of the Blue Dolphins*
George Orwell: *Animal Farm*
K. M. Peyton: *Flambards*
Philippa Pearce: *Tom's Midnight Garden*
John Prebble: *The Buffalo Soldiers*